Bridesmaids

JANE COSTELLO

**SIMON &
SCHUSTER**

London · New York · Sydney · Toronto · New Delhi

A CBS COMPANY

First published in Great Britain by Simon & Schuster UK Ltd, 2008
A CBS COMPANY

This paperback edition, 2018

1 3 5 7 9 10 8 6 4 2

Simon & Schuster UK Ltd
1st Floor
222 Gray's Inn Road
London WC1X 8HB

Simon & Schuster Australia, Sydney
Simon & Schuster India, New Delhi

www.simonandschuster.co.uk
www.simonandschuster.com.au
www.simonandschuster.co.in

A CIP catalogue record for this book
is available from the British Library

Paperback ISBN: 978-1-47117-619-7
eBook ISBN: 978-1-84739-481-1

Typeset in Goudy by M Rules
Printed and bound by CPI Group (UK) Ltd, Croydon, CR0 4YY

MIX
Paper from
responsible sources
FSC® C020471

Simon & Schuster UK Ltd are committed to sourcing paper
that is made from wood grown in sustainable forests and support the Forest
Stewardship Council, the leading international forest certification organisation.
Our books displaying the FSC logo are printed on FSC certified paper.

For Otis, with all my love

Chapter 1

My best friend is due to get married in fifty-two minutes
and the hotel suite looks like day three on the main field at
Glastonbury.

The room is strewn with random items of wedding paraphernalia – and I include the bride herself in that category.
Grace is still in her dressing-gown, with only half of her
make-up done. I, meanwhile, have spent the last ten minutes frantically trying to revive the flowers in her hair after
she trapped them in the car door coming back from the
hairdresser.

I give her curls another generous whirl of spray and throw
the empty can onto the four-poster bed.

'You're sure it's all secure now, Evie?' she asks, hurriedly
applying her mascara in a huge antique mirror. I've used

1

enough hairspray to keep Trevor Sorbie in a comfortable retirement, so am reasonably confident.

'Definitely,' I say.

'It doesn't look unnatural though, does it?' she goes on, picking up a tub of bronzing balls.

I tentatively touch her curls. They feel like they're made of fibre-glass.

'Course not,' I lie, strategically repositioning bits of foliage over some of the thirty-odd hairgrips. 'Your flowers are perfect. Your hair's perfect. Everything's perfect.'

She looks at me, entirely unconvinced.

We're in the bridal suite at the Inn at Whitewell, a timeless old coaching inn, hidden deep in the Forest of Bowland. It is surrounded by countryside so beautiful it inspired Tolkien's Shire in *The Lord of the Rings*, and so tranquil that the Queen herself once said she'd like to retire here.

Outside, there are rolling hills in a palette of lush green, glittering streams of crystal water and a sweeping sky alive with birdsong. Sadly, we've barely even looked at the scenery; there just hasn't been time. It's even difficult to appreciate the suite in this frantic stage – though, for the record, it is gorgeous.

A glamorous four-poster bed sits in the centre of a room stuffed with elegant Victorian furniture, white linen and lavish fabrics. Oak beams stretch across the ceiling towards a dramatic window, from which chiffon ribbons of light spill into the room. There is an Edwardian bath and a peat fire that sits opposite a quirky bookcase smelling of old leather and luxury room fragrance.

It could be the perfect place for peace and contemplation under any other circumstances.

'Great! Excellent. Good! Thanks,' Grace says breathlessly. 'Right. What now?'

Why she's asking me, I don't know. Nobody could be less qualified to advise on an occasion like this.

The last wedding I went to was more than two decades ago, when my mum's Cousin Carol married the love of her life, Brian. Within three years he'd run off with a seventeen-stone painter and decorator. Carol was devastated, despite the undeniably professional job her love rival had done on their hall, stairs and landing.

For those nuptials I wore a puffball skirt and wouldn't let go of the pageboy's hand all day. If I'd known then that that was going to amount to one of my life's most meaningful relation-ships, I'd have tried to remember his name.

Which brings me to the second reason why Grace would be better off asking the grandfather clock in the corner for advice: I accepted long ago that it's highly unlikely I'll ever get married myself.

It's not that I have anything against the idea of marriage, assuming you've met the right person. It's that I don't think I'm capable of it.

I have now reached the age of twenty-seven and have

never been in love, nor indeed come close. Worse than that, the longest I've ever managed to stay with someone is three months. I couldn't even tell you why it doesn't work out beyond that – only that it never, ever does.

At first I thought it was just bad luck. I'd start dating someone feeling full of enthusiasm, certain that the relationship held promise. Then doubt would creep in and, before I knew it, I found them as attractive as a fungal infection.

I soon began to realize that this doesn't happen to other people, at least not with this regularity. Only me. So I can only conclude that the problem is all mine.

On the plus side, it seems I'm unlikely ever to be tied down by a man. Having read *The Female Eunuch* in sixth form (and not shaved my armpits for three weeks), this could be seen as a Good Thing. But is emancipation necessarily so lonely? I don't think a feminist on earth would say it is.

A typical example of this issue in action is my relationship with Gareth. We split up last week. Gareth was – *is* – lovely. Nice smile. Good heart. Decent job. As usual, it started well, with pleasant evenings over a bottle of Chianti in Penny Lane wine bar – near where I live in Liverpool – and lazy Sunday afternoons at the cinema.

But we'd barely been together four weeks when he suggested a three-night caravanning holiday with his mum and dad in North Wales . . . and I knew that it was just too late.

I had ceased to think about the cute little dimple in his chin and couldn't stop thinking about the dirt under his toenails and the fact that the most intellectual thing on his bookshelf was a copy of *Auto-Trader*.

Yet, nothing he did or said was all *that* terrible and, certainly, it doesn't compare with what some women have to put up with. Yet, while I kept telling myself there were worse things a man could do than think that George Eliot was that bloke from *Minder*, I knew deep down he wasn't for me.

Which would be fine except they never seem to be for me. Anyway, after a gap of twenty-two years, I've now got three weddings lined up in one year and I'm a bridesmaid at every one of them. If today's dramatics are anything to go by, I'm not sure my nerves are up to it.

'Shoes!' Grace declares as she stomps around the bedroom, flinging items out of the way.

I look at the clock: thirty-one minutes to go. Grace picks up her lip-brush and hesitates.

'Maybe I should get my dress on now,' she says. 'No, wait, I need my stockings. Oh, hang on, should I touch up my hair with the tongs first? What do you think?'

'Er, stockings?' I offer.

'You're right. Yes. Stockings. Christ, where are they?'

5

Chapter 2

I would like to say it's just the wedding that has prompted today's pandemonium, but this scene is a microcosm of Grace's life over the last five years. During that time, her stress levels have been not just through the ceiling, they've been through three floors, a well-insulated loft and a roof as well.

The onset of this hysteria coincided with her return to full-time work after her daughter Polly was born four years ago. It graduated to a terminal case when baby number two, Scarlett came along last November.

The contents of Grace's bag are chucked onto the floor one by one before she eventually locates her stockings.

'I really must be careful with these,' she says.

Sitting on the edge of the bed, she tears open the packet, removes one, and puts her toe into one leg with all the delicacy of a bricklayer pulling on a pair of Doc Martens. Predictably, her foot goes straight through the end of it with a rip that makes my hair stand on end.

'Oh fff ...' she begins, but as four-year-old Polly walks in from the bathroom, she just about stops herself from saying something she'd regret. 'God!' she goes on. 'They cost eighteen quid!'

'What?' I am incredulous. 'For eighteen quid they shouldn't just be toe-proof, they should be able to withstand a nuclear explosion.'

Twenty-six minutes left. I may be a novice but I know enough to be aware that we should have made more progress than this. The whole place is starting to take on the air of an episode of *ER*.

'Look,' I say. 'What can I do to help?'

'Er, Polly's hair,' Grace shouts, sprinting into the bathroom in search of her necklace.

'Come on, Pol,' I say brightly. But the prospect of smearing Molton Brown hand cream into the carpet seems more appealing to Polly.

'Come on, sweetheart,' I repeat, trying to sound firm and friendly, as opposed to desperate. 'We really need to do your hair. *Really*.'

There is barely a flicker of recognition as she starts on the naran ji handwash.

'Right, who wants to look like a model?' I ask, searching for something – anything – that might persuade her to oblige.

'Me!' she exclaims, jumping up. 'I want to be a model when I grow up!'

This is fortunate. Last week she wanted to be a marine biologist.

I tie Polly's soft blonde curls into two bunches, add a variety of sparkly clips, and look at the clock. Twenty-three minutes to go. My own dress is still hanging on the back of the door and all I've managed to do with my make-up is cover the spot on my chin with some Clearasil.

Deciding that my best tactic is to do a rush job on myself so I can then get the bride into her dress, I go into the bathroom and, perching on the edge of the roll-top bath, I start to apply my make-up.

When it is done – about forty seconds later – I grab my dress from the back of the door and pull it painstakingly over my head, taking care not to leave deodorant snowdrifts down the side. I look in the mirror and survey the results.

Not exactly J-Lo, but I'll do.

And at least my dress flatters my classically English build. Taken overall, my weight is near enough average. It's just that the top half of my body (flat chest) and the bottom half (big bum) somehow look like they should belong to two different people.

My shoulder-length hair is mousy by nature but has been borderline blonde for several years, courtesy of an early *Sun-In* addiction which has graduated these days to full-blown highlights.

Today, it has been painstakingly tousled into a 'natural' look that took precisely two and a quarter hours and enough high-definition hair products to bouffant a scarecrow.

I'm just about to leave the room to attend to Grace, when I spot my bag by the sink and realize I've forgotten a crucial finishing touch. My 'chicken fillet' boob enhancers.

More dramatic than a Wonderbra and – at £29.99 – significantly cheaper than surgery, I've been dying for a suitable occasion to try these out. I shove them down the front of my dress and wiggle them into position, before I turn to look at the results.

I still wouldn't get many tips at Hooters, but it's an improvement on what nature has failed to bestow on me. I'm just about to show my new assets off to Grace when I hear a yell coming from the adjacent room.

The bride is having a showdown.

Chapter 3

'The chocolate favours have what?' hisses Grace, gripping the hotel phone furiously.

'Melted?' she asks, her face growing redder. 'How can they have melted?' She puts a hand on her forehead.

'Okay, how bad are they? I mean, are they still heart-shaped?' There's a pause as steam rises from her cheeks. 'Oh great.' She slams down the phone. 'Arrrghhh!'

'So they're not still heart-shaped?' I ask tentatively.

'From what I can tell, they now look like something you'd find in a litter tray,' she says, forlorn. 'I haven't got a bloody clue where my tiara is. Has anyone seen my tiara?'

'Mummy,' Polly announces, 'I've got no knickers on.' Grace slumps onto the bed. 'This is *terrific*,' she says. 'I'm getting married in about fifteen minutes. I've got a hole in my stockings, I can't find my tiara, I've just found a fake-tan streak on my knee, and now it seems I'm incapable of getting my daughter out of the room with any underwear on. I am the worst bride in the world.'

I sit on the bed and put my arm around her. 'Cheer up. You just need to put things in perspective. It's only the biggest day of your life,' I joke.

She starts laughing . . . then crying. Look, I'm trying.

'What is the point in panicking?' I continue gently. 'It's not like Patrick won't wait for you. So what if you're a bit late? And besides that, whatever you may think, you look *gorgeous*.'

'Do I?' She sounds sceptical.

'Utterly. Now, come on, it's time to step things up a gear.'

I go into bridesmaid-overdrive, assaulting Grace with her toupee tape, bronzing balls, lip gloss, bronzing balls (again), then, finally, the dress, which it takes both of us – plus Polly – to squeeze her into.

Just when I think we're all done, Grace gasps. 'I left my earrings downstairs with my mum. They're my *something borrowed*. Evie, I'm so sorry – could you go and find her?'

I look at the clock again. I am awash with adrenaline.

By the time I've located Grace's mum, secured the earrings and am heading for the stairs, there are about four and a half minutes to go. But as I start dashing up the stairs, something – or should I say *someone* – stops me in my tracks.

He is quite simply one of the handsomest men I've ever seen. With eyes the colour of warm treacle, faintly-tanned skin and a slightly crooked nose that means that he's neither dull nor pretty. He's physically toned, broad shouldered – big but not too big. As a package, he'd make Action Man look like he'd let himself go.

My pace slows as I walk up the stairs, and my heart-rate quickens as I realize he's looking right at me. Brazenly, I find myself holding his gaze as we step closer to each other. Then, as our paths are about to cross, the most astonishing thing happens.

He looks at my breasts.

It's only for a split second, but there is no doubt that it happens. It's so blatant I'd almost describe it as *a gawp*, with eyes conspicuously widened and a faint intake of breath. As he drags away his gaze and continues downstairs, I am rigid with disbelief, appalled that this beautiful man turned out to be a knuckle-dragging Neanderthal. Still, my recent John Lewis purchase is obviously convincing.

I open the door to the bridal suite.

'Ta da!' I say. 'One set of earrings.'

Grace turns around to look and gasps.

'What?' I ask, bewildered.

'I'm not having you in my wedding photos looking like that,' she cackles, barely able to contain herself.

'Like what?' I ask, pleased that she has finally relaxed. But as I look down, the cause of her mirth becomes horribly apparent.

Chapter 4

My cleavage has been attacked by two rogue jellyfish. At least, that's what it looks like. My chicken fillets, the ones I was so very chuffed about, clearly felt restricted inside my dress – and have ridden up to make a break for freedom.

In fact, they nearly made it: my two 'completely one hundred per cent natural-looking' breast enhancers are now poking out of the top of my dress for all the world to see. Or should I say, for him – Action Man – to see. Which feels rather worse than just *the world*.

'I don't believe this,' I say, furiously yanking both fillets from my cleavage. In the absence of a barbecue, I chuck them in the bin.

'Just think of it as God's way of saying you were born flat-chested for a reason,' Grace tells me kindly.

'I'm glad you find it amusing,' I say.

'Sorry.' Grace is clearly trying not to snigger. 'But you must admit it's *quite* amusing.'

I look across the room and see that Charlotte, Grace's other grown-up bridesmaid, is back – having spent most of the morning sorting out flower arrangements – and even she is trying to suppress a smile. It must be bad.

'Don't worry, Evie,' she reassures me. 'I'm sure nobody noticed. They may have just thought they were part of your dress.'

Charlotte is so sweet and lovely that I wish for both our sakes that I was convinced. Unfortunately, the one person who did see it couldn't have noticed more if they'd jumped out and slapped him on both cheeks.

'Thanks, Charlotte,' I say.

I feel a stab of guilt for not having found some time to help her get ready today, to accentuate her pretty features. She's got skin that I'd kill for – smooth and clear like a baby's, with gorgeous rosy cheeks and big, gentle eyes. I remember thinking when I first met Charlotte – years ago now – that she reminded me of an eighteenth-century milkmaid: gloriously soft and round and wholesome.

But while Charlotte does have natural assets, she doesn't make the most of them. To be horribly blunt, there are contestants at Crufts who will have spent longer on their hair than she has today. And although Charlotte wouldn't be Charlotte without her ample curves, she never dresses to flatter them. Her dress is so tight, it looks close to cutting off her circulation.

'It's nearly time,' I say excitedly.

'Yes,' she replies, looking utterly terrified.

'Right, you two,' says the bride, thrusting a bouquet in my hand. 'We can't stand around discussing Evie's cleavage all day. We need to get down that aisle – and quick.'

Chapter 5

It is difficult not to get caught up in the magic of a day like today.

Even the most cynical of souls couldn't deny how incredible it must be to love someone enough to grow old and incontinent with them.

And it's clearly not just the spray tan that has given Grace the glow she's got today. It's Patrick, her groom, and the fact there isn't a doubt in her mind that he's the man for her.

'What's the matter?' whispers Charlotte as we wait outside the main room for the ceremony to start.

'Nothing,' I say. 'Why?'

'You sighed, that's all,' she replies.

'Oh God, did I?' I whisper.

She smiles. 'Don't worry, Evie,' she says. 'You'll meet someone special one day.'

As I follow Grace down the aisle to 'What a Wonderful World' sung by Louis Armstrong, I spot Gareth among the guests and my thoughts swing back to the last time I saw him, sniffing into his napkin as I gently tried to tell him our relationship was over.

I attempt a 'no hard feelings' smile but he sniffs and buries his head in his Order of Service. What's wrong with me? Gareth wasn't that bad.

I glance over to my left and another of my exes, Joe the TV producer, catches my eye and winks. Okay, maybe *he* was that bad. The definition of smug in his Paul Smith suit and sunbed tan, I can smell the four litres of Aramis he's probably bathed in from the other side of the room.

I haven't seen Peter the musician – the third of my flings here today – but I know he's somewhere, playing with his tongue ring and rattling the key chain that I'm convinced is welded to him.

Grace and Patrick meet at the front and exchange nervous looks. I suppose even if you have spent the last seven years together, signing up for potentially the next seventy is enough to make anyone's stomach do back-flips.

My best friend met her groom when they were trainees at the same law firm and, even though that was years ago now, we all knew as soon as we met him that Patrick was the man for her. There was an immediate connection between them – and two kids and three mortgages later – that attraction still radiates from them.

The registrar is an eccentric-looking woman in an A-line

skirt that probably wasn't very fashionable in 1982 when I suspect she bought it. As she introduces the first reading, it suddenly strikes me that there was one person I hadn't spotted as I walked down the aisle. The man I met on the stairs mustn't be a guest at the wedding. So at least one of the most mortifying incidents of my life is something to which I need never give a second thought. I can forget it now. Completely.

My mind drifts to the definition in his features and those dark eyes that seemed dreamier the closer I got. I think about his smell, sultry aftershave and clean skin, and find myself slumping in my seat.

Action Man, where are you?

Chapter 6

Valentina is giving the reading. It's only meant to be a one-and-a-half-minute speech, but you'd be forgiven for thinking she was about to collect an Oscar. She glides to the front and, as she steps onto the platform, conspicuously lifts the hem of her crimson chiffon dress to reveal more of her never-ending bronzed legs than we've already been treated to.

Valentina has been part of our circle since she latched onto Charlotte in Freshers' Week at Liverpool University. They made an unlikely twosome. Poor, desperately shy Charlotte, who'd hardly been out of Widnes. Valentina the Amazon, who'd been everywhere, done everything, and was about as shy and retiring as the average *Penthouse* centrefold.

Valentina tried her hand at various careers when she left university – personal shopper, *Hollyoaks* extra, upmarket restaurant hostess – before finding something at which she genuinely does excel. She is now a professional tennis coach and apparently making quite a name for herself.

Deep down, she's a decent cove, but that's not a universally held opinion and she doesn't help matters when she tells people that she's constantly mistaken for a Victoria's Secret model.

Valentina puts her notes on the lectern and, with a flick of her dark glossy hair, she prepares to address her audience.

'Ladies and gentlemen, before I start my reading, can I just say how *overwhelming* I personally have found it, that two of my closest friends are getting married today,' she gushes.

'When they persuaded me to do a reading I really couldn't have been more touched to play such a significant part in the most momentous day of their lives.'

Grace and Patrick exchange looks. Far from needing any persuasion, Valentina had sulked so much when Grace explained that she wanted to keep the bridesmaids to a minimum that Grace had only agreed to the reading to shut her up.

'The blessing I am about to read is one which has been used in Native American weddings for centuries,' she continues. 'You may be interested to know, however, that the author of it is actually still unknown. It's a beautiful piece of prose and I hope that when you hear it, you'll agree that it is truly fitting for a day like today.'

She composes herself as the registrar looks at her watch.

'*Now you will feel no rain, for each of you will be the shelter for the other.*'

She pauses for effect.

'Now you will feel no cold, for each of you will be the warmth for the other . . .'

After Valentina's performance, the service seems to pick up speed and in no time at all, Grace and Patrick are walking back down the aisle as man and wife, to the rapturous applause of their guests. Polly and I are next in the procession, holding hands as she skips along. Charlotte skulks somewhere behind us.

I try to avoid smiling at the guests, given that there seems to be an ex-boyfriend wherever I look. But just as I am attempting to keep my eyes fixed firmly ahead, something draws my attention to the far corner of the room. He's standing by a window which overlooks some of the most beautiful scenery in the country. But he makes an unbeatable view all by himself.

My pulse starts racing and I grip Polly's hand tighter. It's Action Man. And he's looking right at me.

Chapter 7

I'm trying my best to stay cool but heat blossoms on my neck as I make my way back down the aisle. I instinctively glance down to check my chicken fillets are in situ, and only then remember that I threw them away.

He isn't looking at me as I approach. I catch enough of a glimpse to work out that he is staring ahead, his gaze firmly on the front of the room. Then, when my shoulder is adjacent to his, he turns to me. I instinctively turn to him.

In the infinitesimal moment when our eyes connect, my heart nearly crashes out of my chest. I snap away, quickly bending down to whisper to Polly.

'You were such a good girl during the ceremony,' I tell her brightly, needing something, anything, to focus on other than him.

She looks at me as if to say: 'What *are* you on about?'

I can still feel his eyes burning into me as we almost reach the door. But something is stopping me from looking at him again; instead I focus on Grace's dress and I feel like kicking myself. The fact that I've just noticed I'd done two of her ivory buttons up wrong is the least of my concerns.

When we reach the drawing room, Grace and Patrick kiss while champagne corks pop and the guests pour through to congratulate the happy couple. I grab a glass of bubbly from a passing waiter and only just stop myself from knocking it back in one as I monitor the door, which he's going to have to come through sooner or later.

Not that I know what I'll do when he does.

The drawing room is soon a riot of people and it's difficult to keep track of who has come through the door as there are so many of them. But as I sense someone by my side, my stomach swoops.

Chapter 8

Grace is looking no less stressed than she did *before* the ceremony.

'Evie, listen,' she says, 'I need your help again. Can you get everyone outside? We've got to start doing the photos.'

I look around at the guests tucking into a lavish champagne reception in a cosy drawing room warmed by roaring open fires. My task, if I choose to accept it, is to get them all out – even the ones in strappy high-heeled sandals – onto a wind-swept terrace in February.

'You give me all the best jobs, Grace,' I say. 'I think it might take me until next weekend.'

As she disappears, I hover around the group of people next to me.

'Er, hi,' I say. 'Er, could I please ask you all to make your way into the garden for the photographs? Thanks. Thanks so much.'

I move on to the next group and say the same.

Five groups later I realize that I'd get more response talking to the wedding cake. So I decide to start tapping people on the shoulder as well.

'Er, yes, hi, hello,' I say. 'Really sorry to interrupt, but do you think you could make your way into the garden? The photographer's ready.'

This is starting to get really annoying. I am either invisible or people are more interested in the booze and smoked salmon blinis than standing outside for half an hour being told to say 'chocolate biscuits'.

Hmm. Okay, so I knew it was going to be a challenge. I resist the temptation to stand on a chair, but decide to give it all I've got anyway.

'LADIES AND GENTLEMEN,' I bellow, aware that all I'm lacking is a bell and a town-crier's outfit. 'PLEASE MAKE YOUR WAY OUT INTO THE GARDEN AS THE PHOTOGRAPHS ARE ABOUT TO BE TAKEN.'

The whole room stops talking and turns to look at me as if I'm a stripper who's been booked as the star turn at a Women's Institute meeting.

The poor bloke next to me turns around slowly to discover the source of this outburst and I realize that I've got nowhere to run.

The second I see his face, my heart sinks. At least nobody could accuse me of not knowing how to make a first impression.

Chapter 9

There's only one way to redeem this situation – and that's to say something witty.

I try to conjure up my best, side-splitting line, to lighten the atmosphere and ideally make Action Man want to take me home immediately.

'Er, ah! Er, erm . . .' I splutter. 'Sorry about that.' Move over *Monty Python*.

His face breaks into a smile. 'Don't worry about it,' he laughs. 'Subtlety clearly wasn't going to work in this case.'

'Well . . . people do say I've got a good set of lungs,' I grin, then instantly realize this could be construed as a euphemism. 'I mean . . . I didn't mean that!'

He chuckles into his drink as my face gets hotter. 'Look, it's done the trick.' He nods to the doors, where guests are pouring onto the terrace.

'Thank God for that,' I sigh.

'Is this what being a bridesmaid involves these days?' he

adds. 'I didn't think you had to do anything other than stand around looking pretty.'

'Looking pretty is really my main duty for the day,' I agree. 'That and deafening the guests.'

'Well,' he says, 'you do both exceptionally well.'

I try to stop myself grinning. 'Thank you,' I say instead. 'I'm Evie. Very pleased to meet you.'

We shake hands but before he gets the chance to introduce himself, we are interrupted.

'Evie, you naughty thing! I hope you're not trying to steal my date!'

Valentina is pretending that she's joking, but she now has hold of Action Man's arm in the sort of grip that could get her a job as a parole officer.

'I was just introducing myself to your friend,' he says, turning back to me. 'I'm Jack. Lovely to meet you. And hear you.' Before I can think of anything to say, Valentina beats me to it.

'Jack, there's someone you've just got to meet,' she says, pulling on his arm and giving him little choice in the matter.

So off they go. Bloody, bloody, bloody hell.

Chapter 10

I'd have preferred to discover that Action Man – sorry, Jack – was a trainee monk having just taken a strict vow of celibacy. Or that he was gay. Yes, gay would have been nice. I could have lived with gay.

Instead, he's on a date with Valentina, and that is the worst character reference anyone could have. Every man she goes out with, without exception, is obsessed with looks (his own and hers), hangs on her every word and has the intellectual capacity of a wheelie bin.

Action Man, Jack, Whatever Your Name Is: you can be as beautiful as you like, but unfortunately that's now about the only positive thing I can say about you.

I look over to the bar and realize to my horror that Joe, Gareth and Peter are huddled together talking, apparently having formed an Ex-Boyfriends' Club. They're probably comparing voodoo dolls.

'You haven't seen Grace, have you?' asks Charlotte, her soft voice snapping me out of my trance. 'The photographer is waiting for her.'

'I'll go and look for her,' I say, glad of a distraction.

I finally find Grace in the marquee where the wedding breakfast is being prepared.

'I should be the world authority on wedding etiquette by now, I've read so many bridal magazines, but things are still going wrong.'

My friend is holding a champagne glass in one hand and rocking Scarlett with the other.

'What now?' I ask.

'There has been a mix-up with the table plans,' she says, blowing a stray bit of hair from her face. 'When I sent them over to the hotel last week, the edge was apparently chopped off the top table, including where Patrick's mum and dad were meant to be sitting. Now they've not set up a table big enough to accommodate them and they can't change it without dismantling the whole thing.'

'Didn't they wonder where the groom's mother and father were?'

'I think they assumed they were dead,' she says.

'Well, why don't Charlotte and I just step down from the top table?' I suggest. 'The staff can easily slot us both onto other tables. That way, Polly can still be up there with you, and there will be enough room for Patrick's mum and dad.'

'Don't you mind?' she asks, looking relieved.

'Of course not,' I tell her. 'Rather that than spark a diplomatic incident with your new in-laws.'

'You're a star, Evie,' she says. 'Remind me to ask you to be a bridesmaid at all my future weddings!'

Only after the photos have been taken do I get to have a look at the amended table plan and realize exactly what I've let myself in for.

They've put me next to Jack and Valentina.

Chapter 11

Charlotte and I are heading to our tables when we overhear Valentina talking to one of the ushers.

'Kelly Brook? Oh, that's funny, because most people tell me I look like one of the Victoria's Secret models . . .'

We exchange glances. 'Perhaps she's a little insecure,' Charlotte says.

I launch into a coughing fit. 'Sorry . . . Valentina couldn't be more secure if she were padlocked and guarded by MI5.'

Charlotte giggles.

'Anyway, let's see who's on your table. Oh, lucky you!' I say, nudging her.

Charlotte has been put next to Jim, Grace's favourite cousin. He's a trainee cameraman with the BBC, who has been roped into doing the wedding video today. Although he's a year or two younger than us, he is warm and friendly, with soft fair hair, nice eyes and a face that's pleasing to look at, rather than brashly handsome. Secretly, I have always thought he would make a perfect boyfriend for Charlotte.

'Jim's lovely, you know,' I tell her, not very subtly. Charlotte blushes and looks away. She does this all the time – often for little apparent reason – and I know that she despairs of this trait.

'What's up?' I say softly. 'You have been introduced to Jim, haven't you?'

'Er, yes,' she replies. 'I've met him once or twice before.'

'Don't you think he's nice?' I add.

'Hmm,' she says, her cheeks now the colour of a full-bodied Valpolicella. I strongly suspect my friend has a crush.

'You could do worse, you know,' I tell her.

'I don't know what you mean,' she says, fiddling with sequins on her bag.

Charlotte has only ever had one boyfriend – Gordon, a damp-proofing specialist. I was desperate to like him, but genuinely the man was uniquely lacking in the ability to say a single interesting thing. His one talent was that he could tell you everything you never wanted to know about the differences between dry and wet rot, which, believe me, are many and varied. That was years ago, however, and Charlotte is more than overdue another romantic liaison.

Before we sit down to eat, I go to powder my nose and triple check for cabbage in my front teeth, and that I haven't accidentally tucked my skirt into my knickers. Then I take a deep breath and head back to the marquee to locate table five. Jack is already there by himself. I contemplate making a diversion so I'm not left talking to him alone, but he sees me and raises his eyebrows casually in recognition.

My heart flutters. Then, I remind myself: being stuck next to Valentina's eye candy will be anything but fun.

Chapter 12

'It's the bridesmaid with the big voice,' says Jack cheerfully as I approach our table.

'Am I not going to be allowed to forget that?' I reply uneasily.

'I won't mention it again, I promise,' he smiles. 'So, how do you know the bride?'

I've chit-chatted with enough of Valentina's beaux over the years to know that the next couple of hours are likely to be as excruciating as a dodgy Brazilian wax. But I tell myself to be polite.

'We went to Liverpool University together,' I say, before realizing he appears to be waiting for me to elaborate. 'We shared a house in the last two years.'

'But you're not from Liverpool originally?' he asks, studying my accent.

'Not far,' I say. 'About forty-five minutes north.'

'It's a great city,' he says. 'I love it.'

'So you don't live there yourself?' I ask, annoyed with myself for wanting to know.

'I've just moved there for work.'

Under other circumstances, I'd pursue this as a line of conversation, but instead find myself saying: 'I didn't know Valentina had a new boyfriend.'

He looks surprised at the description.

'Oh, I ... well, we've only been out together once before,' Jack tells me. 'I'm a member of her tennis club.'

I look up to see Valentina flouncing towards us as if she's at Paris Fashion Week, before sitting down and putting her hand conspicuously on Jack's knee. Our conversation comes to an abrupt halt.

'I'm really not sure about this dress,' she muses, inching the hem up. 'Jack, what do you think? I can't decide whether it shows off too much leg.'

She crosses her legs slowly – to show exactly how much leg there is. Jack's eyes are drawn to them momentarily, before he looks away.

The other guests on our table start to arrive, beginning with two of Grace's great aunts. Auntie Sylvia and Auntie Anne are both lovely, tiny women who are dressed today as visions of dusty pink and powder blue, respectively. They both have huge hats, candyfloss perms and meticulously co-ordinated outfits that look like the sort of thing you'd find in a catalogue distributed with the *Mail on Sunday*.

Their husbands, Uncle Giles and Uncle Tom, have spruced themselves up just as much as their wives, although without quite the same panache. Uncle Tom has made a daring attempt at a comb-over, with just a handful of straggly hairs clinging to his scalp for dear life. I'm finding it difficult to tear my eyes away from it.

'Hiya, love,' says a voice I recognize immediately.

I leap up and hug Georgia, another of my old university friends, who is here with her new fiancé, Pete.

Georgia is a millionaire in waiting, but to the untrained ear you'd never guess it.

Her dad grew up on a council estate in Blackburn and is a self-made man who owns one of the largest recycling companies in Europe. They must be the most down-to-earth family on the Sunday Times Rich List. Don't get me wrong, she likes spending as much as the rest of us, but she's also exceptionally generous, knows the price of a pint of milk and sometimes gives the impression that she's not entirely comfortable with her wealth.

'So, how's your practice-run as a bridesmaid been, Evie?' she asks.

'Good,' I tell her. 'I might even have worked out what I'm meant to be doing by the time it's your wedding.'

Georgia and I were briefly in a band together at uni and after we left, although she moved to London, we stayed firmly in touch. We didn't see nearly as much of her as we would have liked, of course, but that's all changed in the last couple of months since the preparations for *her* wedding really got underway.

We have had to meet up for so many dress fittings I'm starting to imagine what it must feel like to be a shop dummy.

'I love your outfit, by the way,' I tell her.

Georgia always looks fantastic. Today she is wearing a cream suit which I'd guess is YSL – her favourite – and a simple pendant with a pear-shaped diamond that sits in her clavicle.

'Cheers, love,' she says. 'It was from Top Shop.'

I smile. If that suit is from Top Shop then I'm a world champion Sumo wrestler. But I'm not going to be the one to 'out' her.

When our first course arrives, Jack turns and asks if I could pass the pepper. But as I reach over for it, Valentina interrupts.

'Don't worry, Evie, I've got one here,' she says, touching Jack's arm as she hands it to him. 'You know,' she says, lowering her voice and closing in on him, 'I've read somewhere that pepper is supposed to be an aphrodisiac.'

I don't know why, but my appetite has suddenly left me.

Chapter 13

'Tell me, Pete,' says Valentina to Georgia's fiancé. 'Are you interested in tennis?'

'I'm what you'd call an armchair fan,' Pete replies as Georgia splutters into her drink.

'What he means is that the last time he played he was so unfit he nearly ended up in casualty,' she says.

'Thanks for your support, love, it's touching,' he jokes.

'I'd be delighted to give you a lesson,' says Valentina, handing over one of her business cards. 'I've done some fabulous work on Jack's forehand, as I'm sure he'll tell you. Not that Jack's forehand wasn't pretty good in the first place,' she adds, flashing a suggestive smile.

We're onto the dessert course when Jack turns to talk to me. He's attempted to do this on several occasions, only to be hauled back into conversation with Valentina as if she's got him on a set of reins. So far, she's asked him to check whether her lipstick is smudged no less than four times.

The only person with whom he's managed a conversation is Pete, when they shared a brief discussion about their passion for rugby. It ended abruptly, however, when Pete suggested he join him in an executive box next weekend. The invitation was for a single spare place.

All of this means that I'm left to talk to Uncle Giles on my right. He seems a lovely man, gentle and softly-spoken, but to be absolutely brutal, if I hear another word about his collection of nineteenth-century shotguns I may have to ask if I can borrow one to put myself out of my misery.

'Vintage shotguns have been my thing since I was a teenager, you see,' he tells me.

'You'd get an ASBO for that these days,' I joke. He frowns and moves on to a long and detailed story about a twelve-bore boxlock ejector, whatever one of those is.

I take the opportunity of this interlude to have a peek at what Charlotte is up to on table fourteen, and am pleased to see that she and Jim are deep in conversation. At least, Jim is. Charlotte is shredding her napkin nervously and is now surrounded by so many bits it looks as if she's just come in from a blizzard.

Chapter 14

Grace's dad looks overwhelmed with relief as he sits down after delivering the shortest, quietest speech in the history of wedding speeches. It was difficult to make out much of what he was mumbling, but we all laughed at the one identifiable joke and clapped furiously at the end.

Next up is Patrick, who is used to public speaking and looks significantly more comfortable than his new father-in-law did. He straightens his jacket – the tails he didn't really want to wear today – and runs a hand through his thick blond hair. Grace looks up at him proudly.

'May I say on behalf of both myself and … *my wife*,' he begins, grinning at Grace's new title, 'how delighted we are that so many of you have made it here today. Grace and I have been together for the last seven years, and I can honestly say that every day I think to myself how lucky she is to have met me …'

The room collapses into laughter at what turns out to be the first of many of Patrick's acceptably lame quips.

Only when he is nearing the end of his speech do I find myself glancing at Jack. I know it's a ridiculous thing to do. His date is sitting right next to him and I've already decided I'm not interested.

But I'm somehow drawn to that perfectly imperfect face as a smile appears on his lips and he turns to me, as the room erupts into rapturous applause.

I snap away my gaze and join in the clapping.

'Have you been a bridesmaid before?' Jack asks, as Valentina has a momentary lapse in conversation.

'Never. Have you?'

He shakes his head. 'I was a pageboy once, but velvet culottes and a dickie bow aren't a good look when you're fifteen. I didn't enjoy it much.'

I find myself laughing. 'Well,' I say, 'it *is* the rule at weddings that everyone else involved in the ceremony has to look rubbish so that they don't upstage the bride.'

He raises his eyebrows. 'So what went wrong with you?'

Before I can even contemplate an answer to this, Valentina grabs him by the hand and whisks him up from the table.

'You still haven't met the bride and groom properly,' she says firmly. Jack has little choice but to go with her, although I'm certain I detect a slight frown as he does so.

'So, Evie,' says Uncle Giles, interrupting my thoughts. 'You were asking about barrels earlier.'

Was I?

I spend the next ten minutes politely trying to extract myself from Uncle Giles and when I eventually do, I head straight for the ladies' where I know I'm safe. Grace is already in there and we go into adjacent cubicles.

'Jack's a bit of all right, isn't he?' she shouts over.

'He's very much Valentina's type,' I say dismissively.

Grace pauses. 'What, you mean thick?' she asks. 'I don't think he is, actually. Val says he went to Oxford and is now the boss of some charity or other.'

I silently unravel some loo roll. Okay, so he's been to a posh university and has a good job. He's probably one of those clever people with no common sense.

'Evie?' Grace says.

'Yeah?' I reply.

'Oh, you'd just gone quiet, that's all.'

We come out of our cubicles simultaneously and she looks at me, narrowing her eyes accusingly.

'What?' I ask.

'You fancy him,' she says.

I take on the indignant air of someone wrongly accused of farting in a lift. 'I do *not!*' I say, and march over to the sink to wash my hands.

'Look, don't worry, your secret's safe with me. Just don't tell Valentina. She's still miffed because I didn't make her a bridesmaid. You getting off with her date would send her over the edge.'

'Grace, I have absolutely no intention of *getting off* with anyone,' I say, slightly exasperated. 'Unless it's escaped your notice, you managed to invite three of my ex-boyfriends to this wedding, so it would hardly be appropriate even if it were true.'

'Only one of them was an ex when we drew up the invitation list,' she insists. 'You've managed to get through two others since then.'

'Well, look, Mrs Smug Newly Wed,' I say. 'Just because you've found a lovely bloke you fancy enough to spend the rest of your life with doesn't mean it happens quite so easily for all of us.'

'So none of the men you've ever been out with have been lovely?'

I frown. She knows she's got a point.

'Look,' she says. 'Maybe you just need to alter your expectations a bit. The initial romance wears off in any relationship.'

'Faster in mine than most though,' I say, feeling thoroughly depressed now.

She smiles and raises her eyebrows. 'Anyway, if you did fancy Jack . . .' she says.

'I don't!' I interrupt.

'Well, I'm just saying *if* you did . . . I wouldn't worry about Valentina too much. He's apparently just split up with his long-term girlfriend. At the most the thing with Valentina will be just a couple of dates, maybe a shag.'

I pause for a second, determined not to give too much away. Grace's words get me wondering though.

'So,' I say idly as we head back, 'you do think they're shagging then?'

Chapter 15

Nice Cousin Jim is taking a break from filming guests and is standing at the bar alone.

'Hi, Jim. Er, where's Charlotte?' I ask. I'd rather hoped by now that he'd be huddled in a corner whispering some of Byron's juicier poetry into her ear.

'I'm not sure,' he says. 'I haven't seen her since dinner. Can I get you a drink?'

'I'm fine.' I pause and sip my wine. 'She's lovely, Charlotte, isn't she?'

'Yes,' he agrees. 'She is.'

'I honestly don't think I've ever known anyone so kind, or generous, or generally fantastic.' I hope I'm not laying it on a bit thick but he laughs.

'She's a really nice girl, no doubt about that.'

'Oh, there she is now,' he says, pointing to the other side of the marquee, where Charlotte is deep in conversation with Grace's mother. I frown.

Oh Charlotte, what am I going to do with you?

'Is everything all right?' asks Jim.

'Er, yes – why?'

'You were shaking your head, that's all.'

'Oh, was I?' I say. 'Sorry. Er, I was just thinking about . . . council tax rises. Tsk, terrible, aren't they? Would you excuse me?'

I begin to cross the marquee when a familiar voice stops me in my tracks.

'Evie, *there* you are.'

I turn around slowly. It's Gareth. And it's the first time we've spoken since our break-up.

'Listen,' he says. 'I really think we need to talk.'

Oh, God. Do we?

'Don't look so worried,' he chuckles.

'I'm not!' I say brightly, though, actually, I very much am. I've been avoiding Gareth all day, because I instinctively knew he'd want to have a discussion about 'our relationship'.

'I really think we need to have a discussion about *our relationship*,' he says.

'I'm not sure now's a good time, Gareth.'

'It's as good a time as any,' he says firmly. We first met through my mum's fiancé Bob, who works with him and, I'll be honest if I'd known it was going to pan out like this I wouldn't have bothered. 'I really do think it's important. The thing is, Evie, I've just got to know something.'

'Oh?' I say, scanning the room for an escape route.

'The reason you split up with me. Was it,' he looks around to see if anyone is listening, 'was it *the underwear?*'

A group of guests a couple of tables away start laughing and, even though I know they can't hear us, I shift uncomfortably. Just the thought of the underwear – his hideous Valentine present purchased from a dubious website under their '*Hot and Horny*' section. I never did try it on but couldn't help thinking that, even with the two big holes in the chest as ventilation, all that rubber had the potential to induce one hell of a rash.

'I can't pretend I wouldn't have preferred La Perla, Gareth. But no,' I add hastily, not wanting to appear cold-hearted, 'it really wasn't that.'

But it's too late. His puppy-dog eyes are looking at me as if I'm a vivisectionist.

'Then what, Evie?' he wails. 'For God's sake, what was it?' Then Gareth begins to sniff, producing a series of long, loud grunting noises that sound like a cappuccino machine on the verge of spontaneous combustion. This can only mean one thing: we're heading for emotional meltdown.

'Don't cry,' I plead, grabbing his hand. I mean it too. And not just because Grace's Uncle Tom and Auntie Anne are looking over.

Gareth produces a threadbare piece of tissue from his pocket and gives his nose the most almighty blow, before chucking it idly on the table next to us. I try to concentrate on what he's saying, but suddenly find it difficult to focus on anything other than the contents of his hankie, which looks like something from *Ghostbusters*.

'I'm not going to cry,' he says with a brave, wobbly smile. 'I'm not going to cry.'

Then he pauses for a second. *'Ohhh! Evieee!'* he blubs.

I pull my eyes away from the tissue, suddenly torn between despising myself and being desperate to get out of there. There is only one thing for it. I turn to Gareth, grab his arm and look intensely into his eyes.

'Gareth,' I say, gripping his elbow. 'We *do* need to talk about this. You're absolutely right.'

He looks surprised.

'Oh,' he says. 'You agree then? That we ought to talk?'

'Absolutely. But the thing is, I can't. Not just now anyway. I've got to go and help Grace's mum ...' I scan the room for inspiration '... with the napkins.'

A frown deepens above his nose.

'What do you need to do with the napkins?' he asks.

'They're a fire hazard,' I say authoritatively. 'You can't just go leaving that amount of paper around the place, it's against EU regulations. One stray spark and this place will be like *The Towering Inferno*.'

He scrunches up his face.

'Sorry Gareth. We'll catch up soon. *Promise*.'

Chapter 16

Charlotte spent the first eighteen years of her life in a dormer bungalow in Widnes, which is Cheshire, but not the posh part where all the footballers live and few of the women's breasts are real.

She had two loving parents who stayed together for the sake of the children for so long they almost forgot they couldn't stand the sight of each other. These days, she works for the Inland Revenue doing ... well, I must admit I've never quite worked out what she does exactly. And, despite her shyness, when you get her alone, she's all those things I told Jim she was – and more.

'So, how come you went off chatting to Grace's mum?' I ask her casually, after I've finally prized her away from an in-depth conversation about why gypsy grass has gone out of fashion.

'Why not?' she asks.

'Well,' I say, wondering how to put this, 'I just thought you and Jim looked like you were having a nice chat, that's all.'

She looks slightly confused. 'Well, we were. But then I had a nice chat with Mrs Edwards too.'

'Okay, what about?' I ask, feeling that this has got to be challenged.

She frowns. 'Sudoku, mainly.'

I pause. 'Sudoku?'

She shrugs. 'Yes. Well, why not?'

'Do you like Sudoku?' I ask.

'Well, no.'

'Have you ever even played it?'

'Um, no.'

'Do you have any interest in it whatsoever?'

'No, but I don't mind talking about it.'

'Charlotte,' I say, 'unless you're going to tell me that Mrs Edwards has a black belt in Sudoku, I can't see how that can be more interesting than talking to Jim.'

She blushes as she realizes what I'm getting at.

'He thinks you're lovely. He told me.'

I can tell I've sparked her interest.

'It's true, I promise.'

'We just sat next to each other, that's all,' she says.

'And so – what was he saying?'

'Okay, okay,' she says, taking a deep breath. 'Well, we were talking a lot about music.'

'And?' I prompt.

'Well, he loves Macy Gray and plays the guitar in his spare time.'

'Just like you!' I exclaim.

'I can't play the guitar.'

'No, but you love Macy Gray.'

'*David* Gray,' she corrects me.

'Don't split hairs,' I tell her. 'Honestly, you were made for each other. Come on, come back over and have a chat with him.'

We are suddenly distracted by some male voices coming from beyond the pillar next to us. It's not that they are being particularly loud – it's hardly quiet in here anyway – but the content of their discussion is something we can't help overhearing.

'It's a shame I'm not a single man any more,' one of them is saying. 'Some of the women here you wouldn't kick out of bed. The one who did the reading was bloody *spectacular*.'

I roll my eyes. The only thing more annoying than Valentina trying to attract so much attention is the fact that she usually succeeds.

'That bridesmaid was a bit of all right, too – the one with the dirty-blonde hair,' says the other – and I realize they're talking about me. 'A bit flat-chested but definitely fit.'

Talk about a backhanded compliment. I tut and am about to go back to my favourite topic of conversation when another voice chips in.

'What about the other one though – the fat bird?' says a voice.

My eyes widen. I know immediately who they're talking about.

'Who, Shrek's ugly sister?'

They fall about laughing and I listen, dumbstruck, as Charlotte's face crumples. I try to think of something to do to stop her hearing what I fear may be coming next.

'I wonder how many pies you have to eat, to fill a dress that size?' someone else sniggers.

'Enough to bankrupt Wigan if she ever gave up!'

Charlotte's cheeks are blazing.

'Right, that's it,' I declare, not knowing exactly what I'm going to say to them, but certain that I've got to do something.

'Evie, please don't,' Charlotte implores me.

'Why not?'

'Because you'll just make it worse,' she says. 'Please don't make me any more embarrassed than I am.'

'*You've* got nothing to be embarrassed about,' I tell her.

'Please, Evie,' she repeats. 'Just leave it.'

I briefly consider not doing anything, but when I hear what comes next, I swiftly change my mind.

'Imagine shagging that. It would be like getting stuck under a giant airbag.'

'Evie,' says Charlotte, her eyes welling up. 'Please don't say anything. I beg of you.'

I step beyond the pillar and come face to face with the three men, still not having a clue what to do. I'm looking directly at them, but they're completely oblivious.

I know I can't betray Charlotte, but I've got to shut them up. Quickly.

What I do next is something spontaneous. You could call it instinct. You could call it madness. Either way, it works . . . on a certain level.

I throw my drink over them.

Actually, it's more than a throw; I shake it up and down like I'm celebrating a Formula One victory, leaving them furious, bewildered and picking bits of lemon out of their hair.

'Whoops! I slipped,' I mumble, spinning round to grab Charlotte's elbow and make a sharp exit. As we start to make our way through the crowd, I soon realize that the crowd has in fact become *an audience*. Grace's Uncle Giles is looking at me as if I'm psychotic. Little Polly's eyes are almost popping out. But the worst is yet to come.

'Did you do that on purpose?' whispers Valentina gleefully, clearly as amused as everyone else is amazed.

'Of course not, don't be silly,' I reply, glancing at Jack by her side.

I wonder if what I've just said would convince anyone. The look on his face would tend to indicate not.

Chapter 17

Common sense tells me I really ought to stop drinking after that little display, but the glass of champagne Grace has just poured for me is about the only thing I've got to take solace in at the moment.

'So you think Charlotte's okay now?' asks Grace, when I've brought her up to date.

'Who knows?' I say. 'I dragged her to the ladies' straight after it happened, but she didn't really want to talk about it, no matter how much I tried. She just kept saying she was fine. Obviously, I could tell she wasn't, but you know what Charlotte's like when she closes up: I don't think even the SAS could get any information out of her when she's made her mind up not to talk.'

I pick up a handful of peanuts from the bowl in front of us and as I start to pop them in my mouth, Patrick appears and tenderly kisses Grace on the cheek.

'Hello, wife,' he whispers.

'Husband. How the hell are you?' she asks, kissing him back.

'All the better for being a married man,' he tells her.

'Oh, for God's sake,' I complain. 'You're putting me off my nuts.'

'We're married now, so if we want to snog in public we can,' Patrick replies. 'It's all official.'

'You're not meant to *snog* in public when you're married,' I tell him. 'You're meant to *row* in public – didn't anyone tell you?'

Patrick sits down to join us.

'So how do you feel?' I want to know. 'Different?'

'What do you mean?' he asks.

'I mean,' I say, 'now you're a married man, do you feel different from yesterday – when you were young, free and single?'

'I was still thirty-four yesterday,' he says. 'But in answer to your question, I'm not sure exactly. I don't think so – not yet, anyway. Although ask me tomorrow – I might thoroughly regret the whole thing.'

Grace digs him in the ribs.

'Do *you* feel different?' he asks Grace, obviously not certain about what he wants the answer to be.

'Yeah,' she says, holding his gaze. 'Good different.'

Grace had had a couple of 'serious' boyfriends before Patrick, one in sixth form and another at university. Both lasted for over two years, but it was obvious that neither was 'the one'.

It's not that they weren't nice. They were probably *too* nice.

Patrick, meanwhile, had a bit of a bad boy reputation. There was always a slight but discernible air of recklessness about him, which was partly to do with the motorbike he rode, but also the fact that he was a serial heartbreaker. There was a time when he dated so many women he'd make George Clooney look like the Pope.

Which has always been heartening for someone like me. Because if Patrick, former confirmed bachelor and committed Lothario, can fall in love, have two children, stay faithful for seven years and get married, there must be hope for someone as hopeless as me.

'Doesn't look like this wedding's going to be consummated tonight,' Grace tells me later, looking over at Patrick as he sways slightly while talking to some guests.

'But it's your first night as man and wife,' I argue. 'It's *got* to be a toe-curler. Those are the rules.'

'Yes, but Patrick's had a skinful of booze,' she says, shaking her head. 'I don't think even my new Agent Provocateur undies are going to be sufficient tonight.'

'I thought those things came with a certificate guaranteeing seduction,' I say, though as he sways again, I realize she might be right.

The only thing that's likely to spark him into action tonight is a defibrillator.

'Mummy, will you come and dance with me?' asks Polly, tugging at Grace's skirt.

'When the disco starts, I promise I will,' she says. 'I've still got to say hello to some people.'

'It's starting now, Mummy,' she insists.

She's about to go with Polly when I say: 'Aren't you supposed to be up there for a first dance?'

'Oh . . . you're right.' She looks down at Polly. 'I promise I'll dance with you next, darling.'

Putting her champagne down, Grace grabs Patrick by the hand. I follow them to the edge of the dance floor, as the other guests gather around and the music for their first dance starts.

'Evie, will *you* dance with me?' Polly pleads, tugging at my skirt now.

'I can't really, sweetheart,' I tell her. 'It's your mummy and daddy's first dance. Nobody else is meant to join in just yet.'

'Why not?'

'That's just the way it is,' I reply, realizing that this isn't a very philosophically constructed argument.

'That's stupid,' she says sulkily. 'Muuummm!' she shouts. 'I want to dance too!'

The guests next to her start chuckling. It's a good job she's cute.

Patrick pulls Grace towards him dramatically and swings her down so her back is arched *à la* Scarlett O'Hara. It's only the fact that he nearly drops her that betrays his state of intoxication. In some ways it adds to the display, although I suspect from Grace's expression that she's concerned he's going to break her neck.

The guests are certainly lapping it up, and the clapping and cheering get louder as Patrick swings Grace across the dance floor, obviously reckoning he'd give Fred Astaire a run for his money.

I look down and suddenly realize I've lost Polly. I'm not overly concerned as she's been running around all day, but I am surprised that she's given up on finding a dance partner so easily.

However, as I look back at the dance floor, I soon spot her little figure.

She's found someone to dance with.

Chapter 18

Jack has lifted four-year-old Polly up by the waist so that her shoes are three feet off the ground.

He's gently spinning her around in a small corner of the dance floor, to make sure they don't upstage the bride and groom. But to be honest, that's a bit difficult. Because the eyes of virtually every woman in the place are glued on him.

They're mesmerized by the strength of Jack's arms as he keeps tight hold of Polly, by his gentle eyes as he smiles at her and the muscular curve of his back through his shirt, now his jacket has been discarded.

At least, I imagine that's what they're mesmerized by.

'Come and join us!' shouts Grace, beckoning Jack and Polly into the centre of the dance floor with them.

Polly looks as if all her Christmases and birthdays have come at once, as Jack twirls her around and around in the centre the dance floor while she giggles uproariously, loving the attention. When the song finishes and Jack puts Polly down, I make a decision. I'm going to go and talk to him.

I know he's with Valentina. I know I've made an idiot of myself today. I know I've got three ex-boyfriends hovering about. But it doesn't matter. I have got to talk to him, if only for one reason: to prove to myself that my instinct was right. That the very fact of him being here with Valentina makes him as dim-witted and shallow as everyone else she's ever gone out with. Regardless of whether he's an Oxford-educated chief executive. Of a charity.

I take a deep breath and start walking towards him. But suddenly, there is a tap on my shoulder and I spin around.

'Evie, I really must insist on five minutes of your time.'

Oh, no.

'There's still so much we need to say to each other.'

This is getting ridiculous.

'Somehow, we've kept missing each other all day,' Gareth tells me, with an expression so pained he looks constipated. 'I don't know how. But anyway, I've caught you now. So we can talk properly.'

'Gareth,' I say, 'I know we need to talk. I know.'

'So, how about it then?' he asks.

'Now just really isn't a good time.'

'I'm starting to get the impression that you're avoiding me, Evie,' he says, narrowing his eyes.

'Me?' I am a picture of innocence. 'Honestly, I'm not. It's just that . . . I need to go and choose some music.'

He screws up his face. 'But they've hired a DJ,' he objects.

'Oh no, the DJ came free with the hotel. They threw him in with the chicken drumsticks. The problem is, he'll only play Neil Diamond tracks unless you tell him otherwise. I mean, I love "Cracklin' Rosie" as much as the next person, but sometimes you just need a bit of Kylie. So I've got to go. Sorry.'

'Wait,' he says, and grabs my hand. 'I . . . I have something for you.'

'What?' I ask, a familiar feeling of dread washing over me. He suddenly looks intense. 'I know you well enough by now to suspect that this is what you wanted all along, deep down. You were just too shy to say it. Some men might think it too soon. But I'm not *some men* Evie.'

'What are you talking about, Gareth?'

But it's at that moment that it dawns on me exactly what he's about to give me. He's got an engagement ring, I know it! He thinks I want to get married. He has that demented glint in his eye.

'Oh Gareth, no,' I gulp, as he reaches into his inside pocket. 'I mean, you've got me wrong. I'm just not ready. I'll *never* be ready.'

'You don't have to fib about it, Evie. There's really no need.'

He smiles and whips out the contents of his pocket like a matador, as all the blood drains from my face.

It's the *Hot and Horny* underwear.

Which is about the only thing I'd rather see less than an engagement ring.

Chapter 19

It's 12.05 a.m. and somehow I feel vaguely sober. Or perhaps the shenanigans with Gareth just sent me into shock.

As we'd stood there in the middle of the marquee, he brandishing *Hot and Horny*'s finest as everybody else bopped around to 'Sweet Caroline', I can honestly say that I have never been more acutely aware of my surroundings.

There was really only one thing for it.

I snatched *the underwear* from Gareth's hand, turned around and ran out of the marquee as fast as my legs could carry me – until, that is, I crashed straight into Auntie Sylvia and Auntie Anne.

They glared at what I was holding and, fortunately, looked bewildered. I'm hoping they assumed it was a bin bag, or some waterproof outdoor gear, though admittedly I have no explanation as to why I'd be walking round with either at a wedding.

The offending item is now stuffed into a sanitary-towel bin in the ladies' cloakroom, which is hopefully where it will stay until someone wearing protective clothing comes to take it away to be incinerated, along with everything else in there. Which I can't help thinking feels like a fitting end for its existence.

I have been laying low for the last couple of hours. Which means that, not only have I managed to give Gareth the slip, but it's also allowed me to quietly witness a number of highlights elsewhere in the party.

Valentina has been the star of the show. In fact, courtesy of her new friends Moët & Chandon, she has provided more entertainment in the last hour or so than a travelling circus. As I sit at a table at the side of the dance floor, perfectly happy to have some solitude, I watch in amusement as she high-kicks her way around Uncle Tom.

'Can I join you?'

It's Jack.

'Yes. Sure. Absolutely. Why not?' I gabble.

As he pulls up a chair, our eyes are drawn back to the dance floor, where Valentina has now moved on to the Can-Can.

'I think you may have stolen the show before with your dancing,' I say.

'It was Polly who stole the show,' he smiles. I'm not so sure. 'So, I believe you're a reporter at the *Daily Echo*?'

I take a sip of my drink and nod, and then look to see what his reaction is. Some people, believe it or not, don't like journalists.

'The reason I ask is that I've been in the *Daily Echo* myself a couple of times,' he goes on.

'You're not a convicted criminal, are you?' I ask.

'They've not caught me yet.' He laughs. 'I work for a charity called Future for Africa,' he explains. 'We create sustainable projects in the third world – helping farmers to help themselves – as well as running refugee camps. Your paper did a fantastic feature about us just over a year ago. It was a double-page spread. We couldn't have bought the publicity.'

Over the next forty minutes, in the amber glow of wedding tea lights, I learn a lot about Jack. And, I'm ashamed to say, that my initial suspicions about him couldn't have been more wrong.

Despite his high-flying job and hard-to-place accent, he went to a comprehensive where the average GCSE grade would only get you a job asking, 'Would you like fries with that?' a hundred times a day.

He was the first person in his family to go to university, and that university happened to be Oxford, where he got a First in History. He travelled all over the world in a gap year, before finally landing a job with the charity at which he is now chief executive.

He is a lapsed vegetarian (the smell of bacon after a night out saw the end of it) who reads about two books a week – everything from Dickens to Lee Child.

The only thing he watches on TV is old episodes of *Frasier*, and instead he listens to so much radio that he's embarrassed to say he knows exactly what is happening in *The Archers* in any given week. He is obsessed with sport, and he loves spicy food (especially Thai), expensive red wine and tortilla chips.

Oh yes, and he's recovering from a broken heart.

Chapter 20

The details about Jack's break-up are relatively thin. It happened recently. They'd been together a while. There's no chance of them getting back together.

I sit and nod, taking it all in, looking as if I empathize thoroughly, as if I know *exactly* what he's going through. But, obviously, nothing could be further from the truth. I haven't got the foggiest what he's going through, since the closest I've ever been to having a 'serious' relationship is with the woman who has highlighted my hair for the last five years.

It hasn't all been about him though. I have found myself over-sharing all kinds of information – telling him about the dad I can't remember, about my pursuit of a great journalistic career, and about the fact that I'd only had time to shave one leg before we walked down the aisle. (I regretted saying this immediately, but fortunately he just chuckled.)

'What's it like, being at a wedding where you hardly know anyone?' I ask him.

'I've enjoyed it. You soon get to know people. There's you, for a start,' he says, and something inside my stomach jumps. 'And Pete and I have become friends for life tonight. I've never met anyone before who's quite as obsessed about rugby as I am.'

'Do you play yourself?' I ask.

'Yeah, I do. I know being wrestled to the ground by fifteen blokes every Saturday isn't everyone's idea of fun, but I love it.'

I can't work out whether it is prompted by this image, or by the fact that I have finally drunk too much champagne, but I do feel very hot all of a sudden.

'You two – together again! Humph. I'm shtarting to think I should be getting jealous!'

You might have thought Valentina would have sobered up now, after all that dancing. Not on the evidence before us.

'I think I've got a bit dirty shomehow,' she says, flopping onto Jack's knee.

'Have you had a good dance?' I ask politely.

She lifts up her skirt to demonstrate that the back of one leg and the front of the other is covered in a black streak of grime. 'Yesh, but I have absholutely no idea how this could poshhhibly have happened. Have you, Evie?' she asks me.

Jack, who is trying to ensure she doesn't fall off his knee and injure herself, looks over to me.

'I think it's because you did the splits, Valentina,' I say.

'The splits? Did I really? Ha!'

She grabs Jack's glass, obviously realizing it's been minutes since she last had something to drink, and almost slides onto the floor in the process. He manages to stop her, but not easily. His temples redden slightly as he helps her to her feet and throws her arm around his neck to support her.

'I think I'd better get Valentina back to the B and B,' he says.

'Yeah. Of course.'

'Jack, I . . . think . . . I think . . . we should go and have a good old dancsh,' says Valentina, her head wobbling from side to side. He pulls her in tighter to make sure he's not going to drop her.

'It was lovely meeting you,' he tells me.

'You too,' I reply.

'Enjoy the rest of the evening,' he adds.

'Oh, I think I'm going to go now anyway,' I shrug.

'Right,' he says.

'Yep,' I say.

'Bye.'

'Bye.'

And off he goes. With Valentina in his arms. Which feels horribly, horribly wrong.

When Jack has left, I scan the room to see if Charlotte is still around and realize that she must have gone to bed, like most of the other guests. The disco man is packing up now and I see no particular reason to hang around, especially as Gareth is still loitering somewhere.

As I lean over to pick up my bag, I spot something on the chair next to me. It's a phone. And it can only be Jack's.

Chapter 21

I manage to get down for breakfast just before they stop serving. Pale morning sunshine filters through the windows of the inn, cascading light across the slate floor and antique furniture. I find Patrick and Grace at a table in the chic, cosy dining room with bottle green walls, a peat fire and stacks of Sunday newspapers. When they've polished off generous helpings of smoked salmon and luscious scrambled eggs, I meet Grace at the juice table.

'How was your wedding night?' I ask.

'I've had more romantic experiences sitting on the tumble dryer,' she says, rolling her eyes as she pours a glass of orange. 'He couldn't even stand up, never mind get it up. Still, we have got two weeks in the Maldives to look forward to, so there's plenty of time for him to make it up to me.'

'Assuming his hangover wears off any time soon . . .' The

70

bags under Patrick's eyes currently look like they could be carrying a week's worth of shopping.

'So, how did you get on after we left?' she asks.

'What do you mean?'

She narrows her eyes. 'You know what I mean,' she says. 'I *mean* you and Jack.'

I look at her as if she couldn't have suggested anything more ludicrous.

'I don't know where you've got this idea from that I fancy Jack,' I say. 'I mean, he's very nice and all that . . .'

'Not thick – like I told you,' she interrupts.

'No, not thick,' I concede.

'Exceptionally good-looking,' she goes on.

I sniff. 'He's certainly what some people might call attractive,' I say.

'Including . . . you?' She raises her eyebrows.

'He's going out with Valentina!' I point out. 'Why are you trying to set me up with him?'

She shrugs her shoulders. 'I don't know, I've just got a feeling you'd be good together,' she says. Then she shakes her head. 'No, you're quite right, I don't know what I'm talking about.'

I pour myself some pear juice.

'So you *don't* think we'd be good together?' I mumble.

She laughs and puts her arm around me.

'He left his phone here by accident,' I tell her. 'So I've got the dubious pleasure of dropping it off at the Crown and Garter where he and Valentina are staying. I tried phoning her but there's no answer.'

Grace stifles a giggle. 'Good luck,' she says.

An hour later, I arrive at the reception of Valentina's pub and am greeted by a hotelier who looks approximately 130 years old.

'You think they may have already checked out?' I ask, Jack's mobile phone in my hand.

'I'm not sure,' he says, doddering over to a large, leather-bound diary. 'Edith tends to look after these things, you see. But she had her varicose veins done on Friday. So it's just me. I'm probably not as on top of things as she is.'

His shaking fingers turn the pages on to February of last year. 'I don't think we've got anybody by the name you're after,' he says. 'Are you sure you've got the right hotel?'

I help him turn the page. 'I think it's *this* February you need to look at,' I say gently, turning it to the right page. I scan its columns silently myself. 'Look, there they are,' I say, seeing Valentina's name. 'Room sixteen. So do you have a record of whether they've checked out?'

He frowns. 'I know I'm meant to,' he says, starting to look around the desk. 'But I think that's in another book. Edith is better at this sort of thing than me. Only, she had her varicose veins done on Friday.'

'Perhaps somebody could go and knock on their door. You know, to see if they're still there?'

'That's an idea,' he says, shutting the book. 'That would solve the problem!'

I smile. 'Great!'

'A very good idea,' he reiterates.

'So, will you ask someone to go up there?' I ask.

He thinks for a second. 'Oh, well I would, but I'm by myself. Edith has had her varicose veins done.'

'Could *you* go?' I suggest.

'Oh no,' he says. 'I need to man the desk in case there's a rush on. You see, Edith has—'

'Had her varicose veins done,' I say, before I can stop myself. 'Sorry.'

'That's okay,' he replies. 'Second door on the left as you head upstairs.'

'Pardon?'

'It's the only solution,' he explains. 'You'll have to go up and see them yourself.'

Chapter 22

The long, guttural snores emanating from room sixteen are audible from the other end of the corridor and bear a strong resemblance to a heavy-duty pneumatic drill. They can only mean one thing: Jack *must* be in there with Valentina.

I take a deep breath and bend down to study the bottom of the door and check if there is a gap big enough for me to slide the phone under and run. But there's a lip on the threshold blocking any such plan. There's no way around this. I'm going to have to knock and get this over with.

I bang my knuckles against the door in a series of short, sharp thuds, before standing back.

But, it's clear after a minute that nobody is coming to the door – and the volcanic snoring continues. Taking another deep breath, I try again, this time hammering with more conviction, before standing back and waiting.

Eventually, I realize this is all in vain. And a more direct approach is in order.

'Valentina!' I shout, pounding on the door with my fist.

The snores come to an abrupt halt. Someone is stirring.

'Um . . . is Jack in there? I've got his phone, that's all,' I say awkwardly.

As the door swings open, I steel myself to get this over with as quickly as possible.

'Jack—' I begin.

But it isn't Jack.

'*What?* Oooh. What time is it?'

Valentina looks as if she has spent the night in the darker recesses of hell having her hair backcombed by a chimpanzee. Her eye make-up is smeared down both of her cheeks and her skin is a colour that I couldn't even describe as grey. It's *off grey*.

'Valentina,' I say. 'I wonder if you could give this to Jack for me? He left it at the Inn at Whitewell last night.'

'*What?*' she says. 'Oooh. Come in.'

'Oh God, no – no, really,' I say, unwilling to come face to face with a post-coital Jack rolling around Valentina's bed. 'Can't you just give it to him for me?'

But as she grabs me by the arm and hoists me into the room, I have very little choice in the matter. Inside is a scene of devastation, with clothes, shoes and bags scattered across the floor, bedsheets tangled up in a ball and a G-string that could be mistaken for dental floss hanging on the bathroom door.

As for Jack, he's nowhere to be seen.

Chapter 23

Valentina's room is generous in size, but the décor isn't entirely in keeping with the age of the hotel: synthetic bedspreads in a vivid shade of lilac, flocked wallpaper and pale pink carpet. She'd have had a fit if she'd seen my gorgeous room.

'Ohh . . . something doesn't feel right. I mean, I'm never at my best in the morning, but something *really* doesn't feel right today.'

'Are you okay?' I ask. I've never seen her with a hangover like this before.

'There's something wrong with my mouth,' she whimpers. 'It's . . . it's . . . *furry*. And it tastes like . . . like I've been licking a pavement. Ohhh no, it's not just my mouth, it's my head as well. My head is *throbbing*.'

'Well, you won't be the only one who feels as if their liver has been pickled this morning,' I point out.

Valentina tries to prize her right eye open, but it's cemented together with a gruesome combination of sleep and four layers of mascara.

'Are you suggesting I'm hungover?'

I pause for a second.

'Valentina, you single-handedly drank more than the average rugby team yesterday and it's taken me nearly ten minutes of banging on the door to wake you up. Call me Miss Marple, but, yes, I think you've got a hangover.'

'I never get hangovers,' she says dismissively as she unsuccessfully attempts to stand up unaided. 'Oh! Maybe I've developed some sort of illness that has caused my tongue to swell up and affect my vision. Maybe Jack gave it to me! He *has* just come back from one of his places in deepest Africa. Where's the bathroom?'

I help her up as she tries to make her way into the corner of the room. But Valentina takes a tumble and bangs her leg on a chair.

'Argghhh!' she screams.

'Oh dear,' I say.

'Argghhh!' she screams again.

'Oh, come on, it can't have hurt that much.' I am starting to run out of patience.

'I'm going to have a huge bruise on my leg now, which means I'll have to wear tights. I *hate* tights.'

'Well, I'm sure you can live with them for a few days if it means covering up such a horrendous disfigurement as . . . as a one-inch bruise,' I say.

When we get into the bathroom, she sits on the loo, unable to stand up in front of the mirror.

'Pass me my make-up bag, will you?' she croaks.

'Is it your chambermaid's day off?' I ask, but I pass it to her anyway.

Valentina starts rifling through her bag, throwing various items of cosmetic creams, powders and formulas onto the floor as she does so. I pick up one of them – an Estée Lauder cellulite serum – and idly examine the label.

'I haven't got cellulite, just for the record,' Valentina tells me. 'I'm taking precautions for later life.'

After surrounding herself in anti-wrinkle formulas, bronzing mitts, facial scrubs and God knows how many more cosmetic concoctions, she finally locates a bottle of Optrex and is about to start squirting it into her eyes.

'Don't you think you'd be better trying to get all that crap off your face first?' I suggest.

'What crap?' she asks.

'Your make-up,' I tell her.

Valentina stops what she's doing immediately.

'*Oh God!*' she squeals. '*WHAT will it have done to my pores?!*'

Valentina scrabbles to the sink and for the first time today sees her reflection. She gasps for air, almost speechless.

'Tell me this isn't happening . . .'

'Don't be ridiculous,' I say, as I pass her a wipe so she can start to take her make-up off. 'It's not that bad.'

'Do you really think so?' she asks pathetically.

'Well, you're no Brigitte Bardot this morning, I'll admit.'

'Ohhh!'

'But a nice shower will sort you out, I'm sure.'

'What's that?' Valentina says suddenly, peering at the back of her leg.

'Ah,' I say. 'You did the splits last night. Perhaps it's muck from the dance floor.'

She peels something away from the sole of her foot and inspects it closely.

'It's a cigarette butt,' she declares, before putting her head in her hands and starting to sob.

Chapter 24

Valentina has showered, dressed, and spent forty minutes applying concealer underneath her eyes. She looks much better than she did an hour ago, but when we go down to reception she is not in what you'd call a good mood.

'All I want is to check out. Sooner rather than later,' she sighs.

'Beautiful morning, isn't it?' smiles the elderly hotelier, not exactly moving at the speed of light.

'Lovely yes.' She lifts up her sunglasses briefly and winces at the light. 'Can we do whatever is needed to check out now?'

He begins slowly rooting through some paperwork. 'Have you managed to do any hiking during your stay?'

I stifle a giggle. Valentina is wearing a pair of £350 Gina shoes with Gucci jeans, and is carrying a top-of-the-range Louis Vuitton travel system.

'No, I haven't done any hiking,' she says, without even the hint of a smile.

'That's a pity,' he says. 'The views from Badger Wells Hill are magnificent.'

'Perhaps next time,' I tell him, gently.

'Is my bill nearly ready?' she asks tersely. 'I really do have to get going.'

'Oh, sorry, dear,' he says. 'Listen to me wittering on while you're waiting. Things will be much better when my wife Edith is back on her feet. She's just had her varicose veins done.'

'As a matter of interest,' Valentina says, 'the man I arrived with yesterday, Mr Williamson – *Jack* Williamson . . .'

'Strapping fellow with dark hair?'

'Yes, him. Has he checked out from his room yet?'

The hotelier thinks for a second. 'Oh yes, he left a long time ago. He was up bright and early, in fact.'

'Was he now?' says Valentina, obviously even less happy now.

'So do you want to take his mobile?' I ask when we get outside. 'I mean, I presume you're going to see him again soon?'

'I doubt it,' she says furiously. 'He's left without even saying goodbye to me. Never mind without *sleeping* with me. I don't know about you, Evie, but that's the sort of behaviour I don't tolerate on a second date.'

'Right,' I say, feeling a surge of optimism. 'I'll have to think of another way of getting it to him. Have you got his address? I'll take it round there myself.'

She thinks for a second, then snatches the phone from me.

'Now you mention it,' she says, 'I am going to have to go

round to see him. I need to arrange his next tennis session. So *I'll* take the phone.'

Valentina opens the boot of her car and starts piling her luggage into it.

'So . . . do you think you'll forgive him?' I ask, unable to stop myself. 'You know, for leaving without saying goodbye?'

She gets into her car, pulls down the visor to look in the mirror. 'Depends on what happens when I go and see him. How do I look? Passable?'

'Well, yes,' I say reluctantly. 'Definitely passable.'

'Then passable will do. I mean, even Penelope Cruz gets bags under her eyes sometimes. Catch you later!'

And off she goes, with Jack's phone on her passenger seat.

Chapter 25

'So, when was it that your pig first started to speak French?' I ask, my notebook and pen poised.

'Ooh, it were a while ago,' says the farmer, who looks as if it's been a while since he washed. 'We 'ad a farmhand from over there, see. We tried to tell 'im to speak proper, but he kept on talking foreign. Lizzie 'ere just seemed to pick it up.'

'Right,' I say, nodding in an attempt to hide the fact that I think this story is the biggest load of swill I've heard all year. 'I don't suppose there's a chance it – sorry, *she* – could let us hear a few words?'

He sucks his teeth. 'She won't just do it on demand, love,' he says.

I feel like saying that, given that a photographer and I have come all the way over here to interview her, surely a little *'Oui'* isn't too much to ask.

'Well,' I say instead, 'do you think we could do anything to help persuade her?'

'A bit of cash might not go amiss,' he says.

Great. So the pig will only speak French if I pay him. So she's a skilled negotiator as well as a linguist.

'Sorry, but we don't pay,' I say. 'We're a local paper – we don't have the budget.' Which is completely true, and even if it wasn't, I can't imagine paying for this story, short of the pig launching into a perfect version of Serge Gainsbourg's *'Je t'aime . . . moi non plus'*.

This really isn't my week, and quite frankly, this story is just about the last straw. I've been a reporter with the *Daily Echo* now for almost eight months, and was starting to feel pretty optimistic about the way my career was progressing. Okay, so at first I was writing little more than two-paragraph 'nibs' – that's news in briefs – about school fetes and car boot sales. None of which, in case you haven't guessed, were threatening the shortlist for any major journalistic prizes.

But, gradually, the news desk started to trust me a bit more, and the two-para nibs became single columns, then the single columns became page leads, and somehow, I started to find my name on the front page every so often, covering everything from court cases to human interest stories.

This week, however, our News Editor Christine – who described me as being 'full of enthusiasm and potential' in my first company appraisal – went on maternity leave.

Her replacement is the terminally sleazy Simon, who can't see my potential because he's too busy looking at my arse. He has bombarded me with school fete nibs and picture stories for what he condescendingly refers to as his 'soft news slots'.

Hence the reason for my being here in a farm 'over the water' at the far end of Wirral – and barely even on the *Daily Echo*'s patch – praying that Lizzie the Gloucester Old Spot will ask someone for a croissant. *New York Times* here I come!

I have also spent the last five days attempting to find out what happened when Valentina went round to Jack's house – and failing miserably. Grace is away on honeymoon, so she's out of the game as far as gossip is concerned. I've attempted to grill Charlotte about it but, bizarrely, Valentina doesn't appear to have told her anything. And I'm certainly not going to ask Valentina herself about it. So I'm going to forget about it. It's not like I'm dying to know. Only . . . I am, aren't I?

I've spent the last five days thinking about it, in between hammering out pieces about bilingual pigs and hamsters with their own YouTube channel.

'What a pile o' shite this is,' whispers Mickey, the photographer. Mickey isn't known for his patience, but he's undoubtedly right.

'Listen,' I tell him. 'We both know this animal can't speak French, any more than I can speak Mandarin. But Simon wants a story about it and I can't go home completely empty-handed. Shall we just try to get the photo done with and then go?'

'She bloody well can speak French,' protests the farmer, obviously having overheard me. 'But she won't do it if she's under stress. And you coming in 'ere telling her she's not capable won't be helping.'

We eventually manage to persuade him to pose for a photo with Lizzie in exchange for a few glossy copies of it to hang on his wall. Mickey, still muttering under his breath, takes it in record time.

'This used to be a paper of record,' he complains to me.

'Don't blame me,' I reply. 'I'm as chuffed to be here as you are.'

'So,' says the farmer, 'when will it be in?'

'I'm not sure yet,' I say. 'It's one of those stories that we call "hold-able". If the city centre is razed to the ground, I'm afraid it doesn't go in until the next available slot.'

Which will be never, if I've got anything to do with it. 'Only I've got the nationals interested too,' he says, 'so you'd better get in there quick.'

'Thanks for the tip,' I say politely, as Mickey rolls his eyes and we head to the car.

Chapter 26

Another Saturday, another dress fitting, this time, for the wedding of Georgia and Pete. And this time, the budget is so big it should be listed on the stock market.

'How much is this wedding costing exactly, Georgia?' asks Valentina as she examines a rail of dresses which, tellingly, don't even have price tags.

'More than my cleaning lady's big day and less than Beyonce's,' says Georgia. 'Not that it matters what it's costing. We could be getting married in Chorley Register Office, for all I care.'

'Thank God it's already booked,' mutters Valentina.

The reality is that Georgia's big day couldn't be *less* like a session at Chorley Register Office. In fact, the ceremony is happening in the Isles of Scilly and is on course to be so lavish, it will make a royal wedding look like something out of *Coronation Street*.

Georgia is having six bridesmaids and we're here today for fitting number two, in a boutique so posh I've held my breath since I got here. Grace, typically, is late following a domestic crisis caused by Polly having fed the rabbit some leftover chicken jalfrezi.

Georgia's two younger cousins are also here and today is the first time we have met them. Beth and Gina are both in their early twenties and so pretty that Valentina could barely hide her disappointment when they arrived.

Then, of course, there is Charlotte, who looks less than cheerful at the prospect of being a bridesmaid again.

'You okay?' I ask, as she sits down next to me on a velvet stool. 'It's not really your sort of thing this, is it?'

'Not really,' she whispers. 'I've put on at least half a stone since Grace's wedding. I've not weighed myself, but I know I have. Only my Evans cords would fit me this morning.'

'I *like* those cords,' I reassure her, as the curtain is pulled back and we both look up.

Georgia emerges in her wedding dress, smiling from ear to ear.

'What do you think?' she asks, twirling around as her gorgeous silk skirt skims the floor. Even Valentina joins in our cacophony of approval.

'You scrub up extraordinarily well,' I say.

'Do you think so?' she says, grinning excitedly.

'Absolutely. I think you should have gone for more frills

though judging by some of these,' I joke, nodding at my wedding magazine. 'Some of the dresses in here look like those little dolls my grandma used to put over her toilet roll.'

'Are you excited, Georgia?' asks Charlotte softly.

'Hysterical might be a better word,' Georgia replies. 'I don't know what I'll do once it's all over though. It's taken a year and a half to organize this wedding. I've forgotten how to talk about anything other than gift lists and table plans. My conversational skills are destroyed.'

'Apparently,' says Valentina, fixing an enormous, elaborate tiara onto her head, 'some couples, once they're married, struggle to find anything in common because all they've talked about beforehand are things to do with the wedding.'

I roll my eyes.

'It's a *well-known fact*,' she says indignantly. 'Ask any psychologist, they'll tell you. I read it somewhere – *Glamour* magazine, I think. Now, what do you reckon?' She turns away from the mirror to show us her tiara.

'It's a bit ... White Witch,' I tell her.

She narrows her eyes. 'Sorry!' I say.

But something has been bothering me about the way Valentina's behaving today, something I've been trying to put my finger on since we got here – and have only just done so. It's been a full twenty minutes and she hasn't mentioned Jack yet.

Chapter 27

Charlotte has the look of someone five seconds away from their first-ever bungee jump. In fact, all she's been asked to do is go behind the curtain with the dressmaker to try on her dress.

'Why don't you go next, Evie,' she says, her eyes imploring me to take the pressure off.

'Yeah, okay, no problem,' I say.

Our dresses are called 'Peony Dream' and are strapless, tea-length numbers in shades of peach and soft coral. As I pull mine on, the fit is, mercifully, near enough perfect – which means that unless I develop a craving for pasties and Big Macs between now and the wedding, I won't have to have another fitting.

I pull back the curtain to murmurs of approval all round. *Nearly* all round.

'You don't think that's a bit saggy at the bust, do you, Evie?' Valentina asks. 'Not everyone can get away with that sort of cut.'

'It fits beautifully,' Georgia jumps in. 'Evie, you look fabulous.'

When I've changed back into my jeans I sit myself down next to Charlotte.

'You know . . . Jim's going to be at the wedding,' I whisper. 'Georgia liked Grace's wedding video so much she's asked him to do hers.'

'I believe so,' she says.

'So, are you going to talk to him this time?' I say, nudging her gently. 'Or just spend the afternoon talking to Auntie Ethel about the tea cosies she's knitted?'

She giggles.

'Oh, do you like Jim, Charlotte?' Valentina is like a heat-seeking missile when it comes to gossip. 'Why didn't anyone tell me? I hate being the last to know these things.'

Charlotte blushes.

'He'd look a lot better with a couple of inches off that hair, you know,' Valentina continues. 'You might want to ask him to consider it if you end up going out with him.'

'I didn't even say I liked him,' she protests, going redder still.

'I think we need a plan of action to get you two together,' Valentina decides.

I groan, really wishing I hadn't brought this up.

'Georgia, why don't you put them next to each other on the seating plan?' she continues, apparently oblivious to how uncomfortable she's making Charlotte feel.

'Do you want me to, Charlotte?' Georgia asks hesitantly.

'No,' she says. Then: 'I mean, if you like. It makes no difference to me.'

Valentina picks up a floor-length Vera Wang number and holds it against her body to admire herself in the mirror. I use the distraction to lean over to Charlotte again, this time whispering so quietly I'm certain nobody can hear.

'Sorry.'

'It's okay,' she says.

'But the thing is,' I continue, 'I only mentioned it because I think he might like you.'

She frowns.

'He certainly seemed to at Grace's wedding,' I add.

'You think . . . really?' she asks.

'Well, he said you were *lovely*,' I whisper.

'So, Georgia,' Valentina says loudly, cutting short my conversation again. 'The guests at your wedding – are many in your sort of social circle?'

Georgia smirks. 'I obviously socialize with them,' she says. 'If that's what you mean.'

'Yes, of course,' says Valentina, pausing. 'I suppose what I mean is do they have a similar sort of, well, demographic?'

'Demographic?' echoes Georgia.

'*Financial* demographic,' says Valentina, begrudging the fact that she's had to spell it out.

'Ah,' says Georgia. 'You mean are there any filthy rich, eligible men? Loads, love, loads. I promise.'

Valentina grimaces. 'Oh, Georgia, I can't believe you think I'd be so vulgar as to only be interested in someone for their money.'

'Are you single again then, Valentina?' I ask, trying to look like I'm only vaguely interested.

She pouts. 'At the moment. I decided I ought to be concentrating more on making some "me time". Jack was very nice and everything, but not really my type. I let him know the day after Grace's wedding.'

'Right,' I say nonchalantly.

'You're more than free to go after him, Evie,' says Valentina smugly. 'He was very upset when we split up, obviously, but you never know – he might be after a meaningless fling with someone to get over it. And I know you like that sort of thing.'

Chapter 28

Valentina doesn't bother closing the curtain to get changed.

She just unzips her dress and lets it drop to the floor so she is completely naked except for a pair of satin high heels and knickers so small they look like they were put on with a pair of tweezers.

Her body is perfect in every way, with high breasts and never-ending legs that she turns to admire from behind in the full-length mirror.

'I hope I've not put any weight on since last time,' she says, running a hand slowly across one of her buttocks. 'I haven't been going to the gym as much as usual lately.'

'It must be terrible to have to live with all that cellulite,' I deadpan. 'There are support groups for people like you, you know.'

'You are funny, Evie!' she hoots and turns around to let the assistant help her get her dress on. As I continue flicking through a magazine, Charlotte nudges me.

'Do you like Jack?' she asks.

'Yes, I think I do,' I reply.

'What are you going to do about it?'

'Good question,' I reply, the implications of what I've heard only just dawning on me.

'Valentina's the only link between us,' I continue. 'Perversely, now they've split up, I can't think of any obvious opportunities to see him again.'

'Thankfully,' she giggles.

But the smile is soon wiped off Charlotte's face. There is only one more person left to try on their dress, and that's her. As she heads behind the curtain, she pulls it back right to the end, checking that there are no gaps anyone could see through.

Finally, I creep over and try to murmur to Charlotte without attracting too much attention from anyone else.

'Are you okay in there?' I ask.

'Wait! Don't come in!' she says, slightly hysterically.

'Okay, okay,' I say. 'I wasn't going to. I was just wondering how you were getting on.'

Suddenly, the boutique door flings open and it's Grace, looking slightly dishevelled and out of breath as usual.

'How's the rabbit?' I ask.

'Rooney? Well, the vet says he's going to have a sore bum tomorrow,' she says. 'But we've managed to avoid major surgery. How's things?'

'Fine,' I say, walking over so I can talk to her privately. 'We're just waiting for Charlotte to come out, but I think she's determined to stay behind that curtain until the wedding is over.'

'Had you better check on her?' she asks.

'I was just about to,' I reply and head over to the dressing room. 'Knock knock,' I say, carefully poking my head through the side of the curtain.

And there she is. Looking completely distraught.

Chapter 29

'I'm sorry,' Charlotte says to Georgia as she emerges from behind the curtain, her lip trembling. 'I really am sorry.'

'But, what's the matter?' asks Grace.

Tears spill down our friend's face and I reach out and squeeze her hand.

'Hey, don't cry,' I say softly.

'Come and sit down here,' says Georgia, gesturing to a velvet footstool.

Charlotte heads towards her obediently as I try to think of something profound to say, something meaningful, to make her pain go away.

'Do you want a cup of tea?' I ask, but she shakes her head silently.

The room takes on an intense quiet as all six of us watch her sad, swollen eyes as she goes to sit on the footstool.

It's then that we hear the tear, a heart-stopping rip that happens before her backside even touches the stool.

Grace and Georgia's hands shoot to their mouths. Valentina and Beth's eyes widen like cartoon characters. Gina's jaw lowers to the floor, and the dressmaker, quite simply, looks as if she's about to faint.

Almost robotically, Charlotte stands up again to look in the mirror at the spectacular rip that runs like a gaping wound right down the middle of the bodice, not even on the seam.

The sheer impossibility of fixing it makes my head spin.

Chapter 30

There is something about being British that makes us ascribe to a simple cup of tea the sort of healing properties you wouldn't even demand from a Harley Street psychiatrist.

It doesn't seem to matter what disaster befalls us, whatever death or destruction throws itself in our path, the reaction is always the same: 'I'll put the kettle on then, shall I?'

'Would anyone like another?' says one of the assistants, popping her head around the door.

'Can you make sure it's Assam this time,' says Valentina, handing back her cup.

The thing is though, it somehow works. At least, it has on Charlotte. Although, admittedly, it might not just be the PG Tips that have done it. Charlotte has spent the last half-hour revealing some of her innermost thoughts to myself, Georgia, the other bridesmaids, and a dressmaker who clearly thinks that if she's going to have to fix that dress, she at least wants to hear all about what was behind its undoing.

The thoughts Charlotte has revealed are ones that she's never, ever told us about before, which is unbelievable really, given that our relationship has lasted longer than the average marriage.

With hindsight, they are thoughts that I probably shouldn't have been surprised about. But the fact is, I *was* surprised. It turns out that lovely, soft-spoken Charlotte – Charlotte who, ironically, never sees anything but good in people – can see nothing but *bad* in herself. And behind the shyness, Charlotte, it appears, *despises* her milkmaid curves and gorgeous rosy cheeks. With a passion.

'I know I've never really said anything, but I have always felt like this,' she says as she sips her tea, her hands still shaking slightly. 'I was teased at school for the way I look, and although people don't say anything to my face any more, I know what everyone thinks about me.'

'Charlotte,' I say, shaking my head, 'what people think of you is that you are a fantastic, *lovely* person who—'

'Well, that's all fine,' she interrupts. 'But don't pretend that even you, even my best friends in the whole world, don't look at me sometimes and think: what a mess she is.'

'Actually, Charlotte, I don't—' I begin.

'I'm not having a go at any of you,' she interrupts. 'I mean, how could I? I *am* a mess. I'm overweight, I don't know how to dress properly and I've never put on lipstick in my life. I wouldn't even know how.'

'We always thought you were just ... comfortable ... with the way you look,' says Grace. 'You should be.'

'No, Grace, I'm not,' she says. 'I hate myself.'

'It does have an effect on your confidence when you feel that you don't look your best,' sighs Valentina. 'I don't want to leave the house sometimes when my eyebrows are overdue.'

Everyone ignores her.

'Charlotte, happiness isn't about being thin,' I say.

'Well, I have enough experience of being fat to know it's not about that either,' she argues. 'I'd love to look as nice as any of you.'

I am about to repeat my reassurances when I realize it's going to be no use. And I suppose, if improving her appearance would make our friend more confident, then why on earth wouldn't we help her do that?

'Listen, Charlotte,' I say, 'I love you just the way you are and so does everyone else here. But if you really feel this strongly about it, we're with you all the way.'

'What do you mean?' she asks.

'I mean, if you want to get fit, we'll help you. If you want us to do your hair and your make-up, we'll help you with that too. Picking clothes, painting nails ... anything you want, we're there. As long as this is what you want?'

'Charlotte,' gasps Valentina, 'I'll introduce you to the director at *Andrew Herbert* if you like! He'll have you looking like Jennifer Lawrence in no time. Oh, this is so exciting!'

'I'm sure it can't be that easy,' she says.

'Actually, Charlotte, I think it can,' says Grace. 'You've got such a pretty face, but everyone looks better with some make-up.'

'I think the biggest problem is my weight,' she says. 'Perhaps I should go to WeightWatchers?'

'Great. We can all come with you for moral support,' I say. 'You'll love it, Valentina.'

'Couldn't you just start throwing up instead?' she says and I tut.

'Do you really think this sort of thing would help?' asks Charlotte.

'Yes!' we all say in unison, and she starts giggling.

'Oh God, but what about this dress?' she says. 'I'm so sorry, Georgia, I really am.'

'What are you on about?' Georgia says firmly. 'It's challenges like this that dressmakers thrive on – isn't that right?'

'Sure, no problem,' replies the dressmaker begrudgingly. 'We'll get another one ready in time. No problem. Yeah.'

Charlotte has a sparkle in her eye and, later, when I catch her by herself I can't resist seizing the moment. 'You've just got to promise me one thing,' I tell her. 'If we succeed in pulling off this makeover, you've got to start putting in some effort with Jim.' This time she laughs out loud.

'Fine!' she says in mock exasperation. 'Whatever you say, Evie. Whatever you say!'

Chapter 31

I only know one person who would even consider getting married in a cowboy hat and feather boa, and that is my mother. 'I think it's quite fun, don't you?' she asks, posing in front of the full-length mirror.

'You look like J.R. Ewing in drag,' I tell her.

'You're so conventional, Evie,' she says, ruffling my hair, something she's done for as long as I can remember and will probably still be doing when I'm collecting my pension.

'Have you thought about something a bit more *demure*?' I ask, thinking back to what the magazines in the bridal shop said. But the second I've said it, I wonder why I bothered.

She doesn't do demure, only demented.

'You mean boring,' she says, continuing to look along the rail. 'Oh, this could be nice.' She picks up a traditional-looking floor-length dress. My hopes rise momentarily.

'I wonder if they'd do it in gingham?' she muses.

My mum is getting married later this year to Bob, who she's been seeing for six years.

He is a bearded philosophy lecturer who wears Jesus sandals even in mid-January; she is a yoga teacher with a fondness for clothes that come in such alarming colours some people risk having a fit if they look at her for too long.

But they are kindred spirits in more ways than their attire. Both spend all their spare time raising awareness of everything from pollution of Formby beach to the treatment of moon bears in China.

They each have a permanently chilled-out expression on their faces, which could give the impression that they've been smoking dubious substances. While I can't testify to what they got up to in the seventies, I think they were just born like that.

I'll never think of Bob as a father, but I'm glad he and my mother are getting married. She deserves to be happy and he'd do anything for her.

But as I've grown up, I've come to realize that, despite her feeding me more lentils as a child than can be good for anyone's digestive system – I was twelve before I had my first Wagon Wheel – and the fact that her idea of a family break was six nights camping at Greenham Common, Mum and I are pretty close.

My dad is a different story. She met him on an Indian ashram and he disappeared when I was two. I sometimes think

I can remember him, but then wonder whether what's in my head are just ideas about him that have been pieced together from old photos and snippets of information I've picked up over the years.

I wouldn't say my mum exactly shies away from talking about him, but the subject rarely comes up and I certainly don't push her on the issue. It can't be easy, having the father of your child simply leave the house one day and never turn up again. He had apparently popped out to buy some LSD, which tells you all you need to know about him. Other people go out to buy a pint of milk and don't come back. My father couldn't even run away respectably.

'I don't think I'm going to go for a wedding dress at all,' she decides. 'I'd just look silly in any of these. They're not me.'

'You haven't even tried any on yet,' I say, getting worried now. 'Oh God, you're not thinking about wearing your usual gear, are you? I'm telling you, Mum, if you wear one of your purple mohair jumpers and painted clogs, I'm boycotting this wedding.'

'Don't be silly,' she says, but she's smirking.

'You need something *special*,' I insist.

'It'll be special no matter what I wear,' she says. 'Who cares what I've got on, really? Besides, I've left it very late now. They probably couldn't even get one ready for me in time.'

'I'm sure they could,' I say. 'Go on, just go and try a few on. For me. Please.'

She pulls a face like a sulky teenager and grabs a handful of dresses from the rail before wandering off behind a curtain. The shop assistant looks at me in the same sympathetic way I've seen people look at Grace when Polly is playing up.

My mum tries on five dresses and by the time she has decided to abandon the sixth one I start to think she may be right. They're all lovely on the rail, but somehow they don't look right on her. They all look weird. By which I mean normal. And, quite frankly, normal isn't her style.

'Shall we just have a little break?' she says hopefully. 'Oh, go on, Evie. *Please?*'

Chapter 32

For proximity's sake, we settle on one of the cafés in the Met Quarter.

I go for my usual flat white while Mum orders a herbal tea that looks and smells as if someone has washed their socks in it. She opens her newspaper, the *Guardian*, which she buys every day even though she has complained about it 'being far too establishment' for the last fifteen years. She also buys the *Daily Echo* religiously, though I suspect from the fact that she asked recently whether we'd given much coverage to a newly-released book of Afghan poetry that she doesn't actually read it all that often.

I pull a copy of one of Grace's old wedding magazines from my bag and turn to the inside back page, where there's a list of things we should have done so far. The reception is booked, so that's one tick at least. Sort of, anyway. The wedding party is being held in a field near Mum's house, and Wendy, her friend who runs a health-food shop, is doing the catering. I'm truly hoping it was a joke when she promised a sumptuous feast of nettle soup and mung bean falafels.

'I suppose I'd be wasting my time asking whether you've ordered the flowers yet?' I say.

'You don't need to do that yet,' she says. 'There are three months left.'

'Two and a half,' I correct her. 'And according to this you do. Mind you, this says you're meant to have sent out cards telling people to expect an invitation soon. What's the point in that? Why don't you just invite people?'

'Capitalism,' she says knowingly. 'They want you to buy two sets of cards. Anyway, we don't need cards. I'll just mention it to people when I bump into them.'

My heart sinks, and not for the first time today.

'Mum,' I say, trying to stay calm, 'you can't do that. I know you don't want things to be too formal, but it's not a sixth-form party.'

'You worry too much,' she says. 'It'll be fine. If you want to send out cards, then do. But I'm not bothered and Bob certainly won't be either.'

I can see that being a bridesmaid at this wedding is going to involve significantly more than it did for Grace's wedding – although it isn't as though I haven't got plenty of people to share the burden with.

As well as myself, my mother has asked nine other people to be bridesmaids, including Grace (who could probably do without the hassle), Georgia (who was looking forward to some wedding-free time), Charlotte (who is traumatized enough with the preparations for Georgia's wedding) and Valentina (who's thrilled – she has a star part again).

'I take it you haven't invited anyone else to be a bridesmaid recently?' I ask.

'No, I haven't actually,' she says. 'Although I don't know why you're so bothered about it. It'll be nice. The more the merrier.'

'I'm bothered about it because, while I'm not saying you ought to be a slave to convention . . .'

She chokes on her tea. 'Heaven forbid.'

'. . . getting married, in case you hadn't noticed, is a *ceremony* – which by its very definition follows certain conventions.'

She frowns.

'You've got to follow at least *some* of the rules,' I say.

'What rules am I breaking?' she asks.

'You're only meant to ask a *select few people* to be your bridesmaids,' I huff. 'My friends would have been happy as guests. I mean, you didn't even go to Grace's wedding.'

'Only because Bob and I were in Egypt.'

'Ah, yes, your Egyptian holiday . . .'

Mum pulls a face to suggest she doesn't want my opinion on this again.

'We enjoyed it, I've told you,' she says.

What's wrong with Egypt as a holiday destination, you may ask. The pyramids, a Nile cruise, Tutankhamun's tomb. Marvellous.

Except, my mum's Egyptian holiday featured none of those and would be enough to give your average Thomas Cook customer heart failure. Her trip was organized by an environmental group and involved my mum, Bob, and a number of other like-minded lunatics waking at 5 a.m. every day to spend six hours picking up tampons and other unsavoury bits of pollution from the banks of the Nile.

'Anyway,' she continues, 'all your friends were really pleased when I asked them to be my bridesmaids. Especially Valentina. Nice girl, isn't she?'

'You won't be saying that when she tries to upstage you on your own wedding day,' I mutter.

I excuse myself to go to the loo, and when I come back I see something that alarms me slightly. My mum has my iPhone in her hand. Technology and my mother are not happy bedmates. This is a woman who thought blogging was something to do with deforestation.

'I tried to answer this for you,' she says. 'I thought it was ringing but I think it turned out to be one of those text thingies.'

'Let me see,' I say, taking the phone from her and narrowing my eyes. I just know this was the newsdesk trying to get hold of me for a big story. I can feel it.

'What did you press?' I ask.

'Nothing!' she protests.

'Well, don't worry about it then,' I say, still slightly

uneasy, but slipping my phone into the pocket of my denim jacket anyway.

She pauses for a second. 'Okay, I might have pressed something,' she says guiltily.

I raise an accusatory eyebrow.

'I didn't mean to, I was just trying to answer it for you.'

'Okay,' I say. 'Was there a message there?'

'Yes,' she says.

'Do you remember what it said?'

'Er, something about a wedding from someone called John. No, sorry, Jack. That's right, Jack. It was definitely Jack.'

Chapter 33

I almost spit out my coffee.

It is now weeks since Grace's wedding and I haven't heard nor seen anything of Jack. Which is exactly what I'd expected, given that he and Valentina are no longer an item – although I'd be persuaded of the existence of the tooth fairy before I'd believe she dumped him.

But one thing's for sure: I haven't stopped thinking about him, even when I've tried to.

I'd be sitting down to bash out a story, when all of a sudden he'd pop into my head, just like that. With his twinkly eyes and big shoulders and heart-stopping smile and . . . well, when you've got a deadline in twenty minutes, this train of thought is very distracting.

Even more concerning is this: Jack and Valentina no longer dating is a problem in itself. As I told Charlotte, Valentina was the only link between him and myself.

The result of this is that since I discovered the news of their break-up, I seem to have spent a disproportionate amount of time musing about all manner of scenarios in which I might 'bump' into him again.

Could I, for example, offer to do a special feature for the paper on his charity? I dismissed that as unethical: I can't just go writing special reports on organizations because I happen to keep waking up in a guilty sweat after dreaming about their chief executive.

Could I take up tennis and join Valentina's club? I'd never be able to act with her hovering about all the time.

So, after spending an annoyingly large amount of time focusing on cunning ideas about how I might get to see Jack again, I'm still doing exactly that. Focusing. In fact, I've been focusing so much I'm starting to develop a headache. Now this: a text message from the man himself. Except my mother has gone and zapped the bloody thing.

'Can you please try to remember what it said, exactly?' I ask, trying not to sound too exasperated.

'Oh, I don't know,' she says. 'Something about a wedding – that was it. I tried to get the words to move down, you know, the way they do on a word processor, but they all just disappeared. Stupid thing, if you ask me. Maybe there's a fault on it.'

I sigh. 'Just think, will you, Mum? This was someone I met at Grace's wedding. Does that help?'

'Not really,' she says vaguely. 'It said something about Georgia and Pete's wedding.'

Why would Jack be texting me about their wedding?

'Is he one of your new boyfriends?' she asks.

'No,' I say grumpily.

She frowns at me. 'You really ought to relax more, you know,' she says. 'You seem to get terribly stressed out sometimes, Evie. Why don't you start coming to reiki with me?'

I scan through my phone book to find the entry for Georgia. When she picks up, it sounds like she's speaking from inside the cylinder of a vacuum cleaner.

'How you doing?' she asks brightly, over the background noise.

'Where are you? I can barely hear you.'

'Flying out for one last check at the venue,' she shouts. 'It's the helicopter you can hear.'

Georgia is getting married in an exclusive hideaway of a hotel on one of the most secluded Isles of Scilly, just off the coast of Cornwall. Which is bound to be gorgeous, but apparently isn't the easiest place to get to and from when you're organizing a wedding.

'I'll be quick, then,' I say. 'Can you think of a reason why the guy who Valentina brought to Grace's wedding would be sending me a text message about your wedding?'

But she's drowned out again by the sound of the propellers. 'Are you there, Georgia?' I shout, and am conscious that the woman on the table next to us must be delighted at me bellowing away while she's trying to have a peaceful cup of coffee. 'Georgia, I can't hear you!'

'I've got you now,' she shouts back. 'It's like *Apocalypse Now* around here. What did you say?'

'I just said, can you think of a reason why the guy who Valentina brought to Grace's wedding would be texting me about your wedding?'

'You mean Jack Williamson?' she says.

'The very same.'

There's a pause. 'None at all,' she says. Great. My mother's got it wrong.

'I mean, I've no idea why he'd be texting *you* about it,' she adds. 'He *is* coming to the wedding though.'

Chapter 34

I can't think of a possible reason why Jack would be going to Georgia's wedding now that he and Valentina are no longer an item.

'How?' I ask Georgia, incredulously. 'And why? You hardly even know him.'

'He and Pete have been to the rugby together three times since Grace's wedding,' she tells me. 'Oh, hang on, you're breaking up . . .'

Her voice disappears again. I put my phone down with shaky fingers.

'Have you sorted it out?' asks my mother.

'Not yet,' I say, and start keying in a text message.

Have you got a number for Jack? Have Forward Planning meeting at work tomorrow and have to do story about charities.

I press Send and fire it off to Georgia's fiancé Pete. Then I take a sip of my coffee, which has now been standing for so long it's almost chilled.

My phone beeps immediately with Jack's contact card – and a message. *Here you go. Forward planning? Family planning, more like!*

I resist the temptation to tell him that *I* wasn't the one who texted first, but I suspect that might not look as cool as I'm hoping to appear. Now I've got his phone number, I'm buggered if I know what I'm going to do with it now.

I start composing a text.

Hello! Had a technical problem. Can you please resend your message?

Oh, no. Far too practical. Aloof, even. I'm missing a trick there, surely.

Hi there, can you resend your text? It's so good I want to read it twice!

God, no. That couldn't be any cornier if it had bunions. None of them feel right, but I've got to pick one. I reluctantly go for option one, although regret it the second it goes. Text was invented for flirting but the one I've just sent is about as likely to set his pulses racing as a party political broadcast.

'Shall we hit the road?' suggests Mum, folding away her paper and leaving it on the table. 'I don't know about you, but I've had enough of weddingy things for one day.'

If I was a better bridesmaid – and daughter, for that matter – I would insist that she continues in the search for the perfect dress. But I've got other things on my mind now.

'Okay,' I say, jumping up from my seat. 'I'll get these.' I'm standing at the counter waiting for my change when my phone pings. I take it out of the top pocket of my denim jacket and see immediately that it's from him. I open the message.

Just wondered if you would be on duty on the 8th, looking pretty and deafening guests?

I immediately become conscious that I am smiling and that the woman standing next to me laden with designer bags is looking at me as if I've just escaped from somewhere. I turn my back and start tapping into the keypad.

Thought you promised not to mention that again...

I go to send it then stop. His message was definitely flirty, so I need to step things up a little. I add the words: *I'll forgive you – just this once.*

Not slutty, but slightly cheeky, I think. I tuck my phone back into my pocket, unable to stop smiling, and pay up before heading back to collect my mum. My pocket vibrates again.

Good. Would not want to be in your bad books. See you at the wedding (looking forward to it).

Excellent. Even flirtier. Right – how to respond?

I decide to do a draft first. Just to make sure that what I write is absolutely right. But for some reason I'm stuck for ideas about how to reply. I start bashing out fantasy texts – ones that I have no intention of sending, but they might just help me work out what I'm really going to write.

Me too. PS. Will you take ME to bed instead this time?

I snort and start to scrub it off. Not in a million years would I send that.

'Evie! I'm starting to think you might be following me!'

Chapter 35

It's Gareth. I have now bumped into him three times since Grace's wedding, a situation with which I am far from comfortable.

'Hello, Gareth,' I say despondently.

'Hi! Mrs Hart,' he adds, as he extends a hand to my mum. 'I've heard so much about you.'

'Oh, it's Ms Hart actually,' she says, smiling as she shakes his hand.

He frowns. 'It's . . . what?'

'Mzz,' she replies, but he blinks, bewildered. 'Mzzzzz,' she says, trying to help him out. 'Not Mrs.'

His mouth opens in perplexed wonder. 'Just call me Sarah,' she says eventually.

'This is Gareth, Mum. He works at the university with Bob. He does their admin.'

'There's a lot more to it than admin,' he corrects me. 'I'm Senior Filing Executive – brackets Postage.'

'Oh, sorry,' I say. 'I didn't mean . . . well, sorry.'

There's another awkward silence.

'So, how *are* you, Evie?' he says, grinning again. 'You're looking really great.'

'You too,' I manage, but sadly, nothing could be further from the truth. Gareth has developed an angry-looking rash on his forehead and hasn't shaved for so long that he's starting to look like Tom Hanks in the last half-hour of *Castaway*.

'Congratulations on your impending nuptials, M*zzzz* Hart,' he says to my mum.

'Oh, well, thank you. Will you be coming to the wedding?' she asks innocently.

'If I'm invited,' he beams. I start having palpitations.

'Oh well, consider yourself invited,' Mum says brightly. Were it not for the fact that she makes her living from teaching yoga, I would kick her very hard in the shin right now. As if sensing my thoughts, she announces that she needs to pop to the health-food shop.

'I've run out of ginkgo biloba. Won't be long,' she adds, leaving Gareth clearly wondering which language she's speaking.

'Evie, we never got to have a proper chat about our relationship,' he says, his forehead starting to crumple.

I've got nowhere to run.

'I'm just not sure there's anything left to say.'

'Well, I've been putting a lot of thought into all this and, well, you've always said you've got a commitment problem. You need help, Evie. And I want to help you with it.'

I try to remain unfazed.

'Gareth, listen,' I say. 'There's nothing you can do to help. It's just the way I am. I'm not ready to make a commitment to anyone yet.'

'But you're going to be thirty,' he says.

'Not for three years,' I protest. 'And besides, it's not 1953.'

'But think of your fertility, Evie.'

The puppy-dog eyes are back. I think he's been taking lessons from a Basset Hound.

'I'd just hate to see someone like you left on the shelf, that's all,' he continues.

I'm tempted to enquire whether he really thinks a comment like that will help his cause but I decide, in light of the fact that his lip is starting to quiver, not to say anything.

'I know I hurt you, Gareth,' I begin.

'You did hurt me, Evie, you really did . . .'

'And I'm sorry,' I continue. 'I am really, really sorry. I'm an idiot. You're a lovely man. You'll find someone who deserves you some day, you will.'

'But I really feel that you and I made a connection,' he says.

I'm not sure I can make this any clearer.

'I'm sorry, Gareth,' I continue. 'I really am. Sorry for hurting you, sorry for not being able to make a commitment to you. I'm just really, really sorry.'

He's about to say something else, but as I see my mum walking back towards us, I decide to make my move.

'Look, here's my mum,' I say. 'I've really got to get her back – it's starting to rain.'

'I've got a brolly,' he tells me.

'Oh, um . . . don't bring that near her. She has a phobia.'

He frowns. 'Of umbrellas?'

I nod. 'Seriously, she goes just *bonkers* around them.'

My mum appears by our side. He hides the brolly behind his back.

'Right, all done,' she says brightly, holding up her shopping bag.

'Sorry we couldn't talk for longer,' I tell Gareth, dragging my mother away.

'But . . . okay, Evie,' he calls out. 'See you at the wedding.'

Bugger, bugger, bugger.

'Mum, do you know what you've just done?'

'What?'

'He was someone I used to go out with,' I tell her. 'He's the last person I want at your wedding.'

She doesn't look overly concerned with this news. 'Oh, sorry about that. I thought he seemed nice,' she says.

'You think *everybody* seems nice,' I point out.

She frowns. 'You're the one who used to go out with him.'

The thought makes my stomach churn. 'I know,' I say grimly.

'Anyway, just because you've split up with someone doesn't mean you can't still be friends,' she says.

'I know.' Although I've managed to comprehensively disprove the theory so far.

I suddenly realize that this diversion has meant I haven't responded to Jack's text yet, and the thought brightens my spirits immediately. I take my phone out of my pocket to reread my message, but as I look at the screen, my stomach lurches. It says Message Sent.

Oh bollocks. My heart starts pounding as I realize I've sent the draft text – and look like a complete tart in the process.

I'm going to have to send him another one immediately, explaining myself. But how the hell do I explain that?

Panicking, I start composing another text. *Sorry – just a joke. I'm not a nymphomaniac, honest!* and press Send immediately.

A couple of minutes later, another arrives. It's from him. One line.

I'll try not to be too disappointed.

Chapter 36

Grace has broken out into a sweat again. Not the soft, glowing sort on the average deodorant advert model. More the red-faced, hair-stuck-to-your-forehead sort.

'I wish I was back in the Maldives,' she groans, bending down to look under the bed for her shoes. 'I could cope with the pace of life there.'

'Is there anything I can do to help?' I ask, looking at my watch and thinking that the entire hen night will have graduated to tequila shots and male strippers by the time we finally arrive.

'Er, yeah,' she says, throwing on her top. 'I'm sure there is. Let me think . . . I know, go and ask Polly if she's seen my shoes. The ones with diamonds on them.'

125

Polly is downstairs watching *Sponge Bob Square Pants* and is transfixed.

'Hey, Pol. How's it going?' I ask.

'Good,' she says, barely blinking.

'Have you seen your mum's shoes?' I ask. 'The ones with the diamonds on them?'

'No,' she says. I can hardly see her lips move.

'You're sure?'

'Hmm, yes,' she says.

'Right,' I say, wondering what to do next.

'Evie,' she says, as I'm heading out of the room. 'Why have they got diamonds on them?'

Now that's more like it.

Why is one of Polly's words *du jour*, along with *What? Where?* and anything else that constitutes a question. Lately, from the minute she wakes up in the morning to the minute she goes to bed, Grace, Patrick and anyone else she comes into contact with is bombarded with questions, questions and more questions. The FBI could take lessons from her.

Tonight, we've covered topics as varied as religion: *Why does God make people and then make them die?* Try answering that one when you're trying to put your eyeliner on; physics: *What is there in the sky after the clouds?*; maths: *How many numbers are there?*; military history: *When did wars start?*; cinema: *Why was Simba – the Lion King – born?*; sex education: *Why was I born?* and a whole wealth of miscellany including: *Who would win a fight between Superman and King Kong?* and *Why does Mrs Harris* (her teacher) *have a moustache even though she's a lady?*

It's proof, according to Grace's mum, that she has 'an inquisitive mind'.

'I think they're there just to decorate them, just to make them look pretty,' I say.

'Why do they need to look pretty?' she asks.

I can see this has the potential to be a long philosophical discussion, and with the taxi booked for 7.30 p.m. I'm not sure we've got time.

When I get upstairs to check on Grace's progress, she is flinging random items of junk out from the bottom of her wardrobe. There's old coat-hangers, plastic bags full of tights, a box full of half-used moisturizers and crusty make-up, and about six or so pairs of shoes, one of which actually has cobwebs on them. Piled up, it is the sort of collection you'd see in the scruffy corner of a car-boot sale.

'Shit,' she says, sniffing the air. 'Can you look at my curling tongs?' The tongs have started to burn a hole in the dressing-table and are emitting the sort of aroma you'd expect from a rusty barbecue. I prop them up next to a bottle of tanning lotion as Patrick shouts from downstairs.

'Is Scarlett's bum meant to look like this?'

Grace takes a deep breath and runs downstairs, followed by me. I'm not sure what light I can shed on the issue, but at least it's getting us closer to the door.

'Hmm,' Grace says as she bends down to examine the evidence. 'She's got nappy rash. Just let her dry out for five minutes then put a load of Sudocrem on.'

'Right,' says Patrick.

'You're obviously not as familiar as I am with the complete works of Miriam Stoppard or you'd have known that,' she adds.

She's clearly joking but I can't help noticing that Patrick flashes her a look, clearly not impressed with whatever he thinks she's implying.

'Are you sure we've got some Sudocrem?' he shouts through to Grace in the kitchen.

'Yes,' she shouts back, having finally found her shoes.

'You're sure?' he asks.

'Positive,' she replies.

'Because there's none in here.'

'There is.'

'There's *not*, I promise you,' he tells her firmly.

'I promise you there is,' she says. 'I bought some last week.'

'Well, you can't have put it in here,' he says.

'I did.'

'You *can't* have,' he says. 'Because it's not here.' His face is thunderous.

I know it's only a low-key domestic, but I'm standing here, stunned into silence, because it's so unlike Patrick and Grace. They just don't row. Not usually, anyway. But *something's* going on here, that's for sure, because there is enough resentment coming from Patrick alone to keep a Relate counsellor going until Christmas.

Grace walks into the living room, moves him to one side and starts rifling through the nappy box, before producing a tub of Sudocrem.

'Oh,' he says. 'I hadn't realized that was the stuff you were talking about.'

'The fact that it's got *Sudocrem* in big letters on the side of the tub wasn't a giveaway?' she jokes. Again, it's a light-hearted jest, the kind both of them usually make all the time.

But Patrick doesn't see it that way. He mutters something under his breath as she heads out of the room but Grace, diplomatically, decides not to ask for a repetition. As it happens, she doesn't need to.

'Mummy,' says Polly, 'what's a pain in the arse?'

Chapter 37

'Is Patrick okay? He seemed a bit stressed,' I say when we eventually make it into a taxi.

'He's fine,' she says dismissively as she attempts to finish tonging her hair while we belt it along the Dock Road. 'He's just being a bit of a grumpy old man at the moment, that's all. It's nothing. Oh, bugger.'

Grace's phone is ringing so she thrusts the curling tongs towards me like some sort of relay baton, to root around in her bag for it. She studies the number which has come up and lets out a long sigh.

'It's Adele,' she says dejectedly. Her boss.

'Well, don't answer it,' I tell her.

She hesitates, biting her lip so much you'd think she was battling with the sort of moral dilemma nations go to war over.

'I've got to,' she says eventually.

'Don't!' I say. 'You're on a hen night. You're meant to be wolf-whistling at barmen and getting so drunk you can't remember your husband's name. This is not the time to be speaking to your boss.'

She bites her lip again and looks out of the window. I know exactly what she's going to do.

'Hi, Adele,' she says cheerfully, as she answers the phone. 'Oh, right. Oh, sorry. Well, I did stay late every night this week and . . .' She pauses to listen '. . . but you see, I thought I *did* get that to you . . .' another pause '. . . oh well, if it wasn't right . . . Yes. Okay, yes. I understand. I'll see what I can do.'

She puts the phone down and lets out another huge sigh.

'What?' I say.

'I'm going to have to go back,' she says.

'Why?' I ask, in disbelief. 'Grace, it's eight o'clock on a Friday night. What can you possibly need to do that can't wait?'

'Oh, it's just a report she'd asked for – I won't bore you with the details. But she needs me to do something else for it tonight.'

Grace is about to lean forward to redirect the taxi driver, and I know I've got to act. Thankfully, I'm faster than she is.

I lean over and grab her phone.

'What are you doing?' she asks.

I open the taxi window and hold my arm – and the phone – out as the wind from the Mersey whistles past it.

'Evie, what are you doing!' she screams. 'Do you know how much they cost?'

'It's a company phone, isn't it?' I reply.

'Exactly!'

'Look, just promise me you're not going back.'

'Evie, *come on!*' she says. 'Give it to me! That's company property!'

'Promise me,' I tell her sternly.

'I can't – I'll be sacked,' she says, almost whimpering now.

'Do you really think that being sacked is a likely prospect?' I ask. 'I mean, how many other employees do they have who would even *consider* leaving a hen night to go and start writing a report?'

She shrugs.

'Come on now,' I say. 'Promise me?'

'So what the hell do I say to Adele?' she asks.

'Here,' I say, pulling the phone back in. 'I'll compose a text message for you. Honestly, leave this to me.'

She rolls her eyes and starts shaking her head, but at least she's starting to see the funny side of it.

Dear Adele, I write. 'Let's keep it vague at this point, I think,' I tell Grace. *I'm so sorry but an emergency has come up and I won't be able to get you the revised report until tomorrow*, my text continues. *I'll explain all on Monday, but I'm afraid it's completely unavoidable. I will however do everything I can tomorrow. Grace.* There, perfect.'

'So . . . what do I tell her on Monday?' she asks.

I shrug. 'You've got two days to come up with that,' I tell her. 'Do you expect me to do everything around here or what?'

Chapter 38

Georgia's hen party is starting off at one of Liverpool's best restaurants, housed in a stunning glass and granite building in the heart of the city.

And while I'm not saying the off-duty city types, sophisticated couples and out-of-towners don't look like they know how to enjoy themselves, I know that if I'd come out for a nice dinner, I wouldn't be entirely thrilled to find myself put next to our gang.

But as Grace and I make our way past the tables and to a private dining room on the first floor, it's plain that we'll be discreetly tucked away – and won't lower the tone elsewhere. Which is a good job. Because as we walk in, Georgia is unwrapping a gift from one of her fellow 'hens' – a ten-inch bright blue vibrator that on first glance looks more like Darth Vader's light sabre.

'We thought you'd never get here!' she giggles, attempting to keep the L-plate pinned on the front of her dress out of her soup.

Tonight may be Georgia's night, but there is one other hen our eyes are immediately drawn to. Charlotte. Okay, so I got a sneak preview earlier after spending the day with her on a mammoth shopping trip, followed by a session at the hairdresser. But with the look now complete – courtesy of a famous Valentina makeover – she is nothing less than stunning.

'Wow!' I say. 'Charlotte, what happened to you?'

'*Fabulous*, isn't she?' says Valentina, admiring her handiwork.

'You look *unbelievable*,' I add. 'Really, you do.'

Charlotte blushes. 'Thank you,' she says, smiling.

As well as her gorgeous new haircut and Valentina's make-up, Charlotte is wearing an ultra-feminine raspberry-coloured jacket, which shows off a cleavage to die for.

Her WeightWatchers diet is also off to a flying start; in fact, she put me to shame. She lost six pounds and was rewarded with a round of applause from the other slimmers and a free packet of low sugar liquorice chews. I, on the other hand, lost 0.2 pounds and was rewarded with a sceptical look from the leader when I told her I couldn't understand it because I'd stuck to the plan religiously. I decided not to mention the curry takeaway I'd had in front of *Game of Thrones* on Thursday.

Grace and I take our seats and I nudge her. 'Hey, I haven't had a chance to tell you what happened.'

'What?' she says.

'Guess who texted me?'

'Who?' she asks, buttering some bread.

I raise my eyebrows and grin.

'*Who?* Come on, we'll be here all night at this rate!'

I check that nobody else is listening then lean closer to her. 'Jack,' I say, trying not to grin too inanely.

'Oh *really*?' She is raising her own eyebrows now. 'Would this be the same Jack who you're definitely, definitely, one hundred per cent not interested in?'

'There's no need to be like that,' I tell her.

'Go on then, what did he say?' she asks.

I pause for a second, then dig out my mobile to show Grace the texts, realizing I'm behaving like a giggly sixth-former.

'You've saved them?' she asks, amused.

'Couldn't resist,' I shrug. And, do you know, I can barely believe it myself.

Chapter 39

By the time we've got through dessert – and a hefty amount of wine – the conversation around the table has turned to the pros and cons of being married.

On the cons side is Leona, one of Georgia's former neighbours, a woman who is expensive-looking in every way and so skinny she could have been on Atkins since birth.

'All you need to know about married life,' she says in between healthy mouthfuls of fizz, 'is that you have more rows and less sex.'

Everyone laughs, but tonight we're all coming down on the side of the bride.

'Oh, for goodness' sake,' she says, laughing. 'Grace, back me up here – marriage is fantastic, isn't it? Go on, tell her – I know I can count on you.'

Grace puts down her cutlery. For some reason she looks lost for words.

'Grace?' I consider prodding her with a fork.

'Oh, sorry,' she says. 'It's great. It's lovely. Yes, it *really* is. Lovely.'

'So, does it bring you closer together?' asks Georgia.

'Er, well, it's difficult to say,' replies Grace evasively. 'We were always close.'

I frown. I can't help thinking we'd all hoped for a little more enthusiasm here.

'Besides, it's different when you've got kids,' she continues. 'Nothing brings you together like they do. Try dealing with a screaming baby at two a.m. when you've both got work the next morning. That's a bonding experience.'

Georgia smiles, apparently happy with this interpretation. 'So you're glad you did it?' she asks.

'Absolutely,' she says, a little too firmly. 'Yes, absolutely. I mean, it was a bloody good party at the very least, wasn't it?'

When the meal is finished we head to Mathew Street which, with its packed bars and clubs, is a far more conventional setting for a hen party. Despite the temperature being only a few degrees above freezing, most of the women are wearing the sort of attire you might expect for the climate of Fiji.

'I hope you don't mind, Evie,' says Georgia. 'Everyone offered to carry some of my hen-party presents in their handbags so I didn't have to cart everything round myself. I think you ended up with the fluffy handcuffs in your bag while you were in the loo.'

'I thought it felt heavier,' I say, 'especially since I have been saddled with Grace's curling tongs too somehow. Still, the handcuffs may come in handy. If that Leona woman keeps going on about how awful marriage is, we could always attach *her* to some railings somewhere.'

Georgia laughs as we arrive at the door to a retro club which was one of our staple nights out when we were students. As the door shuts behind us, we are bombarded with the opening bars of 'Native New Yorker' and Valentina wastes no time in refamiliarizing herself with the dance floor.

Hands on her waist, lips pouting, she flings her coat on a chair *à la Saturday Night Fever* and strides her way into the centre of the dance floor, hips swinging.

'Shall we join her?' I suggest. 'Or do you want to sit this one out at first?' Personally, I'm dying to hit the dance floor. But the get-out clause at the end is for Charlotte's benefit.

But I'm about to be surprised.

'Yes, I'll come with you, Evie,' she says, and I raise my eyebrows in disbelief.

'Why not?' she adds, smiling nervously.

Charlotte might not be the most flamboyant dancer as she sways in time to the music, but three or four tracks in, she actually looks like she's enjoying herself.

'Charlotte,' shouts Grace over the music. 'I know I said this before but you really do look amazing, you know.'

'Thank you, Grace,' she replies. 'I know I've still got a long way to go.'

'I don't think you have, Charlotte. You look like a different person already.'

'I still need to lose a lot of weight,' she says, 'but I'm absolutely determined I'm going to do it.'

'Well, good for you,' says Grace.

'I mean, I'd love to look like you,' adds Charlotte.

'Me?' Grace looks genuinely surprised by this.

'Of course you,' she says. 'You're attractive, you've got a beautiful family. I'd kill to be in your shoes.'

A look of realization suddenly washes over Grace's face.

'I *am* lucky, aren't I?' she says, smiling.

After half an hour of dancing to the sort of tracks that were last in the charts before I was on solids, Grace looks ready for a breather.

'Do you fancy another drink?' she mouths, competing against the Jackson Five.

I nod, and she and I make our way to the bar as Charlotte stays with the others.

'Before I forget, you have still got my curling tongs, haven't you?' Grace asks.

'Yes, I've got your curling tongs, I've got Georgia's furry handcuffs, and in fact I've got enough of other people's junk in this bag to hold a Bring and Buy sale. Now, what are you drinking?'

Just as she's about to produce a twenty-pound note, we can feel someone's presence behind us.

'Let me get these,' says a vaguely familiar voice.

I spin around and hear someone gasp that turns out to be me.

Grace glances at me briefly and smiles as she says, 'Hello, Jack. Fancy seeing you here.'

Chapter 40

Jack isn't as good-looking as I'd remembered. He's better. 'How are you both?' he asks, smiling.

'All danced out,' says Grace. 'And you? I've not seen you since the wedding. Listen, thank you so much for the present – it was beautiful.'

Jack bought Grace and Patrick an Indonesian wall-hanging. Not only is it supremely tasteful and completely unique, but it also has the added benefit of being a great excuse to replace the Whitley Bay landscape that Patrick's mother gave them four Christmases ago.

'I was torn between that and a rather impressive set of garden gnomes.'

'You made the right choice,' she laughs.

'And how are you, Evie? It's nice to see you.'

'I'm great, actually,' I reply, trying to think of something good to say, something that will spark a brilliant conversation and make me sound fabulously intelligent. 'Er, I didn't expect to see you here,' I add.

Marginally better than *Do you come here often?* I suppose.

'It's not one of my usual haunts,' he replies. 'But someone at work is leaving today so I decided to come out for just a pint. That was six hours ago, I must admit.'

'Naughty you,' I say. Oh God, what have I been drinking?

'I'll be back soon,' Grace announces, obviously excusing herself for my benefit. 'I've just got to go and speak to Charlotte.'

She grabs her bag and heads back to the dance floor, leaving me alone with the man who I can't seem to get out of my head lately.

'So, you've heard I somehow made it onto the guest list of the wedding of the year?' he says.

'Georgia told me you'd had an invitation,' I nod. 'Which presumably means that you're the reason Pete has been spending so much time at the rugby lately instead of getting ready for his big day.'

'Ah,' he says. 'Guilty as charged. I hope Georgia will forgive me.'

I find myself drowning in those eyes, feeling blood rush to my face as I watch him talk. I take a sip of my wine and tell myself to relax.

'Is it a big wedding?' he asks.

'You could say that,' I reply. 'Although there are only a few of us out tonight. We went for a great meal and . . . now this.'

'Well, it's a lovely surprise seeing you.'

'Really?' I can't stop myself from saying.

'Yes, really,' he smiles. 'I mean, I had a good time at Grace and Patrick's wedding. If you'd let me, I think I probably could have talked all night.'

A small croak of laughter escapes from my lips.

'Well, I think I probably *would* have let you.'

Jack holds my gaze and my blood starts racing again. The chemistry between us is unmistakable, an unspoken and powerful connection. He can feel it. I can feel it. And it's electrifying.

'Ay, luv, have you gorra pen?' asks a woman next to me, leaning on the bar.

'Mmm,' I reply, making sure I don't take my eyes off him. I'm not about to break this gaze in a hurry.

I reach into my bag to search for the pen I know is in here.

'I pulled the most gorgeous bloke you've seen in your life about twenty minutes ago . . . only my mobile's broken and I can't find anything to write his number down with,' grumbles the woman, but I can't engage in conversation with her. I just can't do anything other than look at Jack.

I dare to smile – the hint of a smile – and he returns it with heart-stopping effect.

Distractedly, I pull Grace's curling tongs out of my bag and put them on the bar to make some room. Then I locate the pen and pass it to the woman.

'Thanks,' she says. Then she just sniggers and leaves. And with a very strange look on her face too.

I think nothing of it as I turn back to Jack. Until I realize he has a very strange look on his face too.

Feeling self-conscious now that the spell between us has broken, I pick up Grace's curling tongs to put them back in my bag. When they are approximately one foot in front of Jack's face I realize something.

I'm not holding a set of tongs after all. I'm holding Georgia's ten-inch vibrator.

Chapter 41

The vibrator was blue in the restaurant. Under the disco lights, it is fluorescent. In fact, it's so fluorescent, you could land a plane with it. I know panicking is the worst possible tactic I could employ in such a situation. But quite frankly, I can't think of anything else to do.

My eyes wide, I grip the vibrator and stuff it firmly back into my bag, hoping blindly that Jack hasn't realized what it is. But the sheer conviction with which I plunge it back in there manages to set something off. And the vibrator starts *vibrating*.

I stuff my hand back into the bag and desperately try to find the OFF button without having to get the vibrator out in public again. But as I frantically feel my way around the thing, my hands sweating and my heart pounding, I realize to my horror that there are at least four different buttons to choose from.

Instinct takes over and I start to press every one of them – my thinking being that *one* of them must shut the damn thing down.

But they don't. Instead, the vibrator launches into an elaborate thrusting movement, the sort you'd expect to see on the production line of an automotive plant.

My bag begins to take on a life of its own, jutting in and out as if it's inhabited by a manic small animal being given a series of electric shocks. I feverishly start pressing the other buttons, the sound of Barry White's 'My First, My Last, My Everything' providing the backdrop to this horrific display. But whatever I press just makes the thrusting get faster and the vibrations get harder . . . and harder . . . and harder.

Conscious of being less than a foot away from the man of my dreams while I wrestle with a ten-inch electronic dildo, my mind starts racing with possible tactics. I am on the verge of throwing the bag over the bar and shouting, 'Bomb!' when finally, mercifully . . . it stops.

Sweating, shaking, I look up at Jack. 'Everything okay?' he asks.

I gulp. 'Er, yes,' I reply, straightening my back and putting my bag on the floor, as if what just happened was the most normal thing in the world.

'Everything okay with *you*?' I ask, realizing immediately what a ridiculous question this is. *He's* not the one who's just had a fight with Ann Summers's finest and lost.

'Yeah,' he says.

'Er, Jack, *ahem*,' I say. 'Obviously, that wasn't mine.'

'What wasn't?' he says.

'That ... that ... *item*,' I whisper.

'You mean the vibrator?' he says.

'It was Georgia's!' I jump in. 'She thought she'd given me the handcuffs, you see, and—'

'*Handcuffs?*' he repeats.

Oh God.

'Fluffy ones,' I offer, by way of an explanation.

Just as I'm about to lose the will to live, I realize something. Jack is smiling. In fact, if I'm not mistaken, he looks thoroughly amused by the whole episode.

'I suppose you think that was funny?' I ask.

'*Fawlty Towers* eat your heart out,' he says, and again gives me that wide, heart-stopping smile.

I laugh, feeling slightly relieved now, which is at least an improvement on just mortally embarrassed. I look over to the dance floor, where Valentina now has her arms draped around the neck of a Tom Hardy lookalike and is grinding her hips like a champion flamenco dancer. Charlotte has somehow ended up with a bloke who looks as if his usual Friday nights are spent rehearsing for a future appearance on *University Challenge*. I start to wonder where Grace could be when I see her battling her way through the crowds to reach us.

'Evie,' she says breathlessly when she gets to us. 'I'm going to have to leave.'

I look up at Jack with a sinking feeling. *For God's sake,*

Grace, I can't go yet, I think. But as my mind races with excuses to stay here with Jack, I suddenly realize her face looks drained of colour.

'What's the matter?' I ask.

'It's Polly,' she replies, clearly distraught. 'She's in hospital. She's had an accident.'

Chapter 42

Grace and I race down the street, towards the main road, as rain belts down onto our faces and seeps into our shoes. Headlights stream past us and squealing groups of girls hurry into doorways to avoid getting wet.

At first glance, Grace and I might look like them, but we're not running to get out of the rain. We need a taxi and fast. So why won't any of them stop?

With each set of headlights I see coming towards us, I hurl myself into the road with my thumb out, but they all just swerve around me and beep. Who wants to pick up two women who look like we do? They probably think we're drunk. We're both as close to sober now as we've ever been.

'Come on, this way,' I say, grabbing Grace's hand. We run for what seems like hours, but is probably less than ten minutes, until we reach a taxi rank. But there is a queue of about forty people. I race to the front and grab the coat of a guy who is getting into a black cab.

'Hey, what the—'

'Please,' I beg. 'There's been an accident. My friend's little girl has been taken to hospital. We need this cab – *please*.'

He looks me up and down, then looks Grace up and down and clearly realizes we're not just two charlatans trying to jump the cab queue.

'Come on, Becky, get out,' he says to his girlfriend inside.

'What?' says the woman, uncrossing her long, fake-tanned legs. She's wearing a tight, unforgiving dress and, despite the rain, her hair and make-up are still perfectly intact. 'I've waited twenty minutes for this taxi. I'm not getting out now.'

'Come on, love, just let them in,' he replies.

When she doesn't move he leans into the car and grabs her by the hand. 'I'll buy you a takeaway on the way home,' he offers and, at that, she tuts and climbs out.

'Thanks,' I say, to both of them and we jump into the back. 'Alder Hey Hospital, please,' I tell the cabbie. 'Accident and Emergency.'

The driver swings the cab around and slams his foot down on the accelerator.

I sit on the fold-down seat opposite Grace and grasp her hands. She still looks stunned.

'So what do you know?' I ask.

'Not a lot,' she says, looking distraught. 'I mean, I'd been texting Patrick all night. First of all to try and make up with him after our spat. But he just wasn't responding. And I was getting so pissed off with him and ... well, then I thought perhaps he'd just fallen asleep in front of the telly.'

She sniffs and tries to hold herself together.

'I told myself just to forget it and have a nice time. So I did. I went to dance with Charlotte and two blokes, but when I went to the loo I looked at my phone. There were five missed calls.'

'And has he left a voice message?' I ask.

She nods. 'Just the same as the text – very brief. He just says that Polly's had an accident and they're on their way to Alder Hey.'

'Well,' I say, 'she might just have twisted her arm or something.'

Grace looks out of the window as we trundle along and her lip starts quivering.

'But she might not have,' she says. I reach over and clutch her hand.

'Patrick is usually Mr Pragmatic when things happen. I panic, he keeps his cool. That's the way it is. But he didn't sound very cool, not this time.'

Even though the most rational part of me is saying that this is probably nothing – a broken arm, a bumped head, maybe – there's another part saying, actually, it might be more than nothing.

I've worked at the *Daily Echo* for less than a year now, but in that time I've covered all manner of horrific stories involving kids. You just assume that that sort of thing happens to other people. Not your best friend's daughter. Not Polly.

Despite the taxi driver's impressive pace, the journey seems to be taking forever.

'Oh, Evie,' says Grace, tears welling up now, 'I can't stop thinking about all the questions Polly asked me today – you know how she does. I was trying to get my hair washed when she kept asking me about why dogs have tails – or something. Do you know what I said?'

I shake my head.

'I said: "They just do, Polly". What sort of a mother says "They just do"? Why couldn't I have taken the time to answer her?'

She bursts into tears, sobbing uncontrollably and struggling to get her breath. I jump over and sit next to her, putting my arm around her as tight as I can.

'Grace, don't be silly,' I say to her as the taxi pulls up at the hospital. 'You're a wonderful mother. And everything will be fine.'

I'm just praying I'm right.

Chapter 43

'I hope she's okay,' says the cabbie, as I hang back to pay him and Grace rushes into the reception. 'Your mate's little girl, I mean.'

'So do I,' I say, handing him a twenty-pound note. 'Oh, I don't want paying, love,' he says.

'But it's a Friday night,' I point out.

'Just go and be with your pal,' he says, pushing my twenty back.

I haven't got time to argue.

'My daughter's just been brought in, in an ambulance,' Grace is saying to the receptionist. 'Her name is Polly Cunningham.' She sounds weirdly calm.

'Just one moment, please,' says the receptionist, as she starts bringing something up on her computer.

'Right,' she says, 'if you'd just like to go through those double doors on the right then follow the corridor along to the desk, they'll be able to help you there.'

We run down the corridor, but before we reach where we're going, I can see Patrick walking towards us, with Scarlett in his arms.

'Patrick!' shouts Grace, and launches into a run.

'I've just come out to try to phone you,' he says when they meet. 'She's *fine*. Just a few cuts and bruises, they think, but absolutely fine.'

The look on Grace's face tells me she doesn't know whether to kiss him or hit him.

It turns out that Polly fell down the stairs. She'd gone into Grace and Patrick's room – something she's taken to doing recently when she wakes in the night – and when she'd seen that neither of them was there, had thought it a good idea to go looking for them.

Which would have been fine, except she tried to do it in the dark and in her new, slightly too long Barbie nightgown. By the time she reached the bottom stair, she was actually unconscious. Patrick phoned for a paramedic and, although she had come round by the time they arrived, they decided to take her into hospital to check her over. In the event, her only real injury is a bruised bone on her arm, for which she needs a sling for a few days.

'I bet you had a shock,' I say to Patrick.

'You better believe it,' he says, shaking his head.

'At least Scarlett slept through the whole thing,' he adds, nodding over at the baby in her portable car seat.

The baby is a vision of peace and contentment, fast asleep with only her little dummy moving as she sucks it.

'I'm sorry we rowed,' Grace says softly.

'Me too.' And Patrick leans over to kiss her on the forehead. I sense my presence is no longer wanted.

'Anyone fancy a coffee?' I ask. 'I'm sure there'll be a machine in here somewhere.'

I do a complete tour of the hospital – twice – before I manage to locate a drinks machine. It runs out of coffee after I've only bought two of them and leaves me with a chicken soup I suspect went in there in powdered form in 1972.

When I get back, Polly is being issued with a sling by the nurse and, to my disbelief, Patrick and Grace appear to be having another domestic.

'Well, I'm sorry, but I think one of us needs to get Scarlett home,' Patrick is saying. 'She's going to want to be fed if she wakes up.'

'I'm sure the hospital will let us borrow a little bit of formula milk to keep her going,' says Grace.

'You can't ask them to do that,' he replies.

'Why not?' she asks.

'Because it's a hospital. They can't just go giving handouts to visitors.'

'I'm not a visitor,' says Grace. 'I'm the parent of a patient that's just been admitted.'

'It doesn't matter,' he says. 'Scarlett isn't the patient, Polly is.'

'Look, I'll pay them for it if need be,' she says impatiently. 'I'm sure they're used to this sort of thing.'

'Don't be so ridiculous,' he snaps.

'I'm not being ridiculous,' she snaps back.

'*You two!*' I leap in, and they both turn to look at me. 'I've brought you some coffee.'

I hand them over, glad at least that I've managed to shut them up.

'Sorry if they look like the contents of a washing-up bowl,' I say.

'I don't mind,' says Grace. 'I'll drink anything that's warm and wet at the moment.'

'Hmm,' says Patrick, sipping his and pulling a face. 'Well, it's definitely wet.'

'Listen, I'm going to get going,' I say. 'You don't need me hanging around.'

'Oh, Evie, thanks so much for coming with me,' says Grace. 'You're a real friend. Sorry as well that you had to leave Jack behind.'

'Don't worry about it,' I say, trying to look on the bright side. 'I'm just glad Polly's okay.'

'See you, Evie,' she says softly as I head towards the door, strongly suspecting they could be on the verge of Round Two.

Chapter 44

Now here's a journalistic dilemma: how do you make a page twenty-three nib about plans to extend the opening hours of an NHS walk-in centre interesting?

I sit and study the press release, the newsroom alive with activity around me. Jules, to my right, is bashing out the splash – a breaking story about a terrorism plot, centred around a Liverpool chippy, which police uncovered only this morning. Laura, opposite, is on the phone to the emergency services, getting a quote for her page one anchor piece about a four-car pile-up on the M56. Even Larry, the twenty-two-year-old work experience guy, is finishing off the caption for the front-page picture.

'It's with you!' shouts Jules, dashing over to the newsdesk, as Simon, the News Editor, opens up his story – ready to give it a quick-fire once-over before it is pinged to the sub-editors.

I look at my press release again and sigh. I can't remember when Simon last asked me to write something for that day's edition – something to get my adrenaline pumping. In fact, I can't remember when Simon last asked me to write something that would prompt anything other than a sudden onset of narcolepsy.

'Evie!' Simon shouts to me after he's sent the last story through. 'Get over here.'

My heart leaps. Maybe I'm about to have my name on page one today, after all! I dash over to the newsdesk, my notepad and pen poised in anticipation.

He settles his eyes briefly on my breasts, then drags them up to my face. 'I wonder if you could explain something to me.'

I hesitate. 'Yes?' I say.

'How you were scooped.'

'Sorry?' I ask, every story I've written in the last two weeks racing around my mind. 'I mean, which story?'

'Our four-legged friend,' says Simon.

'Sorry, Simon,' I repeat. 'I don't follow you.'

'*The pig!*' he snaps, with an expression that tells me I'm about as likely to be handed a hot exclusive today as I am the title of Miss World. '*The pig that spoke Italian.*'

'It was French, actually,' I say.

'I don't give a toss if it was Swahili,' he screams, slamming a paper down in front of me. 'It's in the *Daily Star.*' I gulp as I come face to face with the picture of Lizzie the Gloucester Old

Spot and her owner. I don't know which one of them looks more smug.

'I thought you said that piece was holdable?' he says.

'I assumed it was,' I splutter.

He doesn't look won over by this argument. '*Assume* makes an *ass* out of *u* and *me*,' he says. 'Didn't you ask whether he was speaking to the nationals?'

I cast my mind back to my conversation with the farmer and consider for a second whether there is any point in trying to lie here. Morally, I have no qualms whatsoever about trying to pull a fast one over Simon, who I am starting to think has all the charm of a sewer rat. But lying isn't exactly my forte.

'He did mention that,' I admit eventually, hating myself for being so sheepish. 'But, I've got to confess, I didn't believe him. I never thought the nationals would be interested, short of the pig reciting every verse of the *Marseillaise*.'

Simon shakes his head.

'Listen, girly,' he says, glancing down my top again. 'You've got a lot to learn about recognizing a story. And let me tell you this, in case I've not made myself clear: a talking pig is a good story in anyone's book. It's got a better grasp of languages than half the GCSE students in this country. Get out of my sight.'

When I get back to my desk my eyes bore into my computer screen and I quickly become a seething mass of resentment, imagining all the things I *could* have said to Simon ... but didn't.

Okay, so I messed up. But *Daily Star* or not, this is a story about a talking pig. It's not going to bring down governments or halt the spread of global warming. Besides, I wrote the thing weeks ago. I might have said it was holdable, but I didn't mean until Christmas 2025.

Picking up my press release, I make a vow to myself. I am going to get a page one exclusive for this paper if it's the last bloody thing I do.

Chapter 45

It's quite difficult to drown your sorrows when the person you're with will only drink Diet Coke because there are too many WeightWatchers points in anything else.

'Oh, come on, Charlotte,' I say. 'Just have a little glass of Pinot Grigio with me, why don't you? I'm sure I read somewhere that you burn off more calories lifting a glass of wine to consume it than it actually contains.'

'That's celery,' she says. 'And no, I can't, Evie. I'm determined.'

'Sorry,' I say immediately. 'Don't listen to me – you stay on the straight and narrow.'

'Valentina will be joining us in a minute,' Charlotte tells me. 'She's been on a date. She'll have a glass of wine, I'm sure. It apparently didn't go according to plan.'

Within five minutes, Valentina has appeared at our side and is flinging herself onto the chair next to us.

'I need a glass of water,' she says, putting her hand on her forehead dramatically.

'Not you as well,' I say.

'No, you're right,' she says. 'Can I have a Chardonnay, please?' she asks a passing waiter.

'So come on, tell us,' I say. 'What happened on your date?'

'Zak is the guy I met on Georgia's hen night. And he seemed *perfect*. Six foot four inches of Latin gorgeousness. Runs his own business – as a property developer, he said. He phoned last week to ask me out to dinner and didn't even flinch when I suggested *Le Carriage*.'

I raise an eyebrow. 'Pricey.'

'It's a good first test, Evie,' she tells me. 'So, I arrived fifteen minutes late—'

I raise the other eyebrow.

'You'd have to be *desperate* to arrive any earlier than that,' she says firmly. 'And anyway . . . he wasn't even there yet.'

'Was he stuck in traffic?' I offer.

'No! He just *rolled* in, half an hour late, with no explanation.'

'That must have been annoying,' says Charlotte.

'An understatement, Charlotte,' says Valentina, taking a large gulp of her wine as it arrives. 'I'd made a real effort. I had a microdermabrasion, a manicure and got a Bermuda Triangle on my bikini area the day before.'

I suppress a smile.

'When he arrived,' she continues, 'the waiter asked him what he'd like to drink. Do you know what he ordered?'

I shake my head.

'A Bacardi Breezer,' she says. 'A *green* one. In *Le* goddamn *Carriage!*'

Charlotte and I wince.

'They made him up a cocktail instead,' she says. 'But then, we sat down and he looked at the menu. And I realized he was pulling a face.'

'Oh dear,' I say.

'So he said: "I hate all this foreign shit". Can you believe it? "What foreign shit would that be?" I asked him. "Well," he said, "what's this when it's at home: pow-lett?" He was referring to the *poulet*.

'"It's chicken," I told him. "Oh," he said. "That'll do then. Does it come with chips?"'

I start to laugh, but Valentina appears not to find any of this remotely amusing.

'Oh look, I won't go on,' she says. 'But let me just tell you, he spent the rest of the night shovelling pieces of meat into his mouth like a caveman, he didn't even mention my outfit, and then, to top it all off, he assumed I was paying!'

'It *is* the twenty-first century, Valentina,' I say, but she frowns.

'Somehow, Evie, I don't think that was because he was a feminist.'

Chapter 46

We flew into the main island in the Scillies, St Mary's, yesterday evening, as a red sun was sinking into the horizon and the turquoise water was still and clear. Each tiny island is a feast for the eyes, impossibly green, with a rocky coastline interspersed with soft ribbons of pale sand. It almost looked like we were landing in the Seychelles rather than a part of the UK.

Except, when you do land, there's a chip shop, three pubs and a Spar-type supermarket selling copies of *heat* magazine and packets of Benson & Hedges. But still.

We then travelled by speedboat to a smaller, more rugged island which gives the impression of being virtually uninhabited apart from the hotel. And what a hotel: sumptuous and trendy, with a breathtaking position on the edge of the Atlantic.

Today, there is not a cloud in the sky and as I stand on the bleached-wood terrace of Georgia's honeymoon suite, a soft breeze whispers against my skin. The steps lead down to a private beach, where the sand is fine and soft and the sea is iridescent and shimmering. In fact, the only thing that has disturbed the view all morning is Valentina doing a Pilates routine which involved lots of bending over with her arse in the air.

'This place is gorgeous,' I sigh.

'It's great, isn't it?' says Georgia, who is sitting on the stool at a baby grand piano in her wedding dress, all ready for the ceremony. 'I love it here. It was where we spent our family holidays as a kid.'

'Not Butlins, then?' I ask.

'I'd have enjoyed Butlins too!' she insists.

The suite is furnished in an unfussy, beachy style, with coir carpets, whitewashed furniture and the odd impressionist seascape on the walls.

And, although there are still more than forty-five minutes to go before Georgia gets married, in stark contrast to the scene before Grace's wedding, she seems to have been ready for ages. I can't say the same for my best friend.

'Did you see Grace earlier?' asks Georgia quietly.

She has been heroically attempting not to worry about the fact that one of her bridesmaids appears to have gone AWOL.

'Briefly,' I reassure.

'Because she's getting me a bit concerned now,' Georgia

continues. 'I've been calm all morning and now look at me.' She holds out her hand to demonstrate how much it is shaking.

'She'll be here,' I say, as convincingly as possible. 'Honestly, don't worry.'

Suddenly, the door bursts open.

'Sorry! I know I'm late,' says Grace, wearing that permanently frazzled look she does so well.

'Where have you been?' I ask.

'I've had Adele on the phone complaining about a deal I've just done, I've had my mother on the phone complaining that Scarlett won't eat puréed steak and kidney pudding, and I've had the dry cleaners on the phone complaining that I still haven't picked up the rug I dropped off three months ago.'

'You really need your own personal customer services department,' I say.

'Well, look, you're here now,' says Georgia, throwing the last bridesmaid dress in her direction. 'So just go and get this on and be quick about it.'

'Will do,' says Grace, catching the dress. She turns, striding towards the dressing room, where she collides with Valentina at the doorway.

'Oh . . . Grace,' says Valentina with barely disguised horror at the vision before her. 'Do you need to borrow . . . a new face?'

Grace gives her a withering look. 'Thank you, Valentina, you look gorgeous too,' she says, and barges past her.

'I know,' smiles Valentina. 'I've just been tested for allergies and discovered I have an avocado intolerance. I gave it up last week and my skin is glowing.'

Just then, Charlotte emerges from the dressing room, all dressed and ready.

'Wow! You look great!' I say excitedly, immediately prompting her to blush.

Charlotte is wearing a bridesmaid dress that now fits. As well as the visible weight loss, her hair and make-up – courtesy of the combined efforts of both myself and Valentina – are a vision of sophisticated glamour.

'I'm so pleased with your look, Charlotte,' says Valentina, as if she were personally responsible for everything. 'I don't mean to sound big-headed, I sometimes think hair and beauty could be my number one skill.'

'You said that about fellatio last week,' Georgia points out. 'You told me you could make a man's hair stand on end.'

'Oh yes,' smiles Valentina. 'That too.'

Chapter 47

The ceremony is short and touchingly sweet. Georgia cries, Georgia's mother cries, Valentina pretends to cry and those of us close enough can even see Pete's lip wobbling a bit.

It takes place on an enormous terrace overlooking the bay, with the sun warming our skin and so many guests I feel as if I know what it's like to play the Royal Albert Hall.

I spend the entire ceremony with my back to the guests, wondering where Jack is sitting and whether it's obvious I'm squeezing my bum in to try to make it look smaller.

Like many of the guests, he wasn't due to arrive on the island until this morning, but I know he's here because Grace saw him having brunch. He had fruit followed by scrambled eggs and toast, apparently. Granary. Two slices, no butter. I think Grace has a future career in the Secret Service, if she ever wants one.

I walk down the aisle behind the happy couple, Valentina and Beth, and in front of Grace, Charlotte and Gina.

Suddenly, I feel a prod in the back and glance over my

shoulder to see what Grace is drawing my attention to. I spot him immediately. Looking over at our procession is the only one of my ex-boyfriends here today. Fortunately, it's one of the few I actually don't mind being here.

Seb and I dated for seven whole weeks while at university. That felt like a promising achievement at the time, though if I'd known I'd still be single so many years later, I might not have been so optimistic.

Our relationship eventually suffered the same fate as all my subsequent romantic liaisons, but the whole thing was undoubtedly a more bittersweet affair.

I can't even remember a *precise* reason why we went our separate ways. Just that he didn't call once when he said he would, I didn't press the matter, and the next thing I knew it was the summer break and he was off to Camp America to teach canoeing to twelve-year-olds.

It was a blip in an otherwise predictable pattern. Which means that at least bumping into him for the first time in at least two years isn't the traumatic affair it is with the others.

When he catches me looking at him, Seb smiles and holds up his hand to give me a little wave. I smile back but am prevented from waving both by convention and by the bouquet I'm carrying.

'Seb's a bit of all right these days,' whispers Grace as we get to the back of the room.

I hate to admit it, but she's not wrong.

Chapter 48

Apparently, nobody has informed the photographer that this is supposed to be a celebration. With sideburns like Brillo pads and a ruddy complexion, this guy appears to have taken charm lessons from the Gestapo.

'Right, if you'd just all move a bit closer together,' he bellows. 'Closer, *please!*'

Grabbing the arm of an elderly lady dressed in migraine-inducing cerise, he shoves her towards her neighbour. He seems completely unable to appreciate that getting this number of people into the right position isn't going to happen instantaneously.

'You bridesmaids, you need to move forward. No, not that far!' he shouts. 'Stop there. No, *not* there, backwards a bit.'

Valentina is pouting and for once I can understand why.

'I could have sworn I saw someone like you at the last wedding I went to,' says a voice behind me which I recognize immediately as Jack's.

I hold my hand up to my mouth to try to suppress a smile.

'Bridesmaid on the left, can you put your hand down, *please*,' the photographer trumpets. 'Let's try again, shall we?'

'Behave yourself, Miss Hart, or you'll be sent to the back,' the voice behind me whispers.

'I can do without you trying to get me into trouble,' I murmur through my cardboard cut-out smile.

'It's hardly my fault if you can't do what you're meant to do,' he replies. 'I bet you were always in detention at school . . .'

I'm trying to think of something witty to say in reply when the photographer instructs everyone but the bride and bridesmaids to stand down. The entire wedding party surges towards the hotel.

Jack flashes me an effusive smile. 'I'll catch you later, shall I?'

Yes, please.

One of the things I am starting to learn about weddings is that the photos take such a long time that by the time they're finished, most of the guests are already pissed, and the main wedding party has got leg cramp.

'Have you seen the time?' I hiss to Grace, who is next to me. 'It's gone five p.m. and we haven't even had a glass of fizz yet.'

'You big drunkard,' says Georgia.

'Sorry,' I grin, holding my hands up. 'I wasn't complaining, honest.'

Patently, I was.

'No, you're right,' she says. Then: 'Listen, Bruce,' she tells the photographer, 'from now on, let's just have natural shots, shall we? Come on, girls, where's the bar?'

She marches ahead, leaving Mr Brillo Pads hopelessly redundant, while the rest of us attempt to follow her as daintily as is practical on a beach when you're wearing two-inch heels. When we reach the terrace, I turn to Grace and take a deep breath.

'Is my mascara intact?' I ask her.

She smirks. 'Yes.'

'Hair okay?'

'Yes.'

'How about lipstick?'

'Evie. You look gorgeous. Now let's go.'

Chapter 49

The reception room is magical. Silk drapes fall softly from the ceiling beams, fairy lights snake around the cast iron chandeliers and elegant centrepieces of billowing white roses and eucalyptus branches rise up from the tables.

'Isn't the greenery fun?' says my mother, sniffing a piece of rosemary foliage. 'I must ask Georgia where she got it from. Though . . . I'm thinking big feathers for mine.'

'Really?' I say, sceptically. 'Will that look right . . . given that your reception is in a field?'

'Oh, I wasn't thinking about them for the reception,' she says. 'I thought I could get a headdress. You know, something a bit *Moulin Rouge*. Did I tell you I've found a dress?'

'Really? What colour is it?'

'Slytherin green,' she replies.

Whether the Isles of Scilly were ready for my mother's dress sense, I'm not entirely sure, but her unique style is unleashed on them to full effect today. She has chosen a purple poncho, a floppy sixties-style hat and a skirt so short that it should be illegal for a woman her age.

Don't get me wrong, she's got very decent legs. It's just a shame they're currently sporting a pair of orange paisley tights that make her look as if she is suffering from the early stages of gangrene.

'Hello,' says a voice, and I whirl around, my pulse racing. It's Jack. 'I thought you must have been swept out to sea, you were all outside with that photographer for so long.'

'Tell me about it,' I say, gazing into his eyes.

He looks back at me as if he's trying to tell me something. I just can't quite work out what.

'I'm Jack,' he says eventually, extending his hand for my mother to shake.

Oh God, *my mother*. For some reason I'd had momentary amnesia about her being present. In her mad hat. And hideous tights. And . . . *oh Mum, please behave yourself.*

'Pleased to meet you,' she says, smiling. 'I'm Sarah – Evie's mum. You're one of my daughter's ex-boyfriends, I presume?'

The woman is a liability.

'No, Mum,' I leap in. 'Jack is—'

'Oh, sorry. It's just that she seems to have collected so many of them these days,' she adds, for good measure. 'Everywhere I go, I bump into someone she's been out with.'

'*Ha ha ha ha ha ha ha!*' I blurt out, wanting to throttle her. 'That's a good one, Mum. Anyway, er, right . . . er . . .'

I'm trying to steer the conversation around to a subject that won't let my mother embarrass me. But somehow it's very difficult to think of one.

'Well, it's great to meet you, Sarah,' says Jack. 'Although I'd already guessed you were mother and daughter. You look very alike.'

God help me. I hope he doesn't think I've got a similar wardrobe.

'Excuse me for a second,' says my mum. 'I'm absolutely starved.'

She then almost rugby tackles a waitress passing with a tray of canapés right in front of us. 'You don't know whether any of these are organic, do you?' she asks.

The waitress, who looks like she's barely old enough to have left school, shakes her head. 'I don't. Sorry.'

'Anything with gelatine in?'

The girl shakes her head again. 'Not sure,' she says.

'Anything vegan?'

'Er, I think maybe that's a spinach one,' she says, pointing at something vaguely green perched on top of a square of puff pastry.

'And the pastry ... does the chef use animal fat?'

'I'm not really sure.'

'Mum,' I interrupt. 'Do you really have to ask all this?'

'Of course,' she says. 'And you should too, young lady, with your allergies.'

My allergies consist of one – to shellfish – and even then I haven't had a reaction to that in years.

'Any shellfish?' she asks, right on cue.

The waitress looks as though, if she's asked another question, her head might explode.

'I can go and ask Chef,' she offers.

My mother takes pity on her. 'Tell you what, we'll take our chances.' She then proceeds to load up a napkin with enough canapés for a small family to survive on for two days.

I try to think of something to say to Jack to distract him from this bizarre interlude, but again, I'm struggling to find anything appropriate.

'Is your bedroom nice?' I enquire, and immediately realize he might think I'm looking for an invitation to a private view.

'Not because I want to see it,' I add hastily. 'Well, I mean, I wouldn't *mind* seeing it. But, not because I want to – well, you know.' *Oh God.*

'Er, mine's got a veranda,' I offer. *You prat, Evie.* Even my mother has paused from wolfing down her canapés and is wondering what I'm going on about.

'Yes, it is,' says Jack.

'It is what?' I ask. 'I mean, what is? I mean . . . *what*?'

'Yes, my bedroom is nice,' he smiles. 'And it's got a veranda overlooking the bay. Actually, it's spectacular. I've never been to the Scillies before and I'm starting to wonder why. It'd be nice to come back for a bit longer, sometime.'

'It *is* a beautiful place, isn't it?' says my mum. 'I'm not used to all this luxury. Not like my usual holidays, that's for sure!'

Oh no. Don't mention the week clearing up pollution in Egypt. Don't mention the week clearing up pollution in Egypt. Please don't mention the week clearing up pollution in Egypt.

'I've just spent a week clearing up pollution in Egypt,' Mum announces.

'Funnily enough, a girl I work with did something similar,' says Jack. 'She loved it.'

'You see?' says my mother to me. She then turns back to Jack. 'Evie thinks I'm mad.'

'I know you're mad,' I mutter.

Jack laughs. 'Well, I can see why it wouldn't be everyone's cup of tea. But I'd choose it over a week in Benidorm any day.'

'You see?' Mum repeats to me. 'That's what I think. Evie, you should listen to your friends more.'

I do not like the way this conversation is going.

'Well, yes. *I'd* choose it over a week in Benidorm too,' I lie, 'but there are lots of other places I'd rather go to instead. I'm not one of these people whose idea of foreign travel doesn't extend beyond an 18–30s brochure, as you know.'

'Well, no,' says my mum. 'Plus, you'll soon be too old anyway.'

Chapter 50

The table plan may have been hand-painted with soft peach flowers and intricate calligraphy, but there is one thing about it that I'm not keen on. Jack and I are not sitting together.

Instead, he is next to another bridesmaid, Georgia's Cousin Beth. The sultry brunette with glamorous long hair, perfect skin and a body capable of stopping traffic.

Still, it's not all bad. I am at least sitting next to Jim, which will give me the opportunity to find out whether he has had a chance to appraise Charlotte's new look.

'She's had quite a transformation, don't you think?' I ask as the starter arrives.

'She looks incredible,' he agrees. 'Really different. Although I thought she looked nice before too.'

He's an absolute, grade-A sweetheart.

'Every time I see you, you ask me about Charlotte,' he adds. 'Anyone would think you were trying to set us up.'

'Me?' I say. 'Nothing could have been further from my mind.'

I pause for a second while he raises a sceptical eyebrow.

'All right, if I were,' I continue, 'and I mean *if* – you could do far worse than Charlotte. She's an angel.'

Jim laughs. 'Very subtle. But I don't need any persuasion.'

'You don't?'

'No. I told you last time. I think she's lovely.'

'But?' I ask.

'There's no but. I really like her. There, you happy now?' he laughs.

'But are you interested in her, you know . . . *romantically?*'

Even I think this sounds ridiculously twee, but I can't think of any other way of putting it.

'Yes,' he shrugs bashfully. 'I . . . well, I fancy her.'

'That's fantastic! God, you're made for each other.' I rein myself in. 'Sorry. Getting carried away.'

'Hmm. I'm not so sure,' he says.

I frown. 'What do you mean?'

'I mean, I don't think the feeling's mutual.'

'But it is!' I tell him. 'I promise you it is.'

'Hmm,' he says again, clearly unconvinced. 'I just never got that impression.'

'Oh, that's just Charlotte,' I say. 'She's hopeless. What I mean is, she can be a bit shy. You don't need me to tell you that.'

'And you think that's all it is?'

'Definitely,' I say. 'Leave it with me.'

Chapter 51

I don't actually need to go to the loo. But heading to the ladies' after dessert allows me to make a long and completely unnecessary diversion past Jack's table. I straighten my dress and breathe in as I head in his direction, trying to conceal the alarming and immediate effect a large piece of cheesecake with wild-berry compote has had on my belly.

As I approach, I see Beth leaning on the table towards Jack, laughing as she twirls a lock of hair round her finger. I notice guiltily that she has declined her dessert and attempt to suck my stomach in further as I walk past.

He doesn't look up in my direction and it's not hard to see why. Beth is gazing so deeply into his eyes you'd think she was attempting to conduct an ophthalmology examination.

From the angle I'm at right now, I can't see Jack's face – despite my straining. But from behind, I can't help thinking he doesn't look overly worried about the invasion of personal space. I feel a stab of jealousy. And I don't like it one bit.

I force myself to snap out of it by doing a U-turn and taking another route to the loo, grabbing Charlotte on the way. It may as well not be a completely wasted journey.

'I've got something to tell you,' I say, linking her arm with mine.

'What?' she says.

'Jim fancies you.'

'So you keep saying,' she says, rolling her eyes.

'But this time he actually said it.'

'Oh,' she says.

It's not exactly the reaction I'd hoped for. I can only think that she doesn't believe me.

'Charlotte, honestly, I'm not making this up, or embellishing it, or anything. He *said he fancied you,*' I say. 'As clear as a bell.'

'Okay,' she says, deadpan.

'Well, aren't you happy?' I ask, incredulous. 'I thought you liked him.'

'I do like him, *as a friend,*' she tells me. I think about this for a second.

'You're not telling me that you actually don't fancy him? As in, you *really* don't fancy him?' I ask, scarcely believing this is a plausible explanation.

'Really,' she says. 'I am saying exactly that.'

I frown. 'But he really, really fancies you, Charlotte, and he's absolutely *lovely.*'

'Well, I'm sorry, Evie, but the feeling isn't mutual,' she says, uncharacteristically exasperated. 'I don't know what else to say about this.'

'Okay. I'm not going to flog a dead horse, Charlotte. I'm surprised though. He's good-looking, he's intelligent, he's really nice. What is it you're looking for?'

'You wouldn't understand,' she sighs. Then off she goes into a cubicle, with a piece of loo roll stuck to her heel. Before I've even had a chance to defend myself.

I decide I may as well use the loo after all, and go into the cubicle next to her. Just as I am about to come out, I recognize a voice from outside. It's Beth, chatting to the other bridesmaid, Gina.

'He's actually given you his phone number?' Gina asks.

I take my hand off the lock and decide to listen to this conversation.

'Yes, look,' says Beth, giggling. 'Hasn't he got lovely writing? Who am I kidding, hasn't he got lovely everything?'

Gina laughs now.

I put the lid down on the loo seat and sit on it to contemplate the situation. Why do I have a horrible feeling I know who they're talking about?

'So when are you going to phone him?' asks Gina.

'Depends,' replies Beth, 'on whether or not I manage to sleep with him tonight!'

They both collapse into giggles and, for some reason, I start to feel a bit queasy. That extra dollop of wild-berry compote was definitely a mistake. I'm dying to stay and listen in on more of this but am concerned that if I don't come out soon, someone will think I've collapsed in here and try to break the door down. I turn the lock and walk over to the sink.

Charlotte, it appears, has already gone. 'Hi!' I say brightly to Gina and Beth.

'Hi!' they reply in unison.

'You two enjoying yourselves?' I ask cheerily.

'*She* certainly is,' says Gina, nodding over to Beth, and they both start laughing.

'Oh?' I say, a picture of innocence. 'Why?'

'Oh, nothing,' says Beth. 'I just hit the jackpot on the seating plan, that's all. Actually, the guy I'm next to, Jack – I think he said he knows you, Evie. Vaguely, anyway.'

'Yeah, he does,' I reply, throwing my towel into the bin. 'He does know me. Vaguely.'

Chapter 52

I'm discussing who won the sweepstake on the length of the speeches with a group of Georgia's friends when I feel a tap on my shoulder.

'Long time no see,' says Seb, with a wide smile.

'How are you?' I ask, kissing him on the cheek.

'Brilliant, actually,' he says. 'And you?'

'Yeah, great. How's work?'

Seb studied physics at university and then took the traditional career route for a science graduate – by getting a job in a building society. It's not my idea of fun, but then I write stories about talented farm animals for a living. Plus, if all you were interested in was money, then you really couldn't knock Seb's career choice. The last time I saw him, he'd risen through the ranks so rapidly, he gave the impression that he commanded the sort of salary a journalist like me could only hope to achieve by the time I reach 112.

'Work's really good,' he says. 'And your job – broken the next Watergate scandal yet?'

'One day . . .' I say, really not wanting to get onto the subject of Simon today. 'Are you still living in Woolton?'

'No, I moved last year,' he says. 'I wanted somewhere a bit bigger so I could fit my pool table in.'

I shake my head in amusement. 'Your girlfriend must be very understanding, letting you fill the house with boys' toys,' I say.

'Er, yeah. Well, the pool table arrived after she left,' he says, looking into my eyes. 'We split up last year.'

'Oh,' I say. 'Sorry.'

'No, it's fine,' he shrugs. 'It just wasn't working out so we agreed to go our separate ways. It was all amicable.'

'Good,' I say, nodding.

'It was a nice meal, wasn't it?' he asks.

'Fabulous,' I say, although as I say it, I realize the funny feeling I had earlier when I was in the loo is getting worse. I definitely don't feel one hundred per cent at the moment. I can't put my finger on why, but I'm certainly not firing on all cylinders.

'Well, I must say you're looking fantastic,' I go on, determined not to show that anything's wrong. Besides, this isn't just polite conversation. I mean it. The years since university have been kind to Seb. His once baby-faced features are now more angular and grown-up, and his previously pale complexion now has a light and very becoming tan.

We spend the next twenty minutes reminiscing and discover that lots of things have changed. But lots haven't either.

'I've got to admit,' he confesses finally, 'I was dying to speak to you today.'

'Were you?' I ask. 'Why?'

'I dunno,' he says. 'When I saw you walking down that aisle before, well, you looked incredible. Beautiful. And it made me think.'

'About what?' I say.

'About why I ever let you go.'

Chapter 53

I decide to go for a walk to see if it makes me feel any less queasy.

But after twenty minutes of trying to stop my hair from being messed up in the wind, all the while listening to the wedding party becoming increasingly lively, I realize it hasn't worked. As I head back into the reception, I run into my mother.

'Hi, Mum,' I say.

'Argh!' she exclaims.

'What's the matter?'

'Evie, have you been eating shellfish?' she asks, full of concern.

'I don't think so, although . . .' I bring my hands up to touch my face. 'Oh, God, the canapés!'

Apparently, I *have* been eating shellfish, which is presumably what the unspecified gunk was on the tidbits I ate. It must have been. Because, for the first time in at least two years, it's brought me out in quite a reaction.

'Look. Don't panic,' says my mum, deciding, rather

irritatingly, that she's going to be the calm and rational one. 'Let's go and splash some water on your face. It might take the swelling down. Come on, I'll smuggle you in.'

My mum and I creep through the double doors, attempting, like two very poor amateur cat burglars, to cross the room without being noticed.

I have my hand across my face as if feigning a headache, and Mum is walking three inches in front of me – the idea being that nobody will be able to see past her to get a glimpse of what I look like. Which would be fine, except for the fact that she keeps tripping me up and I've nearly ended up in a nest of meringues.

When we get into the ladies', I take a deep breath and look in the mirror.

'Argh!' I say.

'Oh, come on, it's not that bad,' says my mother unconvincingly.

'So why did you say exactly that earlier?' I grumble. 'It's not even your face we're talking about.'

I won't go so far as to say I look like the Elephant Man, but with my swollen eyes and blotchy cheeks, he would almost certainly win a beauty contest over me at this moment in time. Suddenly, the door swings open, and Grace walks in.

'*Oh my God ...*' she says, her expression that of someone looking at a car crash.

'Just don't scream, please,' I say. 'I can't take much more of it.'

'You look like you've been beaten up.'

'Thank you,' I say. 'I really needed someone to make me feel better. I've had an allergic reaction to some shellfish.'

'I thought you hadn't had one of those in years,' she says.

'I haven't,' I say. 'Probably because I haven't eaten shellfish in years.'

'So why did you today?' she asks.

'I didn't realize— Oh look, it doesn't matter,' I say. 'The fact is, I look like I've just stuck my head in a beehive. What am I going to do?'

My mother sighs. 'There's not an awful lot you can do, except wait for it to go down,' she says practically. 'Besides, there are tribes in Papua New Guinea who find that sort of thing very attractive.'

For some reason, this doesn't feel like much of a consolation.

Chapter 54

In the absence of a paper bag to go over my head, Grace and I find the quietest, darkest corner in the room.

'That girl makes Valentina look like an amateur,' Grace tells me, looking over at Beth.

Despite the fact that she had the pleasure of his company for almost two and a half hours during dinner, Beth seems to have now attached herself to Jack like a leech, albeit a very good-looking one.

'You should go over and get in there,' says Grace.

'Are you insane?'

'I thought you fancied him.'

'Yes, and it's going to do wonders for my chances when he sees me looking like the Phantom of the Opera.'

She takes a sip of her drink and studies my face again. 'It's going down already, you know,' she says. 'How long did you say it usually takes?'

'A couple of hours. I just wish it would hurry up and go

dark.' Grace takes another sip of her drink and looks into the distance.

'Are you all right?' I ask. I can't put my finger on it, but Grace doesn't seem herself today.

'A bit tired, that's all. Scarlett has decided it's a good idea to start waking up for a play at two o'clock every morning, and it's all just catching up with me.'

'You're not in the mood for a sing song at that time of night?' I ask.

'Funnily enough, no.'

Valentina suddenly appears at our table. 'Still puffed up, then?' she asks me.

I frown. 'Why don't you just say, "still ugly"?' I ask.

'I didn't want to hurt your feelings,' she shrugs. 'But: "still ugly"?'

I tell myself just to ignore her.

'How many people are there at this wedding?' she continues.

'Just over two hundred,' I reply.

'Tsk,' she says, shaking her head. 'You'd expect at least a smattering of suitable single men among that number.'

'There are loads of single men here,' says Grace.

'I said *suitable* single men,' she corrects Grace.

'Ah, you mean someone with the looks of Chris Hemsworth and the bank account of the Duke of Westminster,' I offer.

Valentina tuts.

'I don't know why everyone thinks I'm so shallow,' she says. 'But yes, that sort of thing would be a start.'

'Isn't Seb single?' asks Grace.

'Yes, but he's just told me he's having a break from dating,' I say hastily. 'He's just broken up with someone recently and wants some time by himself.'

'I haven't met a man yet who couldn't be persuaded,' Valentina argues. 'Who is this Seb anyway?'

'That guy I used to go out with at college,' I tell her. 'You know, the one who studied physics.'

She pulls a face. If there's one thing certain to put her off a bloke, it's the idea that I've been there before. Hang on a minute. Why am I trying to put her off him? What does it matter to me if Valentina seduces Seb?

Oh, Evie, get a grip.

Chapter 55

Grace is idly chipping away at her nail polish.

'You are sure everything's all right, aren't you?' I ask.

She sighs and looks up. 'Weddings just make you think about your own relationship, that's all. When we'd been to them previously, I would stand there, watching someone else walk past, and try to analyze whether we'd ever do it ourselves. Now that we actually have done it, I've spent the whole of today trying to analyze our marriage.'

'Your marriage is okay, isn't it?'

'Patrick's just in a funny mood lately.'

'How so?' I ask.

She frowns. 'It's nothing in particular,' she says, 'but let me give you an example. This weekend is the first time we've had away together since the honeymoon. So, this morning, we've checked into a gorgeous room with a fabulous view and, I suppose I just expected us to ... I don't know, slot into our usual roles.'

'What are they then?' I ask, hoping she isn't referring to anything involving nurses and doctors.

'Well, ordinarily,' she continues, 'I would be sensible and start to hang up my clothes and then maybe say I was taking a shower to freshen up. At that point, Patrick would throw the bags down, grab my bum, say bollocks to the shower and ... well, you can guess the rest.'

'So what happened today?' I ask.

'I'd completely unpacked and was halfway through shampooing my hair when he came into the bathroom to announce that he was going out and would only be five minutes. So, you know, I said: "Where are you going?"'

'What did he say?' I ask.

'He said he was going for a walk because he had a headache,' she tells me.

'What's wrong with that?'

'The headache's usually my line.'

I frown. 'Look, this sounds like nothing, Grace, it really does.'

'Maybe,' she says glumly. 'But, you know his walk?'

'Yes?'

'It lasted for two hours.'

Our conversation is interrupted by the sound of someone at the microphone and, when we look up, we see that it's Georgia. She's a little the worse for wear, though the champagne today *has* practically been served via intravenous drip.

'I know lots of brides are doing speeches these days, but

I actually hadn't intended to say anything. I mean, you lot have already had to listen to Pete, and my dad and our best man Phil, and I'm sure between them, that was quite enough. But then, as the day wore on, I started to think: Why let everybody off the hook that easily? Besides, anyone who knows Pete and I will know that I never like him to get the last word.'

There is a ripple of laughter.

'People used to say to me, "You'll know when you meet the love of your life",' she continues. '"You'll *just know*". Well, I was sceptical, I have to say. But I've known Pete for over a year now, and during that time, I've discovered a hell of a lot about him. I've discovered that he's generous, he's loving, he tells a good joke, he's clever, he's crap at remembering dates (so I'm not holding my breath for a first anniversary present) . . . and I know he loves me, even on the days when I'm not very loveable. Impossible to believe, I know.'

One or two spontaneous 'aahs' come from the direction of Georgia's aunts, followed by another ripple of laughter.

'But it's not just that,' she goes on. 'The reason I did this bloody incredible thing today – and got married – is that I discovered that all those people were right. I *just knew*. If I was going to spend the rest of my life with one man, then I *just knew* it would have to be Pete.'

She turns to look at her new husband, who is at the very front of the crowd and grinning from ear to ear.

'I love you, sweetheart,' she says quickly.

He steps up to hug her and she throws her arms around his neck, still gripping the microphone.

'I love you too, you soppy bugger,' he whispers.

Grace and I look at each other and smile. Pete is clearly oblivious to the fact that the microphone is two inches from his mouth, broadcasting to the entire room what he believes are entirely private sentiments.

'And can I tell you something?' he breathes, while two hundred guests wait to hear what he's going to say next. 'Your boobs look great in that dress.'

Chapter 56

This really is no good. I'm in possibly the most romantic place in the UK and the man I'm chatting with is my mother's future husband.

The swelling may have gone down ever so slightly, but the blotchiness certainly hasn't. And my desperate attempts to cover it up with Valentina's face powder has just left me with the sort of pallor that would frighten small children.

'Is it just your face that's the matter, Evie?' offers Bob.

'Sorry, Bob,' I say, turning back to him and being momentarily cheered by the sight of his green bow tie and stripy boating jacket. 'It's not just that, no.'

'More boyfriend trouble?' he asks. After six years with my mother, he's familiar with my romantic history.

'Yes. But not really . . . the usual kind.'

'Oh?'

'It's complicated this time.'

He nods and goes back to his tomato juice.

I frown. 'You're supposed to say, "Try me", or something now, Bob,' I tell him. 'You know, persuade me to confide in you. To get it off my chest.'

'Oh,' he says, twiddling his beard nervously. 'Oh, well, obviously I'm all ears.'

'Okay,' I say, taking a deep breath. 'Well, I really like this guy who's here today. That is, I didn't at first because he was going out with Valentina. But then they split up and I realized I did.'

'Oh good,' says Bob.

'Except now someone else seems to have got their claws into him.'

'Oh dear,' says Bob.

'No – wait, that's not all,' I say. 'Now one of my ex-boyfriends is here and says – and I quote – that he wonders how he ever let me go. He's *really* nice.'

'Oh well,' says Bob immediately. 'Go out with him then.'

'I hadn't finished,' I tell Bob. 'I was about to say that he's really nice but I suspect in my heart of hearts he's not the one for me.'

'Oh,' says Bob.

'And that the other one could be. Though I hardly even know him . . .'

'Ah,' says Bob.

I look over to the dance floor, where Beth is currently teaching Jack how to tango. She couldn't be attracting more attention if she cartwheeled across the dance floor wearing nothing but a pair of Mickey Mouse knickers.

'I see,' says Bob, and it's perfectly obvious that he doesn't. Bob's good on vegan cooking and the works of Jean-Paul Sartre, but I think this is going over his head.

'This one you don't think is the one for you,' he says. 'What's wrong with him?'

'I can't remember exactly,' I say. 'It's ages since we drifted apart.'

Bob looks pensive.

'It's not just a question of what's wrong with him though,' I continue. 'I guess the real point is that when I look at Jack my heart does somersaults. When I look at Seb, well . . .'

'Barely a flutter?' he says.

I smile. 'And yet he's lovely and good-looking, and he's got a good job and, he doesn't appear to have any terrible anti-social habits or anything like that. And he obviously still likes me. And I like him enough to not want him to be seduced by Valentina.'

'Hmm,' says Bob, nodding.

'So what do you think I should do?' I ask.

'Well,' he says, thinking carefully, 'have you asked your mother?'

I laugh and squeeze his hand.

'Don't worry, Bob,' I sigh. 'By the way, I've got to know where you bought that jacket.'

'Oh, do you like it?' he asks. 'I thought it was quite dapper too.'

I can suddenly sense someone walking towards us from across the other side of the room, and when I look up, I realize to my horror that it's Jack.

'Oh my God,' I say, leaping up and grabbing my bag.

'What's the matter?' asks Bob. 'You look as if you've seen a ghost. I mean, you look *even more* as if you've seen a ghost.'

I frantically touch my eyes and can feel that they're still puffed up – enough at least for me not to want Jack to see me this way. My eyes dart around the room. I'm desperate to find an escape route. I've got to get out of here. Fast.

Chapter 57

I scramble past the tables and chairs, trying to get to the door as fast as I can. But everywhere I turn, someone blocks my path – and every one of them looks at me as if I've landed the star part in a remake of *Night of the Living Dead*. I start weaving through them, trying not to push, but hoping I could be forgiven anyway on this occasion.

Breathless, I finally get outside into the fresh air, where the sun is setting and the Atlantic waves are crashing onto the shore. Flinging off my Jimmy Choos, and carrying one in each hand, I start sprinting towards the rocks at the far end of the beach. It seems like the most fitting place for me to be at this moment in time: my own rock to crawl under.

I turn back to see if anyone is behind me and to my relief I've managed to lose Jack. I sigh looking out to sea, watching the dark waves as they swell and then retreat, suddenly feeling more relaxed than I have all day. It's great, sitting here with nothing more than the waves and a couple of cormorants to keep me company.

Suddenly, I see something in the water and can tell immediately that it is bigger than a fish. I study the spot where I saw it . . . and it happens again. I cast my mind back to the guide book and realize that it must be a seal. Sure enough, a little head pops up out of the water and turns straight to me. I smile.

'What are you looking at?' I say to him. 'Do I look so bad that I'm now getting dirty looks from you too?'

'Evie,' a voice says. 'Is that you?'

I frown at the seal again for a second, momentarily wondering what on earth is going on. Then I hear footsteps and glance up to see Jack heading towards me.

I immediately put my head in my hands.

'Don't look at me!' I squeal, realizing that this tactic will probably have the direct opposite effect of the one I actually want.

'I just came to see how your allergic reaction was,' he says. 'Your mum told me what happened.'

'Oh God, thanks, Mother,' I say, my head still buried beneath my hands.

Jack sits down next to me. 'Are you going to stay like that all night, with your hands over your face?' he asks.

I lift my head up, my hands still firmly in place. 'Probably,' I mumble.

He bursts out laughing. 'Well, okay, fine,' he chuckles. 'But you must think I'm terribly shallow.'

'How do you mean?' I ask.

'Well, you obviously think I won't want to sit here and have a conversation with someone, just because they've got a few ... spots.'

'They're not spots, actually,' I say. 'They're blotches.'

'Only blotches?' he says.

'Welts, actually. Big, red, hideous looking things.'

'That *does* sound awful,' he says and when I peek at him through my fingers he's suppressing a smile.

'Look, I appreciate the sentiment, but it'd make my life much easier if you just went back to the party and hit the dance floor again.'

'Come on, Evie, be sensible. Let me see you.'

I think about this for a second. Or probably more like a minute. Against all my better judgement, I slowly peel my hands away ... and look into his eyes.

'*Oh – my – God!*' he says.

'Argghhh!' I reply, and put my hands back again.

'I'm joking!' he says. 'Evie, really, I'm joking.'

He puts his hand on my arm, sending a small shockwave through my veins. Then, he slowly pulls my hands away.

'Honestly, that was a joke. I'm sorry,' he says. 'I'm really sorry. Look, Evie, I don't think it looks anywhere near as bad as you think it does.'

I grimace.

'I know you're only being polite,' I say, 'but thank you anyway.'

Jack picks up a piece of rock and starts to play with it as we both look out to sea.

'I think your mum's great, by the way,' he says. I look at him, surprised.

'Do you?' I ask. 'I mean, *I* think she's great too, but most other people would run a mile just at the sight of those tights.'

He laughs.

'Has she invited you to her wedding yet?' I ask.

'She has,' he replies. 'Do I assume from the question that it might not be the most exclusive ticket in town?'

'You could say that,' I tell him. 'I ought to warn you as well that it won't be anything like as civilized as all this. I hope you like nettle wine.'

'It'll be worth it just for that,' he jokes. 'And you're a brides-maid again, are you?'

'Yep, for the third time this year. I'm a serial bridesmaid.' He laughs and looks over to me.

'Anyway,' he says, 'I'm glad to have escaped for a bit.'

'Me too,' I say. 'Although I'd assumed you were taken for the night.'

'You mean with Beth?' he asks.

I nod.

'No,' he says. 'She's very sweet and everything but, no, I certainly wasn't taken for the night. Not with Beth.'

Chapter 58

This should be the best news I've heard all night, but something is still bothering me. Why – if he *wasn't* taken with Beth – has he given her his phone number? I bite my lip.

What has it got to do with me? Precisely nothing, that's what. I'm telling myself this, when something takes my mind off the whole issue anyway.

His hand brushes against mine.

I can't decide at first whether it was just an accident. But then he does it again. This time, his fingers clasp around mine decisively, sending a bolt of electricity through my body. I turn and look at him, our fingers intertwined in each other's, his hand squeezing mine.

'If it's not too personal a question,' he says, looking into my eyes, 'are you seeing anyone?'

I know I should be looking seductive here, but all I can do is grin.

'It's not too personal a question,' I croak. 'And no, I'm not.'
Now he smiles.

'Are you?' I ask.

'No,' he says, shaking his head as a heartbeat passes. 'As you know, I went on a couple of dates with Valentina but that's it since, well, since my girlfriend and I broke up.'

'Oh,' I say, half-wishing that hadn't come up.

There's a short pause while I think about what to say. 'Was it, you know, amicable?' I ask, more out of politeness than actually wanting this line of conversation to develop.

'Hmm. I suppose so,' he says. 'But I don't think that ever makes splitting up less of an ordeal when you've been together for a long time. We'd been an item for over three years.'

'You were in love?' I ask.

'I thought I was,' he says. 'Although when I look back now, things weren't working out for a long time before we split up.'

'You don't think there's a chance you'll get back together again, then?' I ask.

He shakes his head. 'It's taken me a long time to come to this conclusion, but I know now that we were right to go our separate ways.' He pauses for a second. 'That hasn't stopped me making a promise to myself though.'

'Oh?'

'Well,' he says, 'there is no way I'm going to let it happen again.'

'Which bit?' I ask tentatively.

'The being dumped by someone I really care about

bit,' he says. I suddenly feel a little uncomfortable and he clearly notices.

'I just mean . . . something like this makes you put up your defences. It makes you determined not to get involved with the wrong kind of person, someone who's going to mess you about. Do you think that's stupid?'

'No – God, no,' I tell him. 'It's awful when that sort of thing happens – being dumped and everything.'

He smiles. 'You sound as if you speak from experience,' he says.

Christ, do I? How did that happen?

It strikes me suddenly that I've got two choices here. One, I can come clean. I can tell Jack that, in fact, I am the most dysfunctional person he is ever likely to meet when it comes to relationships. Never been in love. Never been out with someone for more than three months. Never come close to having had my heart broken. I am *the wrong kind of person.*

Or I could fudge it.

Option two seems more attractive.

'Well, yes,' I say. 'I mean, I have as much experience as the next person.'

'Go on,' he says.

Oh shit. Can't we talk about something less complicated, like the Arab-Israeli conflict, for example?

'Oh, I don't want to bore you with it,' I say, shaking my head as if the whole thing is all too painful for me to discuss.

He raises an eyebrow and I start to think that if I don't say something soon, he'll smell a rat, and a rather big one at that.

'*Okay,*' I swallow. 'Well, I had this boyfriend . . .'

'What was his name?'

I scan our immediate surroundings for inspiration.

'Jimmy,' I say, hoping any knowledge he may have of the fashion industry doesn't extend to identifying the names of shoe designers.

'And how long were you together?' he asks.

'A while,' I say. 'Yep, a good while.'

'What, two years, three?'

'Yep,' I say.

'Which one?' he asks.

'Hmm?'

'Two years or three?'

'Two and a half.'

He waits for me to elaborate. I pretend not to notice.

'So what happened?' he asks, eventually.

'Well, as I say, we'd been together two and a half years and, out of the blue one day, he split up with me.'

'Right,' he says.

I am painfully aware that the complete lack of detail in this story means it couldn't be more suspicious if it involved Colonel Mustard, a dining room and a bloodstained candlestick. I desperately need to fill in some gaps.

'Basically,' I say in a rush, 'he asked me to go for a walk with him in Sefton Park. Well, we walked and walked until we got to the bandstand and then he turned to me and said, "Evie, I've got something to tell you"'

More detail, Evie, more detail. I take a deep breath.

'I didn't know what he was going to say,' I continue. 'He might have been about to propose, for all I knew.'

My neck flushes red. 'Poor you,' Jack says.

'Hmm,' I add, and am appalled to realize I have developed a sorrowful Princess Di-style expression.

'So he held my hand,' I continue, 'and said, "Evie, I don't want to be with you any more". And you know, I would have cried but the place was swarming with teenagers on skateboards.'

What am I saying?

Jack squeezes my hand as if to say I don't need to go on if I don't want to, and I am torn between disgust at myself and feeling touched by his kindness. Either way, my heartbeat is going into overdrive.

Thankfully, Jack is suddenly distracted by something, and I take the opportunity to breathe deeply and try to force myself to relax.

'Oh, look over there!' he says, pointing into the sea. I scan the water and wonder what I'm looking for.

'I can't see anything,' I say.

'It's a seal,' he exclaims.

I'm about to tell him I saw one earlier, but decide against it, given that he is having to squeeze up close to me to point it out. I search the water but can't actually see a seal this time. Admittedly, this is probably because I am struggling to concentrate on anything other than the fact that his forearm is now around my waist and I can feel the heat from his strong hands through the fabric of my dress.

'I still can't see it,' I whisper. 'You've obviously got better eyesight than me.'

I feel his eyes on me and turn to look at him, at the moonlight raining on his handsome face. We are so close that I can feel his breath against my skin. Then he smiles.

'What?' I ask, wondering whether I've still got some blotches or some wild-berry compote stuck in my teeth.

'Nothing,' he says gently.

My heart starts galloping in my chest as I become aware that our foreheads are nearly touching now, that he's going to kiss me.

His dark eyes drop to my mouth and I'm alive with anticipation as his lips brush mine, so gently that in the moment afterwards I wonder if I imagined it.

'Eviiieee!!' Oh God.

'Eviiee! Is that you over there?'

If I didn't know better, I'd think it was the Hound of the Baskervilles.

'Evie, we need you!'

I could happily throttle Valentina sometimes.

Chapter 59

Valentina had a good excuse to come looking for me, I can't deny that. I'd been carrying Charlotte's key card as it wouldn't fit in her bag and she needed to get into her room for a tampon. Valentina had simply been deputized into the search-party... and managed to ruin the most electrifying moment of my life in the process.

Now, between Georgia's dad stopping for a chat with me, and my mum waylaying Jack for a discussion about Amnesty International's membership fees, I somehow managed to lose him again.

Careless, I know.

'You don't get away that easily,' says a voice behind me, prompting a small somersault in my stomach.

I spin around eagerly, and realize it's Seb.

'Pull up a chair,' I say. 'Have you enjoyed the party?'

'It's been spectacular,' he says.

'Not missing your pool table?' I enquire.

'It's the only thing missing,' he laughs. 'Anyway, listen. Your office isn't far from where I work. We should really go for a drink sometime. Or lunch maybe.'

I hesitate.

'Come on,' he says. 'I've never known a journalist to turn down the offer of a free lunch yet.'

'Oh, you're paying, are you?' I ask.

'Of course.'

I smile. I don't want a romance with Seb again – I'm pretty sure of that much – but being friends could be really nice.

'Sure,' I say. 'We'll definitely do that.'

As I take a sip of my drink I spot Charlotte sitting by herself at the side of the dance floor.

'Would you excuse me a minute, Seb?' I ask. 'I just need to catch up with someone.'

'Can't Get You Out of My Head' is playing and Valentina is in the centre of the floor, jerking backwards and forwards in as close an approximation of Kylie's video routine as someone who is five foot nine can manage.

'Valentina appears to be having some sort of convulsion,' I say to Charlotte as I sit down next to her. 'Do you think we ought to find a paramedic or just shoot her now to put her out of her misery?'

Charlotte giggles.

'Fancy a dance yourself?' I ask.

She smiles. 'Even if I lost ten stone I don't think you'd ever get me dancing like that.'

'I should hope not,' I say. 'There wouldn't be room for two people doing those moves. You'd end up taking somebody's eye out.'

'I just mean I wouldn't have the confidence,' she says, looking now at my mum and Bob, both flailing their arms about like a pair of manic Morris dancers.

'You've got everything to be confident about,' I say. 'You look amazing.'

'I've got a long way to go before I'm a Gold Member at WeightWatchers,' she sighs.

'Sounds like you're determined to do it though.'

She nods decisively. 'Oh, I'll do it all right,' she says, grinning. 'I've not given up my gingerbread lattes and replaced them with this flipping Diet Coke for nothing.'

Suddenly, Valentina bounds over and dramatically plonks herself down next to us.

'I give up,' she says. 'If there is a single eligible man here, I'll be damned if I can find him.'

'Would you like a drink?' asks Charlotte.

'No,' she says. 'I'm taking it easy after Grace's wedding. Strictly between the three of us, I didn't feel so good the next day, although that was probably more down to the beef, which I bet wasn't organic. And I'd had a mouthful of Frisée with my starter which wouldn't have done my enzymes any good. I've told you I've got a lettuce intolerance, haven't I?'

Charlotte nods, then says, 'Well, it's certainly not like *you* to struggle on the man-front, that's for sure.'

Valentina pulls a face. 'You're not suggesting I'm easy, are you?' she asks.

'No!' says Charlotte quickly. 'All I mean is that you usually have them swarming around you.'

This is apparently the right thing to say.

'I know,' replies Valentina, smiling. 'Although, can I let you both into a secret? I'm getting married.'

Chapter 60

'Don't look so surprised, Evie,' Valentina says. 'There simply comes a time in a girl's life when being a bridesmaid isn't enough. And *I'm there*.'

'Well, wow, Valentina, that's wonderful,' I say, though my mind is whirring. Hadn't she just been on the lookout for eligible men?

'It is,' adds Charlotte, as surprised as me. 'It really is wonderful. But who is he?'

'Well,' she says, 'it'll definitely be before the end of next year, although it's early days in the planning process really.'

'Okay, but like Charlotte says – to whom are you getting married?' I ask.

'That's the detail I'm short on,' she says.

Charlotte and I exchange looks.

'So you haven't *actually* found anyone yet?' asks Charlotte.

'Well, no, but how hard can getting married be? I can't believe that with a little application I couldn't manage it.'

'It's not like taking a maths exam,' I point out.

'Besides,' she continues, ignoring me, 'self-confidence is everything. That, and setting yourself clear targets. I'm a firm believer that once you decide you want something, you should go out and get it. That's all I'm doing. You should take a leaf out of my book, Charlotte.'

'Charlotte,' I say, 'for all our sakes, please don't.'

Suddenly, Valentina gasps and sits up straight, focusing on a target on the other side of the room. 'Wasn't he Grace and Patrick's best man?'

Edmund, who was indeed Grace and Patrick's best man, catches us looking over and waves at me. Valentina's man-radar is going into overdrive.

'Yes,' I reply, trying to maintain an expression that says: run for your life.

'I *knew* it,' she says, grinning and opening up her handbag.

I flash a look at Charlotte and she knows exactly what I'm thinking. Edmund may be softly spoken, unassuming and nothing more than a solid average in the looks department. But, as someone who is also due to inherit half of Cheshire, I am amazed it's taken Valentina this long to spot him.

'Do you know, I've just realized – he was looking at my legs when I did the reading,' she tells Charlotte. 'And that can only mean one thing.'

'You had a ladder in your tights?' I ask.

She flashes me a look. 'It *means* he's a man with taste. Now, what else do you know about him?'

Charlotte and I don't reply.

'Well, come on,' she says. 'Spit it out. *Charlotte?*'

'He's a doctor – a surgeon,' Charlotte blusters, buckling under the pressure.

'Really?' purrs Valentina. 'That's *such* a coincidence.'

'Why?' I ask.

'I thought about going into the medical profession once,' she says, 'but then I realized it might involve wiping octogenarians' bottoms. Anything else? Come on now, Charlotte.'

'Well,' says our friend reluctantly, 'I think his father is some sort of . . . *lord.*'

Valentina is now breathless. 'And nobody told me? Nobody *ever* tells me *anything.*'

Her hand is now in her bag, rooting around it frantically and producing such a large and random collection of belongings that its previous owner could have been Mary Poppins.

First is the hand cream, then the eye cream, face cream, spot cream and nail cream. The make-up then emerges, along with the mirror, which she uses to quickly touch up her face. She concludes by giving poor Charlotte's cheekbones a prod with her blusher brush, and commenting on how she should spend more time *accentuating.*

'Right,' she says, pushing the clasp on her bag tightly shut and winking at the two of us. 'I'll see you later. Or hopefully not!'

Chapter 61

Charlotte was determined that she didn't fancy Jim, yet now she's at the bar, sipping her seventeenth Diet Coke of the day, and chatting as if he's the last man on the planet. This sight makes me happier than I can possibly say.

Valentina, meanwhile, has spent the last hour trying to convince Edmund that she's a country girl at heart – having spent one weekend in the Lake District as a Girl Guide – and asking him to give his medical opinion of her hamstring injury. Which obviously involves her lifting her skirt up so she can put his hand on her backside.

Part of me admires her. Because here I am, with Jack again, full of self-doubt and wondering if I entirely hallucinated what happened down at the beach.

'Have the bride and groom left?' he asks.

'I think so,' I say. 'Ages ago.'

'Oh,' he says.

'It's been a long day,' I sigh.

'Yeah,' he agrees. 'It has. A very long day.'

And it's that that convinces me that the moment has gone. Which is bad news for any number of reasons – not least because my blotches have near enough disappeared and if I don't look worthy of a snog now, I never will.

The final bars of Jack Johnson drift across the room and signal that it's the end of the night. Most of the guests have already left. There's a small but hardcore group settling down in the lobby, determined not to give up on the night.

Although the staff are still smiling, they also look weary enough for it to be clear that they can't wait to get to bed.

'Looks like we're about to be evicted,' says Jack.

'I guess so,' I reply, settling my eyes on his lips as my belly swoops. Our almost-kiss on the beach wasn't our only chance, was it?

'Well, I don't suppose the crime rate is very high around here, but can I walk you back to your room?' he asks.

Now my heart thunders in my chest. 'I'd love that. You never know, I might risk getting mugged by a passing seal.'

We head out of the main building and along a stony moonlit path, as we are enveloped by the sounds of the night: the rush of waves against the rocks and the distant laughter of revellers staggering to bed.

'It's been lovely seeing you again today,' he says, looking almost shy.

I can't help noticing that he hasn't tried to hold my hand

again, like he did earlier. I move closer to him so he can if he wants to. But he doesn't.

'Yeah,' I say. 'You too.'

I briefly consider being bold enough to reach out for *his* hand, but surprise myself by deciding against it. I'm obviously not as liberated as I like to think. Mum would be appalled. It is a frustratingly short distance between the main hotel and my suite, and when we reach the door, Jack turns towards me.

'Goodnight then,' he says softly.

'And it's goodnight to you too.' *To you too? What, have I turned into a game show host now?*

'See you in the morning,' he adds.

'Yep,' I say. 'See you.'

It suddenly becomes painfully clear that he is about to leave without kissing me. I root around in my bag for my key card and when I produce it, unkissed, my disappointment is overwhelming. It must show on my face.

'What's up?' he says.

'Oh, nothing,' I reply, looking away and now just feeling embarrassed.

But he puts his hand on my chin and turns me back to him. His hand sweeps to the nape of my neck, where his fingers begin to caress my hairline. My breath quickens as I gaze into the pools of his eyes and he pulls me towards him.

As we sink into a kiss, his mouth is full and soft and tastes faintly of mint. He is gentle and tender, but as he pulls me in tighter, pressing his body against mine, a hunger takes over both of us. Then his mouth is on my neck and my jawline, leaving a trail of kisses on my skin. And when I open my eyes, I find that the stars seem to be twinkling brighter.

Chapter 62

I wake up with a smile on my face. I'm not quite sure why at first, but I just know that yesterday was a good day, that today is going to be a good day, and as for tomorrow – well, I'm feeling pretty damn optimistic about that too.

Rolling onto my back, my eyes flutter open as I pull the sheet up to my chest. The curtains are shut but there is the outline of bright sunlight around the edges. I close my eyes again and picture every tiny feature of Jack's face, up close. The landscape of his skin, the flecks in those brown eyes, the tiny scar next to his cheekbone.

Images of him undressing me flash into my head. His strong hands sliding off my dress, then slipping my bra straps down off my shoulders. Kissing my neck, my belly, the skin on my thighs.

None of that happened last night, I hasten to add. Instead, I'm here, alone. And I would like to say I feel quite angelic about that, except 'angelic' hardly feels an appropriate way to describe my feelings for him.

Suddenly, I realize that the phone is ringing. It can't be so late that they want me out of the room, can it? I scrabble around on my bedside table, and after managing to knock everything off, including a previously untouched glass of water and the Gideon Bible I decided to read last night after I couldn't find my paperback, I finally locate the alarm clock and peer at its display.

9.30 a.m. I distinctly remember reading that check-out was at 11 a.m.

I pull a pillow over my head, but the ringing rattles through my ears like a freight train and I finally resign myself to answering the phone.

'Hhhr?' I say, clearing my throat. 'Sorry, hello?'

'Morning!'

It's Mum.

'Oh, hi,' I say, realizing that my voice sounds as if I've spent the entire night gargling with white spirit.

'Oh, are you hungover?'

'No, I'm not,' I say, though my mouth feels a bit like a bear's armpit, but it's nothing I can't handle.

'I just wondered whether you were coming on the walk this morning?'

I sit up groggily.

'Yes,' I say, remembering that Jack and I had agreed last night that we'd join everyone else after breakfast for the walk Georgia has organized around the island.

'Well, we're all waiting for you,' she says.

'What?' I sit bolt upright. 'I thought we weren't going until ten-thirty?'

'That's the time now.'

I have a vague recollection of attempting to set the alarm last night, but had given up on it and told myself I'd be sure to wake up in time anyway. My technical skills are never at their best in the early hours of the morning and I'd obviously managed to alter the time on it too.

'Don't worry about breakfast,' she continues. 'I put together a little doggy bag from the buffet, so you can have some of that. I've got twelve hard-boiled eggs in my gypsy sling here.'

Putting the phone down, I leap out of bed like a Grand National winner before running into the bathroom to splash my face with some water, scrape off the crusty bits of mascara from last night and brush my teeth.

By the time I'm dressed and out of the door – in less than three minutes – I do wonder whether I should have taken more care over my appearance. But there's nothing I can do about it now.

When I arrive at the main terrace, most of the group have gone. The only ones remaining are Jack and Edmund, who are chatting over coffee. Jack looks in my direction and my stomach does that lurching thing it's been doing constantly for the last twenty-four hours.

'Fresh as a daisy, are we?' His face breaks into an incandescent smile.

'I'm raring to go, I promise!' I say. 'I just had a little bit of alarm-clock trouble. Hi, Edmund. How are you this morning?'

'Great, Evie,' he replies, and I can't help wondering whether Valentina has had something to do with that.

'So, are we all ready to go?' I ask.

'Just waiting for Valentina,' says Jack.

'Well, good morning, everyone!'

We all turn around.

Valentina is tiptoeing towards us in flimsy, thong strap designer sandals, a Stella McCartney yoga vest and a pair of hot pants straight out of *The Dukes of Hazzard*. She is also fully made-up and looks like she's spent two hours tonging her hair.

'You're not coming for a walk in those are you?' I ask.

She frowns at the sandals. 'Why not? They're flat.'

'They're so flimsy though – you could break your neck if you try and walk in them on those rocks,' I point out.

'Thank you, *Mum*,' she pouts. 'If you must know, I have a change of shoes in my backpack if it becomes necessary.' She turns around to display a bubblegum-coloured rucksack with *J'adore Dior* emblazoned across it. 'I have everything in here I could possibly require on an exhilarating morning walk.'

I look her in the eyes.

'You mean your make-up bag, don't you?'

She sniffs and doesn't answer.

Chapter 63

Serious walkers are always looking for their next challenge. They start with the gentle slopes of the South Downs, then go for the trickier crags of Snowdon in North Wales. For the ambitious, it's then on to the Alps and, you never know, eventually they might end up taking on Everest.

But I'm discovering today that they need not bother with any of this.

Instead, there is an item at any outdoor enthusiast's disposal which could turn a very average, unchallenging walk into a positively perilous adventure. Something which could make tackling an otherwise simple piece of terrain a seemingly impossible, nay insurmountable, challenge.

Valentina's shoes.

I can imagine no footwear less suited to a walk around the rocky shoreline of the island than her delicate thongs. It has now taken us forty-five minutes to cover the sort of distance the average toddler could do in five. This is partly because every time Valentina gets one of her toes stuck between a crag, she starts squeaking like a small rodent, before dramatically falling to the ground. At which point Edmund rescues her.

I'm about to suggest to Jack that we leave them to it, when events overtake me. Or rather, Valentina does – she goes jogging ahead, now wearing her Alexander McQueen stud-embellished trainers.

'We can step up the pace now! I've decided a change of footwear probably *was* in order, after all!' she chirps, bobbing up and down.

By the time we finally catch up with the others, they are all on the beach having a rest. My mum and Bob are both sitting with their legs crossed as he shells eggs into a blue bandana and she offers round her flask of dandelion-leaf tea, apparently surprised that there have so far been no takers.

Grace and Patrick are next to them and I'm relieved to see that Grace's beauty routine this morning appears to have been about as cursory as mine was. Charlotte and Jim are also here and, again, are looking very comfortable indeed in each other's company.

Georgia and Pete are holding hands and looking thoroughly loved-up, and as we arrive, the topic of conversation is whether she is going to take his surname or not.

'The thing is, when you've got a maiden name like Pickle, the opportunity to have another surname doesn't seem like such a dilemma,' Georgia is telling us. 'I thought about it for all of three seconds.'

'Yes,' says my mum, 'but as a principle, there are lots of good reasons for women *not* to take their husband's name – not least because of what it meant historically. It's a hangover from the days when a husband was considered to own his wife.'

'I bet life was simpler then,' sighs Pete, in jest.

Georgia clouts him over the head.

'But isn't it just much more romantic?' whispers Valentina, flashing a smile at Edmund.

Bob joins in now.

'Oh, but, Valentina, there's nothing romantic about servitude,' he says softly, although as he sits in his crocheted tank top with bits of boiled egg stuck in his beard, I can't help thinking that the prospect of him ever reducing my mother to servitude seems pretty remote.

'Given that women are well and truly emancipated these days, surely it doesn't hold those negative connotations any more?' says Patrick. 'That's what I tried to tell my missus, anyway.'

All of a sudden, Charlotte pipes up.

'If I ever got married, I *would* take my husband's name,' she says. 'I don't know about historical connotations or anything else, but I do know that if you really love someone, well … why wouldn't you?'

Grace, Valentina and I all look slightly taken aback. Because for those of us who know Charlotte, this has got to count as something of a seminal moment. Charlotte has always hated talking in big groups, and by big, I mean anything more than two people. And yet here she is, actually contributing to a debate. Okay, it may have only been one statement, but this is so far removed from what we're used to, it feels like she's one step away from being a panellist on *Question Time*.

'Well, I admit it,' says Grace, unapologetically. 'I'm with the keeping your own surname camp. It's taken a lot of blood and sweat to build up my name professionally. Why would I want to throw that away now?'

'Hmm,' says Patrick under his breath. 'And that's so much more important than being married.'

Grace looks as shocked at this statement as the rest of us who caught it. But the ensuing silence is broken as Jim stands up and brushes down his combat pants.

'Well, everyone,' he says, 'shall we head back? I'm aware we've all got a flight to catch pretty soon.'

He offers Charlotte a hand, while everyone else starts gathering up their belongings, and we're soon heading towards the hotel.

Jack and I somehow drop back from the group and are soon out of earshot of the others.

'I'd love to get together sometime,' he says. 'You know, just you and me – no wedding or anything.'

'What, you mean you might actually be interested in me

when I'm not in a bridesmaid dress? And here's me thinking you were a satin fetishist.'

He laughs.

'I'd love to get together too,' I add, in case it wasn't obvious.

He smiles. 'Great. Good. Well, we'll swap numbers and go out sometime.'

'That'd be nice,' I say. 'Sometime.'

'Good,' he says. 'Are you free tomorrow?'

Chapter 64

Our speedboat cuts through the waves and leaves a soft spray on our faces. From Valentina's yelping, however, you'd think she was in a canoe during a gale force nine storm. Suddenly the boat bounces off a wave, and we are all thrown upwards slightly.

'Oh!' cries Valentina, and somehow lands in Edmund's arms, despite the fact that everyone else has been flung in the opposite direction.

I feel awash with disappointment when the boat arrives at St Mary's harbour and it's not just because the time to leave this gorgeous place is almost upon us. Jack and I are catching different flights and it's time to say goodbye. Okay, he's going to phone me later to arrange to get together tomorrow, but leaving these islands somehow feels like the end of a holiday romance – admittedly without the tan or huge bar bill – and I just hope things will feel the same back home.

'I'm just going to nip into the shop and buy a paper before I go,' I tell Jack and he waits outside.

The queue at the counter is ridiculously long, not helped by the fact that some poor teenager at the front is attempting to buy some condoms. His nose is pebble-dashed with blackheads and he smells heavily of Persil and Blue Stratos.

'Just the plain ones, is it?' asks the shopkeeper, a man in his early seventies, wearing a T-shirt commemorating Status Quo's 1996 UK tour.

'Hmm, yeah,' says his poor customer, looking at his shoes.

'I think them ribbed ones are on special offer. They're two for one,' the man says.

'Er, okay, whatever,' says the lad, fiddling with his key chain.

'We've also just got some of these new flavoured ones in, if they take your fancy. Melon,' he reads, shaking his head. 'The things they come up with these days.'

The teenager is now the colour of a very ripe cranberry. 'The others'll do,' he says, clearly desperate for this torture to end.

'Quite right, lad,' the man agrees. 'There's sixteen johnnies in there between the two packets – and if that's not a couple of quid well spent, I don't know what is.'

At last, the queue moves forward, but as the shopkeeper launches into his views about whether a Cornish pasty really is a Cornish pasty if it's made of puff pastry rather than shortcrust, I look out of the window and do a double-take. Jack has now been joined by Beth – and she's wearing a pair of denim hot pants smaller than the average bikini bottoms on a Rio beach.

He says something that makes her laugh, which she does

with a flirtatious flick of her long dark hair. She leans forward and puts her hand on his arm, as they both continue laughing. She then twists her waist to remove a piece of paper from the back pocket of her shorts and appears to be consulting him about it. I may be wrong but I'm sure it's the same piece of paper that had his phone number on it yesterday.

I am rooted to the spot, wondering what the hell to do. But with the queue almost grinding to a halt, I decide to abandon my paper and make my way outside, trying to look as casual as possible. There's something about this that makes me uneasy. I want to see what sort of guy Jack really is if I'm going to go on a date with him.

But when I'm still a few feet away, my mum grabs me by the arm.

'Evie,' she says. 'Come on, we've got to get going or we'll miss our flight.'

I look over to Jack and Beth.

'So it's okay if I phone you next week?' she asks him, flashing a set of teeth so white she's like a walking Colgate advert.

'Great,' smiles Jack, who glances up and sees me, then shifts awkwardly.

As Beth walks away, I can't help noticing that half of the people in the harbour have their eyes glued to her perfect back-side, most of which is peeking out of the bottom of her shorts. I walk over to Jack and pick up my suitcase.

'I've had a lovely time,' he says.

'Er, good!' I say, not sure how to handle this.

'So ... are you still on for doing something tomorrow?' he asks.

Maybe there's been some misunderstanding with Beth. Maybe I didn't hear it right. Maybe I should give him the benefit of the doubt. Maybe I'm a complete bloody idiot. Maybe not.

Oh God.

'Sure,' I say. 'Give me a ring later, by all means.'

Suitably nonchalant, but not closing any doors completely. It's the only way to play it. He leans over to kiss me and I find myself turning my head slightly so his kiss lands on my cheek.

'See you,' he says.

'Bye,' I reply. And I walk away in the full knowledge that, sadly, there isn't a single soul looking at my bum.

Chapter 65

'What do you think? Am I being taken for a fool?' I say, taking a gulp of water and putting the bottle on the ground next to me.

'I don't know, do I?' says Grace.

We are sitting outside on the grass waiting for our plane to arrive.

St Mary's hasn't so much got an airport as a field with a terminal the size of a doctor's waiting room. The others – those who are due to catch the first flight with us – are inside drinking tea and eating scones and clotted cream. For some reason, I've lost my appetite.

'You're not being much help,' I laugh gently, but she doesn't seem amused.

'You were the one who was there. Did he *act* like he was two-timing you?'

I ignore her snappy tone and think for a second. 'No. No, he didn't,' I say firmly.

'Well then,' she says, by way of a conclusion.

'At least, he didn't until I saw him telling another woman to phone him. Oh God!'

'Just wait until he rings you later today – that's what he said, didn't he? Then, when you go out with him, if you still feel the need, just ask him straight.'

'Surely I haven't got any right to ask him about this sort of thing?' I ask. 'It's not like he's my boyfriend. We just, you know, kissed.'

She shrugs.

'If he's worth his salt he won't mind you asking,' she says. 'As long as you ask in the right way. You know, like you're not really bothered but just . . . interested.'

Problem is, I am bothered. I'm very bothered indeed.

Chapter 66

There is either something wrong with my phone, or there is something wrong with *me*.

When Jack said he would call, I assumed he meant earlier than this. It's now 9.30 p.m. and, no matter how hard I try to relax, I suspect I couldn't achieve that without the help of a tranquillizer dart right now.

I switch on the TV and catch the tail end of a piece about some Brits being taken hostage somewhere in the third world – a story that will undoubtedly dominate the papers tomorrow. I switch channels to some trash TV, a programme about extreme cleaning.

I pick up my mobile and scroll down to his name. Maybe I should phone him.

Or maybe not. No. Or maybe yes.

No. Definitely not.

237

I put the phone down and decide I need to do something to occupy myself. I settle on cleaning out my food cupboard, which bears an alarming resemblance to that of a family of fifteen from Hackney who have just been told by the show's presenters that they have an estimated 42 billion dustmites living in their carpet.

My flat isn't particularly dirty, it's just averagely disorganized. Until today, the food cupboard hasn't really been on my radar.

I pull out a 'power spray' from under the sink, which I can't help thinking sounds like something you'd find at a nuclear processing plant.

When I open the cupboard door, I am confronted by an array of foodstuffs that ought to have been condemned a long time ago. A packet of Bird's custard powder that has split in the middle. White wine vinegar that's gone a slightly strange colour, a bit like a urine sample. Loose Earl Grey tea which has never been opened and that I could only possibly have acquired by mistake instead of bags.

This is the cupboard that time forgot. No wonder Jack doesn't want to phone me. Why would a guy like him want to go out with a woman who has spilled desiccated coconut at the back of her shelf?

Depressed by this thought, I go to have another look at my mobile again, just in case it accidentally went into silent mode without me knowing. Sadly, my phone screen refuses to humour me. I go to the contacts book, scroll down to Grace's mobile and press Call.

'What's up?' she asks, when she answers.

'Can you do me a favour?'

'Of course. What is it?'

'Can you just phone my mobile?'

'Why?' she asks.

'Er, because I've lost it and think it might be under a cushion or something.'

'But you're phoning me from it now,' she says. 'Your number's just come up.'

'Ah,' I say, realizing I've been well and truly rumbled. 'Look, Jack's still not phoned, and I want to dismiss even the tiniest possibility that there's something wrong with my phone before I go away and slit my wrists.'

'Don't be so dramatic,' she says. 'I'll do it now.'

I put the phone down and wait. And wait. And I keep waiting until at least a minute goes by. This is starting to look promising. I look at my clock and decide I will time it. If three minutes pass without Grace phoning, there really must be something wrong with my phone.

They feel like a long three minutes but, sure enough, the clock ticks by and eventually they pass. I feel ridiculously jubilant. There *is* something wrong with my phone, after all! Which means Jack hasn't gone off me. In fact, he probably still likes me very much indeed. My mind starts spinning with the thought of him frantically trying to get hold of me to tell me he's booked a table at a romantic restaurant or that he's cooking a candlelit dinner round at his place. Who am I kidding? I'd be happy if he were planning a date at a sewage works.

Oh joy! Oh Jack! You still like me. You still want to go out with me. You still want to walk along beaches with me and hold my hand. You still want to let me look into those deep brown eyes. You still . . .

The phone rings. I look at the display to see that Grace's number has come up and I answer it.

'Bugger,' I say despondently.

'Charming,' she replies.

'Sorry.'

'No, sorry it took me a while to phone back. I was busy having a domestic.'

'Is everything all right?' I am thinking back to Patrick's barbed comments in the Scillies when he accused Grace of caring about work more than her marriage.

'It's nothing. I've got to run, Evie,' she says. 'And don't worry about Jack. He'll phone.'

Chapter 67

He hasn't phoned.

It's now 6.30 p.m. on the day we were supposed to be going out together, and as far as I can tell, I have two choices. I can sit here moping all evening about the destitute life of spinsterhood I have in front of me. Or I can phone Jack. Part of me thinks this is the grown up thing to do; the other thinks it makes me look like I make bunny stew in my spare time.

Not very appealing, I'm sure you agree.

It has taken me nearly twenty-four hours of contemplation, but I decide, finally, to phone him. It's the twenty-first century, after all – and at least I'll know where I stand.

I go to the contacts book on my phone, scroll down to his name and quickly press Call before I get the chance to whip myself up into a nervous frenzy.

But the phone doesn't even ring; it just goes straight to his messages, indicating he's either on the phone to someone else (probably someone significantly more gorgeous, intelligent and witty than me), or he's switched off (probably because he's with someone significantly more gorgeous, intelligent and witty than me).

'Hi, *you've reached Jack's mobile . . .*'

Oh God, do I leave a message?

'*. . . but I'm not available at the moment.*'

Yes, I'll leave one.

'*Just leave a message after the tone . . .*'

No, I won't.

'*. . . and I'll get back to you as soon as I can.*'

Oh bugger.

'Er, hi, Jack, it's Evie,' I splutter. 'Just thought I'd give you a ring because, well, you know – to see how you are. And because we were supposed to go out, if you remember. And, well, I didn't hear from you. I don't want you to think I'm a stalker or anything – that wasn't why I phoned. Er, so why *did* I phone? Well, just to say that if you don't want to go out with me, then that's just fine. But if you do, then that'd be great – even better, in fact. And in that case, well – here I am! But, well, clearly you don't, otherwise you would have phoned. So, I'll go now.'

I go to put the phone down, but hesitate.

'Whatever happens,' I add, 'I had a nice time this weekend. Just thought I should say. Bye.'

I put the phone down.

I've been stood up. I don't believe it.

That's it for me and Jack, then. Over before it even began. But what I don't understand is that he seemed so keen. *Until you saw him flirting with another woman, Evie.*

But all the signs seemed to point to him really liking me. *Apart from him giving his phone number to someone else.* But didn't he kiss me and tell me we'd get together today?

Yes, but how many other women has he done that with?

I'm simply going to have to pull myself together. This is not worth wasting another thought over. I'm just going to forget it right now. Not mention it to anyone, not allow myself even to think about it.

There, I feel better already.

Chapter 68

I feel terrible.

Chapter 69

I can't believe I even considered phoning my mother to confide in her about this.

But after almost twenty-four hours of thinking about nothing else, I've just got to get a few things off my chest. But, Grace has a deadline and, according to Patrick, she has told him not to call her to the phone unless it's God on the line to say He's decided to make her a millionaire.

Charlotte, meanwhile, appears to have been at the gym all night, Georgia has very inconsiderately buggered off on her honeymoon, and as for Valentina ... well, not even if I plummeted to the depths of despair would I consider confiding in her.

'I got the impression that he liked me,' I tell my mum.

'There is always the possibility that something's come up,' she says.

'He still could have phoned, couldn't he?'

'Well, maybe he's been in an accident,' she says

cheerfully. 'You never know what sort of state he could be in. It does happen.'

'So, you're trying to make me feel better about this by telling me he might be injured or dead?'

'Oh, okay,' she sighs. 'I'm not much good at this, Evie. You've never asked me about these sorts of things before.'

That's because it's never really happened before. The only positive thing I can possibly say about the fact that it is now late on Monday and Jack still hasn't phoned, is that my taps are now gleaming. I've spent four hours scrubbing limescale off them with a bit of old potato and some washing-up liquid, and to the cleaning programme's credit, they really have come up a treat.

I'm starting to worry for my mental health though.

Chapter 70

I can't leave another message on his answer machine. I'm just going to have to forget him. I mean, it was only a kiss. And he's only a man. So what if he's got gorgeous eyes and a body to die for and is generally lovely in every way? I wish I'd slept with him now. I'd at least have the memories . . .

Argghhh! No, I don't. Oh, for God's sake.

Chapter 71

Wednesday, still no call, and I have resorted to Valentina.

'Some men just seem to think it's impolite not to say they'll call after they've snogged you,' she says, sagely. 'They just say it to fill a gap in conversation when they've got no intention of actually going through with it. Not that I've experienced this personally, of course.'

Chapter 72

I am getting over my failed romance by plunging myself into my career.

What's more, I have realized that there is only one way I'm going to get a front-page splash – and that's by going out and getting it myself. Because it is now perfectly clear that Simon is about as likely to feed me a decent story as he is to offer me a pedicure.

So, in between knocking out nibs about the quarter-finals of an OAP crown green bowling competition and the fact that the gas supply in Skelmersdale is going to be switched off for an hour on Friday, I have been doing something else. Phoning my 'contacts'.

Okay, so not all of them have been fruitful. No, that's an

understatement. The only thing which has even approximated a story was a tip about some theft allegations at the distribution depot of a toilet roll firm – which turned out to be completely and utterly false.

But, now, I am sitting in my favourite Liverpool café, opposite Uncle Benno, aka Detective Inspector Gregg Benson – aka my mum's second cousin. And things are looking up.

'There is *something* that might make a story for you,' he tells me, polishing off one of the three muffins I've just bought.

'*Really?*' I am trying to retain an air of professionalism – rather than just looking pathetically grateful. I push muffin number two towards him.

'Yep,' he says, taking a bite.

I haven't exactly specialized in crime reporting, but I've met enough police officers since I started this job to know that Uncle Benno isn't exactly following the rules by talking to me about work. They teach officers on the media training courses to avoid talking to journalists off their own back and instead refer everything to the press office.

But I'm family, so I guess I'm different.

He tells me confidentially that the story goes like this: Pete Gibson, the Liverpool-born pop star with a squeaky-clean image and a string of Top Ten hits under his belt, has been arrested and bailed on suspicion of supplying cocaine.

He was caught at it during a drug-fuelled orgy involving

several other celebrities – models and footballers. *Something* it undoubtedly is.

'You can't run the story yet though,' says Benno.

'Oh. Okay,' I say, feeling my first ever decent story slipping from my hands.

'Thing is, we suspect Gibson isn't the only one up to no good.'

Benno has reason to believe that Gibson has been attempting to bribe a police officer to 'lose' some of the evidence that will be used against him in court. If that is the case – and he succeeds – then there is a seriously dodgy copper to deal with too.

'Can't you just arrest them both?' I ask.

He licks icing sugar off his fingers. 'There's protocol to follow, Evie. We need to catch them at it. So, we're following Gibson. The guy can't have a crap without us knowing about it. If he turns up at our man's door with a brown envelope in his back pocket, we'll be in there like lightning.'

'So how long will that take?'

'I promise you, Evie, you will be the first to know about it.'

I have a terrible feeling this just isn't going to happen. There's no way this story is going to stay out of the nationals.

'Definitely?'

'I can speak to the press office when it happens, if you like. See if you can come and take a picture of him being brought in. Would that help?'

My eyes widen again.

'Uncle Benno, if this story comes off, you will be, without question, my favourite journalistic contact *and* my favourite family member.'

'Good,' he laughs. 'How about another of those buns then?'

Chapter 73

I head back into the newsroom with a spring in my step.

'Evie,' Simon says, chucking a press release onto my keyboard, 'we need some grout for page thirty-nine. Bash out a bit of that, will you?'

I pick up the press release and look at the headline: *Blood donor sessions – time change.*

As I dejectedly start to type out a piece about how the planned blood donation sessions at Childwall Library will now take place at twelve noon, and not 12.30 p.m. as initially advertized, I look up and notice the buzz around me. There is a big story breaking.

'What is the splash?' I ask Jules, next to me.

He nods over to BBC News 24 on one of the television screens. It's the story about the hostage crisis that has been on every news bulletin and in every paper for the last couple of days.

'A load of hostages have just been released in Sudan,' he says. 'One of them is from our patch. Graham's doing it.'

I look over at Graham, frantically typing out some copy with his phone perched next to his ear, and feel a stab of jealousy. Graham has been here a year longer than me, but the stories we're assigned differ so monumentally in quality, it could be twenty years. I look up at the big screen in the newsroom to see what the BBC have got to say about it.

'One British hostage, who was released this morning, is forty-two-year-old Janet Harper, an aid worker from Lancashire,' says the correspondent. 'Her release marks the end of a terrifying ordeal which began three days ago when she was seized outside a camp in Darfur by a gang of militia men.'

The correspondent continues: 'I have with me Jack Williamson, who runs Future for Africa, the British-based charity Miss Harper was working for when she was seized.'

As the camera pans out, my jaw almost hits the floor.

It's Jack. My Jack. Jack – who I have been cursing for standing me up. Jack – who, it would appear, has a pretty bloody good excuse for standing me up.

'Mr Williamson, have you been in contact with Janet Harper since she was released?' asks the BBC correspondent.

Jack is unshaven and looks tired, but he's still so handsome he'd make a nun reconsider her career choices.

'I have,' he says. 'I spoke to her about an hour ago.'

'And can you confirm what sort of condition she is in?' asks the correspondent.

'Physically unhurt, but obviously very shocked,' Jack tells

him. 'She's receiving treatment in hospital at the moment and is doing very well under the circumstances.'

'There has been some criticism of your organization for not pulling their aid workers out of this area earlier, in the light of the unrest,' says the correspondent.

'I'm aware of that,' says Jack, as a pulse appears in his neck. 'We were monitoring the situation carefully back home and, to be honest, we were getting increasingly concerned about it. I spoke to Janet's project director two days before she was kidnapped, and we agreed that if the situation deteriorated any further, we would act. Clearly, events overtook that. And I'm just desperately sorry we misjudged the situation.'

As the piece comes to a conclusion, I rush over to the newsdesk.

'Simon,' I say breathlessly. 'You've *got* to put me on this story.'

Chapter 74

Simon looks at me as if he's just realized that an irritating bout of piles he thought he'd got rid of has come back.

'It's traditional in newsrooms for the reporters to do what the News Editor tells them,' he says curtly. 'Unless, of course, you've finished that press release already.'

'No,' I say. 'No, I haven't. But I know that guy on the telly!'

'Who?' he says. 'Michael Buerk?'

I decide not to tell him that this particular BBC Africa correspondent is about twenty years younger than Michael Buerk and happens to be Asian.

'No, Jack Williamson – the boss of the aid agency the hostage works for.'

Simon shrugs. 'Who's interested in him? It's the woman we want.'

'But—' I begin.

'Look,' he continues, 'unless you're telling me you can get

an interview with the woman's family and the first pictures of her in time for the second edition, then please, don't bother.'

We both know he's asking the impossible.

'I'll do my best,' I declare.

He raises an eyebrow and looks down my top.

'Good,' he says. 'Otherwise I've got another story here that's right up your street. It's about a missing parrot.'

My first port of call is the obvious one: Jack's mobile. I'm not expecting much, given that every time I've tried him previously it's gone straight onto messages – and now I know that he's in the middle of the desert, it's clear why. I think he's found the last place in the world where there isn't a mobile-phone mast in sight.

'Hi, Jack,' I say, when I get his message service. 'I've known blokes to go to some lengths to avoid going on a date with me, but this is ridiculous.

'Er, seriously,' I continue lamely, 'I've just seen you on TV and well, believe it or not, I'm covering this story for the *Echo* and I wondered if you'd be prepared to give me a ring about it. I'll understand if you don't want to – you're probably being bombarded with press enquiries at the moment. But if you were able to, I'd be really grateful.'

I'm about to say goodbye, but something makes me hesitate.

'Just one more thing,' I say, and wonder how I can best put this. 'I'm sure you're more than capable of handling yourself but, well . . . I just hope you're okay out there. Do me a favour and take care of yourself, won't you? Bye.'

I put the phone down and don't stop to think before I pick it up again.

'Who are you trying now?' asks Graham, sitting opposite me.

'The charity's head office,' I say.

'Don't bother,' he replies. 'I've already done it. They're being completely unhelpful.'

I decide to give it a go anyway. Surely when I tell them I know Jack, it'll open some doors. When I get through to the charity's offices, a woman with a youngish-sounding voice answers.

'Hi,' I say. 'I'm phoning from the *Daily Echo* and was just wondering who was handling your press enquiries over the Janet Harper kidnapping?'

'What is it you want to know?' she asks.

'Janet is originally from our patch, I was wondering if her family would be prepared to give us an interview.'

'Right,' says the voice at the other end. 'I'll have to pass it on to our Press Officer – I'm just taking messages. What was your name again?'

'Evie Hart,' I say. 'I'm from the *Daily Echo*.'

'Okay,' she says. 'Got it. I'll pass the message on.'

There is something about the tone in her voice that makes me think I'd have more success if I directed my press enquiries to Lassie.

'Hang on. There's something else.'

'Yeah?' she says.

'I'm a friend of Jack Williamson, your boss,' I tell her.

There's a short silence.

'And?' says the woman at the other end of the phone.

'Well, if he phones in, will you tell him I'd love to speak to him? My name is Evie Hart.'

'Yeah,' she says. 'You already said.'

Chapter 75

Graham has already contacted the Foreign Office, the UN, the British Embassy and a handful of other aid agencies working in Darfur to try for new leads.

But all anyone is giving us is a succession of uniformly bland press statements which manage to ramble on for four hundred words and say precisely nothing. More importantly, there still isn't a sniff of a picture of Janet Harper.

'We need to get back to basics,' Graham decides.

'How do you mean?' I ask.

He picks up a phone book and throws it at me, coming alarmingly close to knocking me out.

'Let's split the Harpers between us and phone them all.'

'But there are loads of them,' I object.

'I know,' he replies. 'We'd better get cracking.'

Just as I'm about to phone the first one, a new Foreign Office press release comes through and as I scan it, something immediately jumps out at me.

'Hang on, Graham,' I say. 'This may not have to be as laborious as we thought. Are there any Harpers in that phone book from Ormskirk? That's where the FO are now saying she's from.'

'Brilliant,' he says. 'Er, let's see ... two of them. Let's give them a go.'

I phone the first number, while Graham takes the second. But after two minutes of it ringing out, I realize I'm not going to be in luck.

'No answer,' I tell him.

'Me neither,' he says. 'I guess we need to get out there.'

At the first address, the door is answered by an old lady with luxuriant facial hair and curlers.

'What do you want?' she shrieks, peering around the door.

'Sorry to bother you, but we're from the *Daily Echo*,' I tell her. 'We're looking for the family of Janet Harper. She's been working in Sudan, in Africa, now but was born in Ormskirk. I don't suppose you're any relation, are you?'

'What?' she shouts again, holding a hand up to her ear.

'*I said*, we're looking for Janet Harper,' I say, significantly louder. 'Do you know her?'

'You're not from that Church of the Latterday Saints, are you? If you are, you can bugger off. I gave up on God when Robert Redford got married.'

'No,' I say, 'we're not,' and she appears to be able to lipread that much.

'Well, if you're conmen, I'm warning you – don't even try it. I can do self-defence. I'll have my fingers in your eye-sockets before you get a chance to scream for help.'

Suddenly something dawns on me.

'Is your hearing aid on?' I ask, pointing at my ear.

'What?' she hollers.

'YOUR HEARING AID?' I holler back.

A look of comprehension washes over her face, and she reaches behind her ear to fiddle with something.

'IS THAT ANY BETTER?' roars Graham, making me jump.

The old lady winces. 'There's no need to shout. What is it you want?'

'We're looking for Janet Harper,' I say. 'She lives in Africa.'

She shakes her head. 'My niece Janice lives in Aberdeen. Is she any good?'

Chapter 76

As we arrive at the next address, it is clear that this is the hot favourite. Because, sadly, we are not the first here – far from it. There are four journalists outside already and it's almost certain there will be more on the way.

'Any luck?' I ask Andrew Bright from the *Daily Mail*.

He shakes his head. 'Nobody's in there, but our news desk has told me to wait until they return.'

Which is, I fear, exactly what we'll be doing.

Twenty minutes later, I look at my watch and know that Graham's earlier version of the splash will have made it onto the front page of the *Echo*, with a few late lines added in by the news desk, but not a single exclusive revelation, and certainly not a picture or interview with the family.

I've missed the second edition, along with my (admittedly impossible) deadline. The only way I could possibly make up for this is to get something mind-blowingly brilliant for tomorrow. Although, judging by the conversations outside the

Harper family home, that's looking as unlikely for me as it is for everyone else.

Suddenly, my phone rings, and I'm on full alert.

'Evie Hart,' I say, sounding hopeful, possibly desperate.

'Evie. You still outside that Harper house?'

Great. It's not the new love of my life, it's my least favourite News Editor.

'Yes,' I say. 'Although I was planning on leaving Graham here to head back to hit the phones again. No point in two of us being here.'

'You said it,' Simon says. 'Get your arse back here. You've wasted an entire bloody morning.'

I'm sitting in a taxi on my way back to the office when my phone rings again. I'm coming as fast as I can, but Simon obviously doesn't realize that the firm that runs our company taxi account isn't exactly famed for its sense of urgency.

'I'm on my way,' I say, as soon as I pick up the phone. But there's no reply. That man really is charm personified. When it rings again, I decide to try a bit harder.

'Hi,' I say, but know I'd probably sound more pleased to be speaking to the clap doctor.

'Evie, is that you?'

I almost jump out of my seat.

'Jack! Bloody hell! Are you all right?'

'I'm fine,' he says, 'but this line is terrible and I've got to be quick. I'm so sorry about the weekend.'

'Don't worry,' I say. 'I can hardly be annoyed at someone who's valiantly jetted across the world to rescue hostages.'

'I'm not sure I did anything that heroic,' he says. 'Look – I'm due back the day after tomorrow. I'll phone you then, if that's okay. And in the meantime, I really am sorry. If there's anything I can do to make it up to you, let me know.'

I grip my handset. 'Now you mention it, Jack, there could well be something . . .'

Chapter 77

My story is the lead item on our website and every national newspaper in the country seems to be on the phone seeking a copy of the picture of Janet Harper. The chat with the family is also widely sought after, but it's my interview with Janet herself – conducted on Jack's mobile from her hospital bed – which has got everyone the most excited.

Everyone, that is, apart from Simon, who couldn't have been more begrudging in his praise if somebody had been holding a gun to his head. Not that that matters. The Editor himself sent one of his 'hero-gram' emails around the newsroom, telling everyone how great they'd done. And he singled *me* out in it. *Particular thanks go to Evie Hart* it said, *who has proved in spectacular style just what hard work, determination and brilliant contacts can do. Well done, Evie.*

Janet was lovely when I spoke to her, and has agreed to do a follow-up interview with me when she returns home in a couple of weeks.

She was also full of praise for Jack.

'There is no way the Foreign Office would have jumped into gear that fast if Jack hadn't been on their back from the word go,' she said. 'He really is wonderful.'

Chapter 78

Alma de Cuba, Liverpool city centre

Seeing Jack prompts the most unusual physical reactions in me. I'm talking the sort of symptoms for which other people might seek a doctor's appointment: churning stomach, racing pulse, raised temperature, that sort of thing. I could, in fact, quite feasibly be diagnosed with the early stages of malaria.

I'm pretty certain I haven't got malaria, though. I'm pretty certain that what I've got is . . . well, I'm trying not to get ahead of myself. But as I sit opposite Jack, on an unusually balmy April evening, it's difficult.

His skin is a shade darker after Sudan and his hair has been cut into a style which, on anyone else, would look boyish. But, as I glance at the swell of his biceps, it strikes me that boyish is the last word you'd use about Jack.

'So, I helped then?' he asks.

'Very much so,' I say. 'I suspect if you hadn't spoken to Janet

268

Harper for me I might have been begging for a traineeship to serve burgers somewhere by now.'

He chuckles.

'I'm exaggerating, obviously,' I add.

'That's a shame,' he says. 'I'd have enjoyed thinking of ways for you to repay me.'

It's a week later than originally planned, but now I'm sitting opposite him, I have all the composure of a giggly schoolgirl.

There are no speeches to interrupt us now. No wedding cake to be cut. No bridesmaids looking for spare tampons. This is just Jack and me.

'Do you want another drink?' he asks.

'Please,' I say, draining my glass.

He picks up the cocktail menu. 'Well, you can have a Singapore Sling, Mai Thai, Sea Breeze, Cosmopolitan, Daiquiri, Cuba Libre, Long Island Iced Tea, Klondike Cooler or indeed, any exotic combination of fruit and alcohol you want.'

'I'll have a beer,' I say.

He goes to order, but then hesitates. 'You don't fancy going somewhere a bit less . . . fancy?' he asks.

As we walk out into the street, where throngs of people are making their way from bar to bar, Jack takes my hand and I huddle up to him as if to keep warm – despite the fact that I'm actually perfectly cosy already.

In recent years, the city centre has been overtaken by lots of hip bars attracting painfully fashionable clientele and not a packet of pork scratchings in sight. Tonight we're in the mood for something different, something simpler, and as we reach a familiar door I know exactly what it is.

'The Jacaranda!' I exclaim, pulling Jack towards the bar. 'I haven't been here for years.'

'Me neither,' he smiles. 'And for good reason.'

'You mean you're not a fan of the open mic?' I ask.

'You wouldn't get me up there for a night with Elle Macpherson.'

I frown.

'Okay, a week,' he says.

As we enter the bar, we are struck by a combination of heat, noise and a heady perfume of booze and sweat. It isn't a bar for posing, or picking up, just one for drinking old-fashioned booze (the kind in a pint glass) and, if the mood takes you, *singing*.

Tonight at the Jacaranda is open mic night. This is not 'Like a Virgin' territory; it's for proper musicians and half the performances I've seen in here have been better than most signed bands.

One of the reasons I love it so much is that I used to come here to sing too. In those days, when I was at university, I fancied myself as a musician, although I was never really a serious one. I always knew my days as the lead singer of Bubblegum Vamp would eventually peter out when I got a proper job.

These days, the only exercise my vocal cords get is singing in the shower and occasionally in the car, although I do less of that since I noticed the looks I attracted from other drivers. Grace saw me at some traffic lights belting out 'Suspicious Minds' once and told me afterwards that I looked as if I was having a fit.

'This brings back memories,' I say, as we dive towards two stools at the bar when a couple stand up to leave.

'You're not a singer, are you?' Jack asks.

'Don't sound so surprised,' I say. 'As a matter of fact, I used to be in a band. A long time ago, admittedly.'

'Then you must have a go tonight,' he says, clearly with some degree of amusement.

'No *way*,' I shake my head vigorously. 'It's been forever since I sang in public.'

'Well, then,' he says, 'I'd say it's about time you gave it a go again.'

'I don't think so.'

'Oh, go on.'

'Believe me,' I reply. 'I'd only embarrass you.'

'You won't embarrass me,' he says. 'If you're crap I'll just pretend I don't know you.'

Chapter 79

Oh God. What am I doing?

I've sung in front of all sorts of audiences: parents and teachers at school, students at university, and many a time in front of the crowd in this place too. But after an hour of Jack attempting to persuade me to do this – and eventually succeeding – I suddenly feel overcome with nerves.

My palms are unpleasantly clammy, my stomach feels very like it does after a dodgy curry and, now I'm up here, all I can think about is what on earth possessed me to agree to this. Okay, the glass of wine and two bottles of beer probably had something to do with it.

At least the band are pretty good, so much so that I'm amazed they agreed to get up here with me.

As the opening bars begin, I realize immediately that the song I've chosen is all wrong. I saw Ruby Turner sing 'Nobody But You' live on Jools Holland's show years ago and fell in love with it immediately. But I should have remembered one of the fundamental principles of singing in public: no one should attempt to emulate Ruby Turner unless they're Ruby Turner.

A spotlight suddenly shines in my eyes and I wonder if everyone in the audience is aware, as I am, of the bead of sweat moving slowly down my forehead.

Too late to worry about it now. I take a deep breath, and the second I start singing those beautiful words, my anxiety starts to drift away.

'No one ever gave me anything . . .'

I glance up and realize that people are looking up at me, and none seem to want to run a mile. I close my eyes and imagine myself singing in the bathroom, with no inhibitions, no audience, only a crackly radio and a load of empty conditioner bottles to keep me company.

It may be misguided, but as I hit a high note, I feel a surge of confidence. I sound okay. No, forget that, I sound *great*!

'No one ever held my hand . . .'

I look over at the bass player and he nods his approval. My nerves are forgotten. I feel on top of the world.

'Nobody. Nobody but you.'

My eyes fix on Jack as I sing to him with all my heart and soul. But as I'm about to start on the second verse, someone else catches my eye. Someone at the front. Someone waving.

Oh my God.

It can't be.

It bloody can. It's Gareth.

'*Every time that I felt lost . . .*'

Oh shit. That was really wonky.

I'm trying desperately to concentrate, but I can't keep my attention on anything other than Gareth, who smiles and looks suddenly like Jack Nicholson in the final scenes of *The Shining.*

I'm trying my very best to sound soft and husky, but now I just sound like I've got a cold. And as people start to turn away, I look over once again to the bass player for some moral support. This time, he avoids making eye-contact, obviously wishing that he was with someone with more vocal ability. Like the Cheeky Girls, for example.

Gareth is now right at the front of the crowd and is the only person in the room swaying in time to the music, his eyes glued on me. I glance anxiously at Jack, on the far side of the room. When he sees me, he smiles encouragingly. For some reason it brings to mind the expression of my Sunday school teacher after I broke wind conspicuously in the middle of a nativity play when I was six. Even at that age, I was painfully aware that the Virgin Mary was simply not supposed to fart – at least not publicly – and no matter how sympathetic my teacher looked, my humiliation wasn't going to just go away.

As the song reaches a crescendo, I close my eyes, desperate to block out any sight of Gareth and determined that, as I reach the final, most difficult line, I'm going to give it everything I've got.

Bridesmaids

'No ... body ... but ... YOUUUUU!'
I gave it all I've got all right.
Shame I sounded like a chicken being slaughtered.

Chapter 80

My hands shaking, I put the mike back into its stand and make my way down the steps of the stage. The applause consists solely of an embarrassed smattering – with the exception of Gareth, who is cheering me on at the front as if he's just seen Shania Twain on the final date of a world arena tour.

As I reach the bottom step, my head is swirling with all manner of thoughts: how I'm going to get past Gareth, how I'm going to get Jack out of here, and not least how I'm going to live down a performance that, a couple of centuries ago, would have been a hanging offence.

It's with these thoughts spinning through my head that I suddenly become incapable of placing one foot in front of the other. Instead of gliding off the bottom step and into Jack's arms, as I'd hoped when I first got up to sing, I make the sort of manoeuvre that you might expect from a knock-kneed ostrich on Jägermeisters.

Gareth dives out of the way as my legs twist around each other and the ground hurtles towards me – until I am face down on the floor with two prawn cocktail crisps and a Budweiser bottle top stuck to my cheek.

'Evie, are you all right?!' gasps Gareth as he helps me up.

'Fine,' I tell him, brushing myself down. Nothing is broken – except my pride – although as Jack is getting the next round of drinks in at the bar, at least he didn't appear to see my fall.

'You were amazing,' Gareth breathes.

'No, I wasn't,' I say, thinking I'd have preferred him to have tried to break my fall instead of trying to flatter me now.

'Evie, you *were*.' His is now angrier looking than ever. 'Your voice has such a haunting quality,' he goes on. 'Very Geri Halliwell.'

'Oh, er, well, thanks,' I say. 'Anyway, I must run.'

'I've been meaning to give you a ring,' he continues.

'Right,' I say. 'Why's that?'

'Because I've been thinking a lot . . . *about us.*'

My heart sinks. 'Gareth, all this thinking will make your nose bleed if you're not careful.'

He ignores me. 'I know we talked about this commitment problem you have . . .'

Not any more I don't.

'And how I feel I can help you get over it . . .'

No, thanks.

'And, well, I know what you said last time . . .'

I couldn't have been clearer, as I remember.

'But the upshot is . . . I'm willing to give you a second chance.'

Chapter 81

There is a slight pause as I try to work out whether I have heard Gareth correctly. He's certainly looking immensely pleased with himself.

'I've come to the conclusion that nobody is perfect and that your emotional detachment from just about anything or anyone is something we can work through *as a couple*.'

I glance up and spot Jack on the other side of the room. 'Gareth, we no longer *are* a couple,' I say politely.

He pulls a face. 'Evie, I *know* that. And there's no need to speak to me like I'm some sort of psycho, either. I'm not. I'm just a guy, standing in front of a girl—'

'Yes, I know the line,' I snap.

He looks hurt.

'I know you're not a psycho,' I say gently, even if Norman Bates does seem like a more attractive proposition at the moment.

'Gareth, look,' I continue, aware that I've got to get back to Jack. 'I know it may look like I keep trying to avoid you, but I'm truly not. I just really have got to go.'

He lets out a long sigh.

'I tell you what,' I add, thinking of the only thing that might appease him, 'I'll give you a ring next week and we can talk about it then, okay?'

He perks up. 'I'd like that, Evie.'

'I'll see you then,' I say, finally about to make my exit. He grabs me by the arm. 'Before you go,' he says, 'I want you to have something.'

'What?' My mind flashes back to the last parcel he decided to give me in public.

'Don't look so suspicious,' he chides me. 'Just take it, please. As a present. From me.'

He hands me a little box wrapped up in silver paper and a shocking pink ribbon. I start shaking my head. I have no idea what this is, but accepting any gifts from Gareth at the moment feels dodgier than a cupboard full of porn in a vicar's garage.

'I can't accept this,' I say, and I have never meant anything more in my life.

'You can, Evie. *Please*,' he says. 'It's the earrings you wanted. You saw them when we were out together once and I remember you saying how much you liked them. I was going to buy them for you for Grace's wedding, but then you dumped me.'

I feel a stab of guilt.

'Gareth, that really is lovely of you,' I say, 'but I mean it, I just don't think it's . . . appropriate.'

'You can be so cold,' he says, narrowing his eyes.

For someone supposedly in love with me, Gareth is very good at his put-downs.

'Look, I'm sorry, but I don't want this.' Feeling terrible, I hand the box back. It would only lead to trouble.

But he doesn't take it from me; he just turns around and starts walking away.

'Sorry, Evie,' he says, with an expression about as genuine as a runner-up at the Oscars. 'I've really, really got to go now.'

And before I know it, he's gone.

Chapter 82

'Are you sure everything's okay?' asks Jack as we jump into the back of a taxi.

'Fine. Honestly, I think I've just had a bit too much,' I say, crossing my eyes to emphasize how drunk I am and immediately realizing how completely unsexy this must look. But he grins.

'Lightweight. Well, I thought you were incredibly brave anyway, getting up to sing like that.'

'Brave or stupid.'

'Seriously,' he goes on. 'I mean, there is no way in a million years you'd ever get me up to do it. People think there's a tom cat fighting when I sing. I even mime the hymns at weddings.'

'Ah, well, I wouldn't know that, would I?' I say. 'I'm always at the front with a bouquet in my hand. Anyway, you should try it one day – you might enjoy it.'

'Evie, you could persuade me of many things, but never that.'

'What a spoilsport,' I sigh. 'And after I've just been through all that.'

His hand suddenly finds mine and my heart flick-flacks in my chest. His eyes search my face and he gently pulls me closer towards him. As we begin to kiss in the darkness of the taxi, our bodies pressed against each other, my pulse is in overdrive.

I silently become aware that Jack's hand is on my leg, moving slowly upwards, gathering the fabric of my skirt on my thigh. His kissing slows as he tries to work out whether I'm happy about it or not. I kiss him back in a way that leaves him in no doubt.

'Is it quicker going around the park?' the driver shouts into the back, and Jack and I jump apart.

'Er, yeah, that's probably the best way,' says Jack. We look at each other and smile conspiratorially.

The taxi trundles along for a couple of seconds, before Jack moves towards me again so I can just see his features lit up by the orange flicker of streetlights. His lips brush against my ear and send a shiver of electricity through me.

'Only someone I had in the back last week wanted me to go down the Dock Road,' says the taxi driver, and we jump apart again, stifling giggles.

'I think you're definitely right on that one,' says Jack.

'Well, that's what I thought,' says the driver. 'I get all sorts in the back of here, you wouldn't believe it.'

He proceeds to tell us a story about a woman whose King Charles spaniel went into labour in his cab while he was trying to struggle through a mile and a half of roadworks on Smithdown Road.

Jack leans over again, but not to kiss me this time. Holding my hand, he puts his mouth next to my ear. 'At the risk of sounding unoriginal, would you like to come in for a coffee?' he whispers.

Unoriginal sometimes has a lot going for it. So I kiss him briefly on the lips and say simply:

'I thought you'd never ask.'

Chapter 83

'Hey, Charlotte!' someone shouts as we're heading into the gym.

Charlotte and I turn around and one of the instructors is jogging towards us, clutching some leaflets. He's one of those annoyingly athletic people who never seem just to walk, but instead move from place to place with a permanent skip.

'Oh, hello, Shaun,' says Charlotte brightly.

Six months ago, the idea of Charlotte being on first-name terms with a gym instructor would have been unthinkable. Now they're all practically her best friends.

'I tried to catch up with you yesterday but couldn't find you,' he says.

'I just had a dental appointment, that's all,' she explains. 'I've been every day this week, apart from yesterday.'

'You're a walking advert for this place,' he smiles. 'Anyway, the reason I was looking for you was that I'm organizing a

285

charity challenge for next year. I'm trying to get a group of people together to do a bike ride across the Atlas Mountains.'

Charlotte is completely taken aback, but he misinterprets her look.

'No, I didn't know where they were either,' he says. 'Morocco, apparently. Anyway, the point is, it'll be great fun and we can raise money for charity. Have a think about it, won't you?'

'Er, okay,' she says. 'I will.'

As Shaun and his impossibly muscular legs skip off again into the men's changing room, I turn to Charlotte.

'Do I not exist or something?' I say. 'Don't *I* look capable of cycling in the Atlas Mountains?'

She shrugs apologetically. 'I think it might just be the regulars they're asking to join them,' she says.

'Hmm. I suppose I haven't been for a while, have I?'

She smiles. 'I think that's what happens when you find someone you want to spend every minute of the day with,' she says.

'Is it that obvious?' I feel a flash of blissful Jack-induced happiness, combined with a very definite undercurrent of guilt. I've been neglecting Charlotte. And Grace, for that matter. Valentina I haven't seen for ages – although she does have her own blossoming romance with Edmund Barnett.

'So, Charlotte,' I say. 'The Atlas Mountains. Are you going to do it?'

'Do you know,' she says, 'I just might. It can't be any harder than shifting all this weight.'

'You're doing that all right,' I say.

In the ladies' changing rooms just how much Charlotte is doing that becomes immediately apparent. As she gets undressed, this time, she no longer hides behind a towel. She happily walks around in her underwear, which is now lacy and fashionable – a far cry from her old granny pants.

It's not just her underwear though. Charlotte now owns an item of clothing she has coveted for her entire life, in the same way that other people covet Gucci jeans. A trouser suit from Next. It might not sound flashy. But, for the first time ever, she doesn't have to go to a specialist store selling larger sizes. She can just stroll down the high street, walk into any bog-standard shop, and buy one of the first things she sees.

'How much did you lose this week?' I ask.

'Another five pounds,' she says, glowing. 'Everyone warned me that the weight loss would start slowing down soon, but that just hasn't happened. It seems to be falling off now.'

Knowing that she's another five pounds lighter makes Charlotte run faster on the treadmill. She presses the buttons until she gets to 9km an hour and is striding away on it.

As I look up into the mirror in front of me, a familiar face walks through the door and I turn to Charlotte in amazement.

'Is that Jim who's just come in?' I whisper.

She nods. 'He joined shortly after Georgia's wedding,' she says. 'I recommended it. He doesn't come as often as I do though.'

'No one does.'

'Hello, you two,' grins Jim, approaching us. 'How are you, Evie?'

'Brilliant,' I say, still taken aback to see him. 'You?'

'Yeah, great,' he says. 'I'm starting to think you live here, Charlotte. You seem to be on that treadmill every time I walk through the door.'

She presses a couple of buttons on the machine and slows it down to a gentle walk.

'I promise you I do go home at night,' she says, breathless. 'Although they have to throw me out sometimes.'

'You put me to shame,' he says. 'I tell myself every Sunday night I'll come here a minimum of three times in the following week, but I've not hit that target once yet. I enjoy the pub after work too much.'

Charlotte giggles.

'Speaking of the pub,' says Jim, 'I don't suppose ... well, I don't suppose I could tempt you to come with me one night, could I?'

She hesitates.

'Oh, it doesn't have to be the pub, it could be anywhere you like,' he says. 'The cinema, a restaurant – whatever you want, really.'

'Yes,' she says. 'That would definitely be nice.'

'Great.' He looks pleased.

I knew it. I bloody knew it.

'I'm really busy over the next couple of weeks,' continues Charlotte, as my smile dissolves. 'What with the wedding and everything – there's only three or four weeks to go until that. And I've got a lot on at work. But sometime we'll do it, yes. Definitely.'

Jim smiles softly but he obviously knows what she's trying to say.

'I'm not trying to give you the brush-off,' she adds.

But it looks suspiciously like that's exactly what she's trying to do.

Chapter 84

A funny thing happened last night. Jack and I have been going out together an average of about five times a week since Georgia's wedding and, while the general state of euphoria I'm in at the moment is in many ways priceless, it is not having a positive effect on my bank balance.

'Let's just stay in then,' Jack said. 'We can watch a movie and cuddle up on the sofa. If you're okay with that.'

'Fantastic,' I said. And, bizarrely, I meant it.

Before now, it was exactly this sort of thing which counted as one of my 'triggers': those little things which might seem perfectly innocuous to a bystander but were enough to make me start plotting my bid for freedom.

I had loads of these triggers. From the sight of someone's socks in my washing basket to the suggestion of dinner with the parents, anything that could reasonably be deemed 'coupley' was enough to make me run for the hills. I'm told my dad was exactly the same, though that isn't a great deal of comfort.

Still, as of last night, staying in to watch a movie is apparently a prospect I consider to be more exciting than a front row ticket to the Oscars.

I loved eating the dinner Jack had cooked for me, I loved watching the crap film we'd picked from Netflix, and I loved cuddling up on the sofa. No, I *really* loved cuddling up on the sofa.

There was, in fact, only one downer on the whole evening – something I can't quite get out of my mind, even now. Jack went to the bathroom and while he was out of the room, his mobile started ringing. I was about to answer it for him, when I saw the name flashing up on the screen. *Beth.* My eyes widened as I sat there, letting it ring, wondering what the hell to do. It rang off as he was walking back into the room.

'Er, you just missed a call,' I managed, as my palms slicked with sweat.

'Oh,' he said, looking at the phone. 'Thanks.'

I scrutinized his expression, but he wasn't giving anything away.

'Aren't you going to ring them back?' I asked as casually as possible.

'No, it's not important.'

I couldn't just go launching into a full-scale interrogation.

Relationships are about trust, or so every magazine I've ever read in the hairdresser's has told me.

Tonight, I ring the doorbell to Jack's flat at seven having shaved my legs again (they haven't been this smooth for such a sustained period since I was three months old) and put on just enough make-up to cover any blemishes but not so much that I look over the top for an evening in front of the telly.

He answers the door wearing jeans and a T-shirt which shows off the definition in his arms to such a distracting degree I know immediately I won't be able to look at anything else tonight.

'Come in,' he says, taking off my coat as I am enveloped in a fantastic aroma, which for once isn't coming from him. 'I hope you like Thai food?' he says as we go through to the kitchen so he can stir his sauce.

'Love it,' I say.

Then somehow, and I honestly don't know how, something happens which brings our conversation to an immediate end. It might be the spices invading our senses or, more probably, the simple fact that I am overcome with desire. Whatever it is, within seconds of my arrival Jack and I are in each other's arms, kissing – no, not kissing, *devouring* – each other.

With our mouths exploring each other's and his body pressing hard against mine, we stumble across the room until we find ourselves next to the breakfast bar. Jack lifts me up onto a stool, kissing every inch of my collarbone as I wrap my legs around his waist. Something takes over me as I grab his T-shirt and lift it over his head to expose the muscles of his torso.

Item by item, we undress each other until we are both almost naked and swept away in a bliss I can confidently say I have simply never experienced before.

The Thai red curry frantically boils over and the rice turns into mush. Dinner is certain to be inedible.

But, to be honest, neither of us care.

Chapter 85

We didn't move from Jack's flat for two full days, surviving on nothing but toast, black coffee and a healthy helping of lust.

Tonight, I've been on a late shift at work and so we've agreed we won't see each other until tomorrow. Apart from anything else, there is a big part of me that thinks I really ought to spend a night by myself just to prove I can.

That was the theory. It's now almost 10 p.m. and as I open the door to my flat and flop in front of the television, the news is on and I wonder if he's watching it too. I immediately shake the thought out of my head. I am concerned that I'm becoming a bit pathetic now.

Tonight, when I was covering a story about a protest by animal rights activists, it made me wonder where Jack stood on this and a host of other issues. When I went to the ladies' and looked in the mirror, it made me think about him kissing my forehead last night. I even found myself doodling his name on my shorthand pad when I was meant to be taking down some quotes from a local councillor. The last time I did that with a boy's name, Take That were in the charts. I've been thinking about Jack Williamson more or less constantly.

But it's not all been good. At the back of my mind I still can't shake the nagging feeling about that phone call from Beth. Should I challenge him about it? Or would that make him run a mile? I'm thinking about this very issue – again – when my mobile rings.

'Just thought I'd phone to see how your evening was,' says Jack.

Despite what was going through my mind a second ago, the sound of his voice makes me smile. I couldn't look less cool if I was wearing Clark Kent's glasses.

'Oh, fabulous,' I tell him. 'I had a succession of nutters on the phone. One wanted me to do a story about him being ripped off by a guy who'd sold him some dodgy cannabis.'

Jack laughs. 'What did you tell him?'

'I advised him to contact Trading Standards,' I say. 'What about your night?'

'Nothing like as exciting,' he says. 'I was torn between catching up with a load of work, fixing the skirting board in the living room and watching old episodes of *M.A.S.H.*'

'It'd have been Hot Lips Houlihan all the way for me,' I say.

'Yeah, well, she pretty much won the day,' he agrees. 'But I have to say, I had a better night last night.'

I smile again, this time from ear to ear.

'Me too,' I purr. 'In fact, if you don't think it's too forward, I'd like to do it again sometime.'

'I *do* think it's forward,' he tells me, 'and I'm very glad you'd like to do it again sometime, because as far as I'm concerned, you can do so as often as you want.'

'But will I get breakfast in bed every time?' I say.

'Is that all you want me for – bagels?' he asks, sounding hurt.

'Hmm, bagels and your body,' I tell him.

By the time the conversation ends an hour and a half later and I'm climbing into bed, I have to force myself to think about some of the other things I'm meant to be thinking about at the moment. Uncle Benno and his story about Pete Gibson's goings-on (which I'm still plugging away at), Polly's fifth birthday next week, my mother's wedding … *Oh God, yes – my mother's wedding!*

Only three weeks to go, and while she's sorted out a woman to dye her headdress and someone to apply her henna tattoos, there are still other matters she's 'working on'.

Like invitations and transport and music. Just the little things, really.

Chapter 86

I answer the door to Valentina, who is grinning madly and carrying a suitcase so big that if it had wheels you'd call it a caravan.

'Are you embarking on a round-the-world trip?' I ask, grabbing the handle of her case to help her hoist it up the stairs.

'If you're referring to my case,' she says, 'Harvey Nicks have some far less modest ones. I have got both myself and Charlotte to attend to today, which means I had to bring double the amount of cosmetics. We have completely different skin tones.' She pauses and looks at me. 'You look very nice today, Evie.'

I study her expression for a second. 'Is everything all right?'

I've never seen Valentina smiling quite so broadly before; she's usually worried about triggering premature wrinkles.

'Oh yes,' she replies mysteriously. 'Oh yes indeed.'

We finally get up to my mother's bedroom which, with its riot of batiks and ethnic throws, looks like a cross between a charity shop and an opium den. The overall feel of the place is shabby chic without the chic. And with six people crammed into it, it's also already starting to feel a little bit claustrophobic. 'Valentina! Lovely to see you!' says my mum, kissing her on the cheek.

Mum has spent all morning in her dressing-gown, with her red hair pinned up in tight kiss curls, which I strongly suspect are going to make her look like a Muppet when they come out.

'Thank you, Sarah,' beams Valentina, squeezing her hand. 'And how are you today? Nervous?'

'Oh no,' says Mum. 'I don't tend to get nervous. I've done too much yoga over the years.'

'All that dope you smoked in the seventies probably helped too,' I suggest.

The doorbell rings again and Valentina jauntily offers to go and get it, although she's probably glad to get away from all the joss sticks, which must be clashing dreadfully with her DKNY Be Delicious perfume.

It's Charlotte, Grace and Gloria Flowerdew, my mum's friend and another of her many bridesmaids, wearing her trademark dungarees. What with my two younger cousins, Deborah and Jasmine, as well as Denise – who works on reception at the place where my mum teaches yoga – the number of people in the room is now starting to give it the air of a third-world bazaar.

'Right, Charlotte,' says Valentina, guiding her over to the edge of the bed. 'How shall we do your make-up today?'

'I don't mind,' says Charlotte. 'You always do it nicely. Just do what you think.'

'Right,' says Valentina, looking for some reason as if this wasn't the response she was expecting.

'What do you think, Grace?' she adds, tilting Charlotte's chin upwards. 'Soft apricot swept across her eyelids would really bring out her colouring, wouldn't it?'

Grace, who is rummaging around in her handbag, looks up momentarily.

'Definitely,' she says, before going back to trying to locate her mobile.

Having grinned more than a Cheshire cat since she got here, Valentina, for some reason, is starting to look unhappy. This time, she turns to me as I'm putting my own make-up on in the mirror.

'Evie,' she says, 'those colours you're using might be nice for Charlotte too. What do you think?'

Then she does the weirdest thing. She places both hands on my shoulders and leans down to look at me in the mirror as she's talking. It's the sort of chummy physical contact you might expect between two pals in their third year at Mallory Towers.

'I'm sure you're a far better judge of these sorts of things,' I tell her.

She pulls away and crosses her arms, now looking really annoyed.

'What's the matter?' I ask. 'There is something the matter, isn't there?'

'Well, let me *think*,' she says, hand on her chin.

'Come on then, spit it out. What is it?'

'*This!*' she squeals, thrusting her left hand in front of my face, as the room falls silent.

On the third finger along she is wearing a diamond ring so big it could double as a paperweight.

Chapter 87

'Oh, wow!' comes a cry from the other side of the room.

It's Denise, and she is rushing towards us. Grabbing Valentina's hand, she examines the ring while Valentina at last looks mildly satisfied.

'I was going to get one of those!' exclaims Denise in tones that make Coleen Rooney sound as if she's had a lifetime of elocution lessons.

Valentina's face drops. 'I don't think you were,' she says.

'I *was*,' insists Denise.

'No,' insists Valentina back, snatching her hand away. 'No, you weren't.'

'Honestly,' continues Denise innocently, 'it's *Diamontique*, isn't it? They had them on that shopping channel last week. They are *gorgeous*. You lucky thing.'

'Would you like to sit down?' asks Charlotte diplomatically. 'You look a little faint, Valentina.'

Our friend perches herself on the edge of my mother's bed.

'This is *not Diamon-icki-ticky*-whatever,' she says firmly.

'*Diamontique*,' corrects Denise, oblivious to the distress she's managing to elicit.

'This is a genuine five-carat diamond, perfectly cut and one of a kind. Master craftsmen have toiled away for months to create the most beautiful, the most unique and perfect engagement ring anyone could ever hope to find. *More importantly, it cost an arm and a leg!*'

Poor Denise is finally silenced.

'You're *engaged*?' asks Grace, incredulous.

'Is that so hard to believe?' Valentina purrs.

'Yes – I mean *no*,' Grace flusters. 'What I mean is, you've only known Edmund for weeks, haven't you? Isn't it a little soon?'

'We're *in love*,' growls Valentina.

Charlotte leans down to give her a hug. 'Well, I'm delighted for you,' she says simply.

This, for some reason, seems to snap everyone into action and they all start fussing and congratulating her. When it dies and people begin to concentrate on their curlers and mascara again, I go over to Valentina.

'Well done,' I say. 'It's fantastic news, brilliant. So when did he ask you to marry him?'

'Yesterday,' she says. 'It was *very* romantic.'

'Did he get down on one knee?'

'Between you and me, not exactly,' she whispers. 'We were

in bed at the time, in the middle of a technique I'd read about in *Cosmopolitan*. I was only expecting an orgasm from it and ended up with a fiancé. What more could a girl ask for, from a quiet night in?'

Chapter 88

The others first started to wonder about the nature of this wedding when my mother announced that we were all just to bring our own bridesmaid dresses. There were no fittings, no months of wading through bridal magazines, nothing more in fact than a simple instruction: wear purple – if you like.

There are so many of us that we are in danger of looking like a walking bunch of grapes. But it's only now we're all here that I realize just how many shades of purple actually exist. Still, everyone's made an effort, especially me. I've had a manicure, my hair done by a half-decent stylist and I've bought a dress that has sent my overdraft into freefall.

Charlotte, meanwhile, is also a revelation in the *size 12 dress* that I helped pick out with her. Grace looks nice, if slightly dishevelled because she was in such a rush this morning. Although she's not pleased that Valentina has spent all morning offering her Eye Rescue Treatment.

Valentina is sporting her usual look – footballer's wife meets high-class call girl – and is already dazzling everyone in sight with the bling on her finger.

She doesn't look entirely at one with my mum's friends – especially Gloria with her 1970s maternity smock and Penelope with her culottes. God love them all, but if the fashion police turned up today, some wouldn't just be convicted, they'd end up on Death Row.

Still, nobody will be surprised about this when they see the bride herself. As we reach the front of the register office, I sit down with the other bridesmaids and the guests have the opportunity to see Mum's wedding dress in all its glory.

Bob turns towards her and smiles as if she is the most beautiful person in the world. I've always known he was slightly mad and this has just confirmed it. Because everybody else just gasps.

The most striking element of the bride's dress is that it is green and when I say green, I mean it could start traffic. The bottom half is fine – full-length, swirly – but the top has a peculiar neckline that involves an alarmingly low-cut halter neck *and* collars.

It is the sort of thing Margo Leadbetter of *The Good Life* would have worn. The look is embellished further by a headdress made from a single enormous peacock feather. Bob looks her up and down approvingly, then smiles, enraptured.

The aged registrar straightens his tweed jacket.

'Good morning, ladies and gentlemen,' he says meekly. 'May

I start by welcoming you here on this very special day. Today, Sarah and Bob are here to offer each other the security that comes from legally binding vows, sincerely made and faithfully kept. You are here to witness this occasion and to share the joy which is theirs.

'But before we begin the main part of the ceremony, there will be a short reading by Ms Gloria Flowerdew.'

Gloria nearly knocks everyone out with the overpowering pong of patchouli oil as she walks past.

'Er, hi, everyone,' she says, holding up her fingers to make the peace sign, and begins to recite the words to some poem.

It all sounds strangely familiar, but I can't quite put my finger on where I've heard it before. It's only when she reaches the main body of the text that I actually realize what she's reading.

'Thank you, Gloria,' says the registrar, at the end. 'That reading was an extract from "Light My Fire" by *The Door Knobs*.'

Someone giggles.

'*The Doors*,' Mum whispers. 'Just *The Doors*.'

'Oh, ah, right – *Just The Doors*,' he corrects himself.

Chapter 89

Outside the register office, the sun is shining and the guests are in ebullient mood.

'You look really happy,' I tell my mum, feeling a swell of affection.

'I *am* really happy.'

I kiss her on the cheek.

'What was that for?' she laughs.

I shrug. 'I'm just really happy for you too.'

I've turned soppy lately. Even though my mother looks as if she's been playing with the contents of a dressing-up box, when she and Bob were saying their vows earlier, I had a tear in my eye.

As the guests start pouring out of the register office, we find ourselves in a blizzard of confetti which is, my mum spends a long time reassuring everyone, one hundred per cent biodegradable.

Charlotte appears at my side.

'You look amazing,' I say.

'Thanks, Evie,' she replies with a bashful smile.

In the space of a few months Charlotte has given herself a crash course in all those skills it usually takes a lifetime to accumulate: how to wax legs without the need for an epidural, how to apply lip-liner without looking like Boy George, how to paint the nails on your right hand without covering your whole hand in polish.

Today is the culmination of all this, but I don't simply mean she's slim and pretty. This is not about how she looks; it's about how she holds herself. She's glowing with confidence and self-assurance – and that combination is far more powerful than anything toned abs and a nice dress could achieve.

There are throngs of people on the tiny driveway and it's clear that it would be best for everyone concerned not to hang about here too long.

'Mum,' I say, grabbing her arm, 'you need to throw your bouquet before we go.'

'Ooh, right you are,' she says.

Within seconds of Mum getting into position to throw the flowers, a group of female guests gather to join in the fun.

To my surprise, someone is missing.

'Valentina!' shouts Grace to our friend as she talks to Jack and Edmund on the other side of the drive. 'You'll miss this if you're not careful!'

As the bouquet flies through the air, narrowly avoiding an

entanglement in my headdress, there is a surge forwards, some good-humoured jostling and laughter.

But nobody here has the athleticism – or determination – of Valentina, who has hitched up her skirt and is sprinting towards us.

In the process, Grace's mum's powder-blue hat is knocked off, Cousin Denise's bouquet flies out of her hands, Gloria's kaftan ends up over her head. And, finally, looking very like an Olympic volleyball player, Valentina dives for the bouquet. Somehow, miraculously, everyone manages to get out of her way at this crucial point. Everyone but me.

With Valentina flying through the air, it is almost in slow motion that I can see her engagement ring getting closer, like a small comet heading straight for a crash landing . . . on my face. As it makes contact, squarely in the socket of my eye, it takes my breath away as I am flung to the ground.

It takes me a second to work out what has happened as I contemplate the tiny droplet of blood at my nose, and the deep throbbing in my eye-socket.

I look up, expecting a fuss, but nobody has even noticed what has happened to me. They are all too busy looking at the flowers. Watching, dazed and confused from my vantage point on the car park floor, I can just about see through the crowds.

Patrick is there – dressed more casually today than he was at his own wedding to Grace – and is grinning at Charlotte.

'You must be next down the aisle, Charlotte,' he teases gently, as he puts an arm around her shoulders. He points at the flowers her hands are gripped around, having beaten Valentina to them seconds earlier.

'Have you been keeping someone secret from us?' he says, laughing softly.

Charlotte looks up at him, blushing even more furiously than usual, before breaking into an enormous smile. I decide to try to stand up to go and congratulate her.

It's at this point that I pass out.

Chapter 90

'You really ought to go and see a doctor, you know,' says Jack, dabbing a piece of damp cotton wool on my eye.

'I don't need a doctor,' I say miserably. 'I need a paper bag to put over my head.'

'I know the swelling's bad now but these things tend to go down really quickly. It'll surprise you.'

I've had rather enough of surprises. Like the one I saw when I looked in the mirror just now. Having spent the entire morning tarting myself up for Jack's benefit, my face now looks as if I've just done ten rounds with Mike Tyson.

She *has* apologized – in fact, she was so shocked by what she'd done, she did look genuinely sorry. But that doesn't change the fact that my eye is so swollen I can barely see out of it, and I have now had the indignity of my boyfriend insisting on wiping the crusty blood away from my nose.

'You still look lovely,' he says, and as he kisses me on the lips I feel like crying. And it's not just because my head, even after enough painkillers to anaesthetize a shire horse, feels as if someone is jumping up and down on it.

Jack and I have now been together for exactly eight weeks. Under other circumstances I might have considered this an achievement, which it undoubtedly is, given my past history. But I'm just not thinking about it in those terms. Hitting the eight-week mark has happened so effortlessly that I can't imagine not hitting the ten-week mark, twenty-week mark, or any other mark after it.

It's not just that I'm not sick of him. It's that my heart leaps when I see the soap bag he now keeps in my bathroom. It's that when we wake up on a Sunday morning and he suggests we spend the day together – *again* – I can barely contain myself. It's that when he phones me at work and mentions that he can't wait to see me that night, it's the highlight of my day.

In short, I think I am cured. My relationship issues are a thing of the past. The only downside is that it's taken me until today to realize just how much I've abandoned other people in my life. Outside work, the only person I've spent much time with lately has been my mum, and this was largely out of necessity, given how haphazard her wedding planning has been.

Still, with the exception of her daughter looking like she's been brawling in the street, things haven't worked out too badly. The reception is being held in a field near her house, which sounds bad but I'm staying optimistic. I keep reminding myself that bohemian weddings are all the rage these days.

Bridesmaids

Okay, so the marquee doesn't have chiffon curtains and trendy lanterns — because it's a former cider tent from the Reading Festival. And so there's not much in the buffet if you have a particularly strong liking for red meat . . . but if you like mung beans and dried papaya, you'll be in heaven.

No, it's not really my mum I'm concerned about. It's Grace. She's been my best friend for as long as I can remember, and she doesn't need to spell it out for me to know something's going on between her and Patrick. I don't know what because she's not given a great deal away aside from the odd moan.

If there's one thing I am determined to do today, it is to broach this subject as soon as I possibly can.

Chapter 91

I suppose it had to happen. I knew it had to happen. I'd just pushed it to the back of my mind to try to pretend it wouldn't. But Gareth is the sort of person who just can't help himself, much as I wish he would.

'Evie!' he shouts, as I'm heading towards Grace on the other side of the marquee.

My heart plummets.

'I was trying to catch your eye during the ceremony,' he tells me, 'but ... what's happened to you?'

'Oh, nothing,' I say, touching my eye, but I feel like asking the same question of him. Gareth's skin is now so bad it looks like he's been exfoliating with a cheese-grater.

'Are you ... all right?' I ask.

'Of course,' he replies, picking at one of the drier bits on his chin and flicking the resulting debris to the ground. 'Why wouldn't I be?'

'I don't know, you just don't look terribly well, that's all,' I dare to say.

'I'm on top of the world. Though you never did phone me like you said you would, did you? Still, I won't hold it against you. Have you been wearing my earrings?'

The earrings he gave me in the Jacaranda are currently burning a hole in the bottom of my chest of drawers as if they're made of Kryptonite. I don't want them there, I just don't know what to do with them. I'm certainly not wearing them, but throwing them away seems a bit callous.

Especially as a part of me can't help feeling bad about the effect me dumping him has clearly had.

'You shouldn't have bought me the earrings, Gareth,' I say, trying my best to sound firm and kind, as opposed to bossy and slightly irritated. 'I know you meant well.'

'But you wanted them, didn't you?'

'That's not the point,' I say.

'What *is* the point then?' he asks, scratching his jaw.

'The point is, we're no longer together,' I tell him gently. 'And we're not going to get back together.'

'Not *yet*,' he smiles.

Before I get the chance to disabuse him of this fantasy, Bob appears. It was Bob who first introduced me to Gareth and I can't help but feel immensely relieved that someone else is now here to share the burden of his presence.

'Bob, congratulations!' says Gareth, patting him on the

back with such force he nearly knocks him over. 'How are you keeping?'

'Um . . . very good,' mumbles Bob. 'How are you? Have you found a new job yet?'

I had no idea Gareth wasn't still working with Bob at the university.

'Oh, I've got lots of irons in the fire, put it that way, Bob,' he replies, glancing at me.

'When did you leave?' I ask.

'A few weeks ago,' he says. 'I, er, decided it was no longer for me.'

Now Bob is frowning.

'Anyway, I'm going to go and tuck into some of that lovely food,' Gareth continues. 'Catch you later, Evie, Bob.'

As he heads off towards the marquee, I turn to Bob.

'What was all that about?' I ask.

'Hmm, funny business really,' he replies. 'He wasn't exactly sacked, but the rumour is that the Vice Chancellor and he came to a mutual agreement that he would leave and never darken their door again.'

'Why?' I ask. Gareth may be as much fun to be around as a plague of dustmites at the moment, but I never had him down as the type to be sacked.

'No idea, but I get the feeling they've been trying to get rid of him for ages. He's just a bit of a difficult person to work with. He's . . . sneaky. But what the exact circumstances of him going were, I'm not exactly sure, except that he had a huge row with one of our media professors – a nice lady called Deirdre Bennett. Big bottom and terrible teeth, but nice. He just seemed to go after that. No one misses him much, I must say.'

'Oh well, remind me never to rely on you to introduce me to eligible men in future,' I say.

He looks over at Jack, who's talking to my mum inside the marquee, and nods.

'It doesn't look much like you'll need it in future, does it?'

Chapter 92

Patrick is trying to give Scarlett and Polly a kiss goodbye before Mrs Edwards takes them home. Trouble is, he's clearly seeing four of them.

'Wheresh my besht girlsh?' he says, stumbling, before scooping both of them up.

'Are you drunk, Daddy?' asks Polly.

'Don't be shilly,' he says, trying to pat her on the head but missing.

'I'm not sure you fooled her,' Grace tells him after they've gone, but he ignores her and takes another liberal gulp of his beer.

As dusk starts to descend, the lights in the marquee are turned on and the four of us – Grace and Patrick, me and Jack – watch as the band prepares for their big performance. They are friends of Bob's, who look and sound like a souped-up version of Simon and Garfunkel.

'Hey, everyone,' says the lead singer, a middle-aged man in a Hawaiian shirt and with hair like a mad scientist. 'Before we start, can I just say congratulations to Bob and Sarah. I can't think of a . . . cooler . . . couple.'

Everyone cheers as the band launch into the song the bride and groom have chosen for their first dance – 'Let's Spend The Night Together' by The Rolling Stones.

Bob grabs Mum's hand and leads her onto the dance floor in a half-skip as their heads bob up and down manically in time to the music. He swings her around in wild abandonment and, with both of their arms flailing like they're performing a rain dance, they set the dance floor alight in their own unique way. 'Other people choose Ed Sheeran for their first song,' I say, shaking my head.

'Well, they're entertaining if nothing else,' says Grace, laughing. 'You've got to admit that.'

'Yep, they are,' I laugh. 'Listen, I was thinking. We four should get together soon, you know.'

'What, you mean a double date?' says Grace. 'I've not been on one of those since I was about eighteen.'

'I wasn't going to suggest we go ten-pin bowling,' I laugh. 'I thought a bit of dinner might be nice though. Jack's a great cook.'

'Tsk, Jack,' says Patrick, as he starts to sway backwards and forwards. 'It starts off being invited out and ends up with you doing the bloody cooking. I wouldn't stand for it, mate.'

There is an unhappy-drunk edge to his voice that Jack is polite enough to pretend he hasn't noticed.

'You're right,' he says. 'Maybe we should get the girls to do the cooking instead. The only trouble with that is that I've tasted Evie's Pasta Puttanesca and I'm a bit worried I might not survive the experience twice.'

I hit him playfully on the arm and he responds by pulling me towards him and gently kissing the top of my head. As we move away from each other, I turn to look at Grace and Patrick and am a bit shocked by what I see. They are standing apart from each other and look so uncomfortable with our display of affection, neither of them appears to know where to put their eyes. Then, something strange happens. Patrick drains his glass, turns on his heel and walks away. Just like that.

'Are you going to the bar?' Grace shouts after him.

But he ignores her and continues with his swaying march away from us.

'I hope you weren't expecting to get lucky tonight,' I say. 'I haven't seen Patrick this drunk since your wedding night.'

'Hmm,' she says, forcing a smile. 'Well, I'm starting to think if I can't beat him I may join him. Can I get either of you a drink?'

We both shake our heads. As she walks away in Patrick's direction, I grab her by the arm, out of earshot of Jack.

'Grace,' I say. 'What's going on? Do you want to talk?'

'No, honestly,' she says. 'It's no big deal.'

But it is starting to seem like a very big deal to me.

Chapter 93

If I thought Patrick was acting strangely, that is nothing compared with Charlotte.

This is the first time she's drunk anything other than saccharine-packed fizzy drinks since the start of her WeightWatchers regime, and it has had an immediate effect. When I shared a Portaloo with her earlier she was swaying so much trying to hover that she nearly toppled the thing over.

'Oooh,' she says, throwing her head back wildly. 'The first proper drink I've had in ages and it's made me go really squiffy. Still, it's not unpleasant. In fact, it's quite nice.'

As Charlotte and I head back into the marquee, the band are in full swing – and so is Valentina. Apparently not put off by the fact that they're playing a Van Morrison track, she has dusted off her old Spice Girls routine and is giving it its first outing since 1999. Edmund couldn't look more proud.

'You know,' says Charlotte, out of nowhere, 'people look at you differently when you're thin.'

'*I don't*,' I say determinedly. 'I mean, you look great and everything, but you're still the same Charlotte to me. I've always thought you were lovely and I always will do.'

'Yes, but not everyone's like you, Evie,' she says. 'Take my mother ...'

She swallows a large gulp of her wine.

'Do you know what she said on Sunday? "*There's barely a pick on you*," was what she said. I'd gone round for lunch and passed on the Yorkshire pudding and gravy. She nearly fainted!'

I smile.

'But it's not just my mother,' she continues, running her hands contentedly over her new dress. 'It's ...'

'Who?' I ask.

She looks up at me and smiles conspiratorially.

'Men,' she giggles.

'Men?' I echo, grinning. 'Go on, who've you been flirting with?'

'Ah,' she says, taking another liberal mouthful of wine. 'That would be telling.'

'Charlotte,' I say, slightly amazed, 'stop teasing. Come on, tell me.'

She shakes her head. 'No, I can't,' she says.

'Charlotte!' I squeal. 'Who are you talking about? Tell me this bloody instant!'

She giggles again. 'Maybe ... maybe one day.'

'Okay, okay.' I am desperate to know, but don't want to make her clam up completely. 'But has anything ... happened?'

She looks into her wine glass and smiles again. 'Oh yes,' she says dreamily.

I frown. 'What?' I ask.

She shakes her head again, apparently enjoying teasing me with this story as much as the story itself.

'So, have you kissed?' I ask.

She smiles privately, then – so subtly I wonder if I've imagined it – she nods.

'Look here, you,' I laugh, exasperated, 'I am a journalist and I will get this out of you sooner or later – I promise. So, look, are you seeing him again?'

Charlotte's smile suddenly disappears and she looks very serious, and very drunk.

'I hope so,' she says. 'I really do hope so. But, I'll be honest with you . . . it's complicated.'

Chapter 94

Patrick has always been what you'd call a happy drunk. A harmless drunk. The sort of person who, after a few jars on a Friday night, does silly things and gives sloppy kisses to his male friends. He's never obnoxious. Although on the evidence of his behaviour earlier, something's clearly changed on that score.

It is because of this that I've left Jack chatting to my mum about mudslides in Guatemala to go off in search of Grace, who I find talking to Jim near the bar.

'Hi, you two,' I say brightly, not wanting to arouse any suspicion that I've come in search of a deep and meaningful conversation. 'The band are good, aren't they?'

'Brilliant,' says Jim. 'Although Valentina threw them earlier by asking if they knew any Christina Aguilera numbers.'

'Listen, Jim,' I say, 'I hope you don't think I'm being rude, but I wonder if I could borrow Grace for a few minutes?'

'Sure,' he says. 'I was going to try and persuade Charlotte to come and dance with me anyway.'

Grace and I go in search of a quiet table in the corner away from the dance floor. I can't help noticing as we pass that Valentina's dancing, which always involves a fair amount of arm movement anyway, tonight involves so much conspicuous waving of the hand with her ring on it that she could be directing traffic.

'What's up?' says Grace as we sit down in a suitable spot.

'I was about to ask you the same thing,' I say.

But before she gets the chance to answer, my handbag starts ringing and I realize it's Jack's mobile which, since he abandoned his jacket earlier, I've been looking after. Normally, I'd take it straight to him, but now is really not a good time so I just dig it out and press the silence button.

'What do you mean?' she asks.

'Look,' I say, 'I don't want to pry or anything, but I've noticed that you and Patrick both seem a bit ... I don't know ... not really yourselves.'

She bites her lip and considers this for a second. 'Nothing gets past you, does it?'

'Is something the matter?' I ask.

She sighs. 'I think there is, Evie. But it's hard to put my finger on.'

Suddenly, the phone goes off again. I dig it out of my bag, and press Silence again, before nodding at her to go on.

'It's hard to put my finger on because it's no one big thing,' she continues. 'We've not had a huge row over money, or the kids or, well, anything. But we are at each other's throats a lot. Everything I say seems to offend Patrick at the moment. And he just *never* seems happy.'

'Do you have any idea what's caused it?' I ask.

'Being married to me, apparently,' she says miserably.

'Don't be daft. I mean ... it can't just be that ...'

Her head snaps up. 'Does that mean you think he's having an affair?' she asks, her eyes welling up.

'No!' I say hastily. 'I don't think that for a second.'

'Don't you?' she says. 'I'm not so sure. I'm really not so sure.'

Some people, when they cry, look like they do in the movies, with a single tear cascading poetically down porcelain skin. Grace, like me, isn't one of them.

Her cheeks now resemble corned beef, her eyes are almost as puffy as my own and her nose has acquired that special beetrooty tinge that comes from excessive blowing on a six-ply napkin.

'Patrick loves you, I know it,' I say. 'God, you only had to see the way he looked at you at your wedding. Things can't have just gone from that to what you're talking about in a few months.'

'You wouldn't have thought so,' she says, sniffing into her napkin again. 'But that's what it feels like.'

'I take it you've tried talking to him about it?'

'It's hard to bring up. I haven't wanted to confront him,' she admits.

'Well, you should,' I say firmly. 'Confront him, talk to him, tell him you love him.'

I see the hint of a smile.

'For someone who has never had a long-term relationship, you're actually pretty good at this advice stuff.'

I put my arm around her. '*Had* is the operative word,' I say. 'Commitment is my new middle name.'

'Well, I'm glad,' she says. 'I really am.'

Suddenly, Jack's phone rings again. This time, for the sake of shutting the damn thing up, I decide to answer it.

'Hello, Jack's phone,' I say.

'Er, oh, hi,' says the voice of a young-sounding woman on the other end. 'Is Jack there, please?'

'Not at the moment,' I say. 'I mean, he's around but I'm not sure where he is right now. Can I take a message?'

'Yeah,' says the woman. 'Can you tell him Beth rang. Just let him know he's still got my T-shirt. I forgot to take it with me when I left this morning and I wanted to know whether I could come over and get it tomorrow.'

I freeze.

'Er, can I take a number?' I ask.

'Oh, he's got it,' she replies.

I am suddenly unable to think about what to say or do.

'Hello?' she says.

'Er, yes, no problem,' I say, and end the call.

'What's up?' asks Grace, leaning over. 'Evie, you're as white as a sheet. Whatever's the matter?'

Chapter 95

I'm an idiot. No, worse than that. I'm a gullible idiot.

I'd known the second I saw Jack talking to Beth on that jetty in the Scillies that something was going on. Then there was the phone call to his mobile the other week. And now this. So how could I have been so stupid?

I know exactly how. I've been swept off my feet; every ounce of common sense with it. I managed to convince myself I hadn't even *noticed* anything was going on.

Which is absolutely ridiculous because I *knew* this was happening and just chose to ignore it!

'I can't believe it,' I tell Grace as I storm across the floor of the marquee.

'Are you sure there couldn't be an explanation?' she says, trying to keep up with me.

I spin around. 'What explanation could there *possibly* be? I saw it coming at Georgia's wedding. He gave her his phone number. I saw them flirting. Then, I saw her name come up on his mobile a couple of weeks ago. Now Beth has apparently left an item of clothing at his flat when she left ... this morning!' Grace is obviously trying to think of something to say but is just opening and closing her mouth like a frustrated goldfish instead.

'So you weren't with him last night, then?' she asks finally, clutching at straws.

'I was helping my mum get ready for the wedding,' I continue, ranting. 'Which was obviously the perfect opportunity. I just don't see what possible explanation there is apart from Beth having stayed over for an all-night sex session.'

'Okay, so she clearly has stayed over. But it might have all been innocent,' says Grace weakly, though it's clear she can't imagine how.

My face crumples as I teeter on the edge of tears, sniffing them back furiously. Instead, I let anger build up in me – it feels like a far better approach than blubbing.

'If it was innocent, why wouldn't he have mentioned it?' I say angrily.

'I just don't want you to do anything you'll regret, Evie,' she says, grabbing my arm. 'I know how much you like him.'

'*That* was before I discovered that he was two-timing me.'

Leaving Grace next to the entrance of the marquee, I continue to look for Jack. But my mother gets to me first, calling my name out as she skips towards me, her peacock feather now bent over in a perfect right angle.

'I've hardly seen you all night,' she beams.

'Oh! Sorry, yes,' I say, forcing a smile that she's clearly not convinced by.

'What's the matter?' she asks.

'Nothing,' I tell her. 'Have you seen Jack anywhere?'

'Oh, he *is* lovely, you know,' she enthuses. 'If I'd tried to speak to some of your other boyfriends about the humanitarian crisis in the Republic of Congo they'd think I was speaking another language.'

'Hmm,' I say. 'Have you seen him?'

'And he seems very fond of you,' she continues.

I'm starting to think *I'm* talking another language. 'Yes,' I say patiently. 'But have you seen him?'

'Yes,' she says. 'I left him talking to that chap you know.'

'Which chap?' *Honestly, Mum!*

'You know,' she says, 'the one with the unfortunate complexion. I told him he ought to get that seen to. I met someone with a rash like that when I lived in India and he fell into a coma a week later.'

'You don't mean Gareth, do you?' I say.

'That's the one,' she says brightly.

Chapter 96

I feel an instinctive stab of horror at the fact that I've failed to keep Jack and Gareth apart. But I remind myself that this is now irrelevant under the circumstances.

As I head towards them Gareth is smiling one of his increasingly creepy smiles that have started reminding me of the Child Catcher in *Chitty Chitty Bang Bang*.

Jack, on the other hand, isn't smiling at all.

'Can I speak to you a minute, please?' I say to him.

'What?' he says, distractedly. 'Yeah, sure.'

'Having a nice evening, Evie?' Gareth enquires as we walk away, but I can't bring myself to do anything other than ignore him.

When we are a safe distance away, I turn to Jack and produce his phone.

'There,' I say, slamming it into his hand. 'There's your mobile. Beth phoned. She left a message asking you to ring back.'

'Right,' he says, taking the phone from me without showing even a flicker of embarrassment.

'That's right,' I add for good measure. *'Beth.'*

'I heard you,' he says.

'Oh, *did* you?' I am aware that my voice is starting to sound slightly wobbly in an I'm-actually-hysterical-but-I'll-be-buggered-if-I'm-going-to-show-it kind of way. 'Oh, you heard me, did you? Right. Right then. O-*kay.'*

He just ignores me, which I can't help thinking is unbelievable. Positively shameless, in fact.

'I need to ask you about something, Evie,' he says instead.

'Oh?' I cross my arms huffily. 'What?'

'About something that—' But he stops midway through his sentence. 'Why are you doing that?'

'What?'

'Pulling that funny face?' he says.

Now I really am annoyed.

'Because *I'm upset,'* I say, trying to sound dignified though it comes out like Miss Piggy throwing a tantrum.

'In fact, I'm *bloody* upset, you deceiving . . .' I want to say *bastard*, but am concerned that might be some way short of the dignified approach '. . . you deceiving . . . *so and so.'*

But even I think that sounds ludicrous.

'What are you talking about?' Jack looks mystified.

'I'm talking about the *thing* you're having with Beth,' I grind out.

He furrows his brow.

'Don't look like that,' I say, my head banging again. 'I know you gave her your number in the Scillies. I know she's been phoning you because I saw her name come up on your mobile. And now she's just phoned to say she left her top at your place this morning. You must think I've got the intelligence of an amoeba.'

'Evie,' he says calmly. 'You don't know what you're saying.'

'You're denying it then?'

'Yes,' he says. 'I am denying it. But while we're on the subject of deceptive *so and sos*, I wonder if you could clear something up for me?'

'Fire away,' I tell him, crossing my arms so tightly now my wrist has gone dead.

'You know how you told me that heartrending story on the beach in the Scillies about how you'd just been dumped? Who was it, by Jimmy, who you'd been seeing for two and half years?'

I can feel the heat rising to my neck now. 'That was a load of rubbish, wasn't it?' he says.

I'm trying to think of a suitable response but nothing is springing to mind.

'I've just been told that you've never – not once – been out with anyone for longer than a few weeks because you dump them unceremoniously before then.'

Again, words are somehow failing me. Which is not something I'm used to, I'll admit.

'So I can only assume that's what this is all about. Why did you lie to me, Evie?'

I consider this carefully and try to remember again why I did.

'It wasn't exactly a lie,' I try.

'Wasn't it?' he asks.

'Look, I don't have to justify myself to you. I had my reasons. But let's not change the subject. I want to know how long this thing between you and Beth has been going on.'

He shakes his head. 'There *is* no thing between me and Beth.'

'I don't believe you,' I say.

He doesn't say anything, just looks at me, his eyes blazing. 'Are these ridiculous accusations your way of splitting up with me?' he asks. 'Why don't you just have the guts to come out and say it?'

'Oh, they're ridiculous, are they?' I say, refusing to get drawn into anything other than the most important matter here.

'Yes,' he says, 'they are. But let me save you a job, Evie. I'm happy to go quietly.'

'Fine,' I say. 'Go!'

Neither of us move in the second that follows. And as his eyes soften on my face, hope rises in me that something, somehow, is going to turn this situation around.

But instead, he takes a step back. And I watch as he spins round and walks away from the boom of music, away from the party, away from me.

Chapter 97

In a strange way, I feel like I did on the day I lost my virginity. I remember the sensation distinctly as I walked through town, idly looking in shop windows. I felt as if a fundamental part of me had changed for ever. And I couldn't help getting an eerie, if illogical feeling that people could tell. From the shopkeeper who asked me if I had change of a twenty-pound note to the woman sitting next to me on the train reading an article about HRT, I felt as if they knew that something earth-shattering had just happened to me, that it must be written all over my face.

As I jump into the back of a taxi, I wonder whether the driver can tell that I've just been dumped by someone – someone I actually care about. I wonder if he realizes how this event, so completely alien to me until now, has changed everything.

'Have you been in a fight?' he asks, studying my black eye in his mirror.

'Yes,' I say. 'I mean no . . . no, my eye was just an accident.' I stare out of the window, really not wanting to talk.

'Have you come from that wedding down the road?' he asks.

'Yes,' I mutter.

'You're the third one I've picked up from there,' he says, and only then do I realize just how late it is. 'Christ, I've seen some sights. The last one was wearing a poncho. Looked like she'd just stepped out of a Spaghetti Western.'

So maybe he doesn't know.

My head spins as I lean back on the seat and block out the sound of his voice. *Just take me home*, I think. *Just leave me alone.*

My daze is broken as the taxi beeps and swerves around something, or somebody. As I look out of the window, I realize we've just narrowly missed Grace and Patrick as they walk down the middle of the road.

'Can you stop a minute, please?' I say to the driver, and as he pulls in I push the window down.

'Do you want a lift?' I ask.

They're holding hands, but Patrick won't look at me. 'No, no,' says Grace. 'Honestly, we're going in a completely different direction. We'll flag our own one down. Is everything okay, Evie?'

I hesitate.

'I'll speak to you tomorrow, okay?' My voice is wobbling.

'Sure,' she says.

She huddles up to Patrick, but I can tell from his face that something still isn't right. I don't know what. And at this moment in time I don't really care. Somehow I can't bring myself even to think about Grace and Patrick's problems any more.

As the journey continues, it strikes me how quickly my rage, the rage that was so forceful such a short time ago, turns into something else: a dull, rising ache which already feels far more potent, and far more painful, than plain old anger. Or the lingering effects of Valentina's left hook, for that matter.

Tonight marks the end of something which, just four hours ago, I thought was the best thing that ever happened to me. It's the end that I, recklessly, never thought would come. The end of me and Jack. Jack and me. My one and only steady relationship. Almost.

I try to blink away the heat from my eyes and swallow a hard, bitter lump in my throat.

I think of Jack tenderly kissing my swollen face earlier and telling me I was still the most beautiful woman he'd ever known. I think about how safe it made me feel. How special. How loved.

The tears that have pricked my eyes now spill onto my cheeks and a silent howl builds inside me.

I look out of the window but can't focus on anything except an image of Jack's kind face, with its warm eyes and oh so soft mouth. It strikes me that I may never see that face again.

Bridesmaids

I put my head in my hands and, despite my attempts to hide the fact that I'm crying, a sob escapes from my lips.

'You're not going to be sick back there are you?' says the driver, looking in his mirror. 'Cos it's an extra twenty-five quid if you are.'

Chapter 98

I wake up with a hangover mouth, a throbbing eye and a very odd feeling about the night before. I know immediately that something is wrong, but it takes a half a second before I recall exactly what it is. My stomach lurches so hard it feels like I've been kicked by the hind legs of a donkey.

In some ways, it's no surprise I feel like this, given the amount of coffee I drank when I got back last night. On top of the alcohol I'd been drinking all day. On top of the painkillers I'd taken in the afternoon. On top of the smack in the head by Valentina's sparkler.

And yet, I know that what I'm feeling isn't caused by that lot. Because nothing is making me feel more nauseous than the recollection of Jack's words.

Are these ridiculous accusations your way of splitting up with me? I'm happy to go quietly.

Just remembering them makes my head spin almost as much as my stomach, my thoughts being thrown this way and that in a desperate attempt to make some sense of what happened. He looked so sincere. Yet how could he be, given what Beth told me? God, I want to believe him – which can only make me a bloody fool. But what if he was telling the truth? Is it too late now anyway?

I look up at the ceiling and focus on an impressive cobweb cascading between my Ikea lampshade and the top of my curtains. I close my eyes and try to think about all this rationally.

As far as I can see, there are only two possible explanations for what happened:

Jack *has* been lying and two-timing me with Beth as I suspected. In which case, he's been acting like a horrible, deceiving rat for months, with no regard for my feelings. And I'm an idiot.

Or

Jack *hasn't* been lying or two-timing me with Beth. In which case, I publicly accused him of doing just that – immediately after he discovered, not just about my past, but also that I've been telling monumental fibs about it. And I'm an idiot.

I'm struggling to find anything positive in either scenario.

Chapter 99

'Jack, it's Evie. We need to talk.'

No, no, no, that's all wrong. I sound like someone from a bad daytime soap. I have now practised so many deep, meaningful and often pathetically tearful conversations with Jack – with everything from my shower head to my steering wheel – I'm starting to wonder if I need therapy.

The problem is, I just don't know where to start. Because I have no idea whether or not he and Beth were getting it together, I just don't know what approach to take here. Do I confront him again? Or do I beg for forgiveness?

There has also been something else nagging at the back of my mind and it's this: it has now been five days since our fight and it's not as if he's banging down my door to try to patch things up. In fact, I haven't heard a solitary word from him. And I am now absolutely sure that he hasn't attempted to contact me as I have taken my mobile into the phone shop twice since Monday to check whether it needs servicing because it never seems to ring (or at least *he* doesn't). Apparently my mobile is in such rude health it is currently on course to out-survive me.

It's been a weird few days. A numb, horrible, sick-to-my-stomach few days. And although I can't deny I've had a continual stream of visitors – everyone from Charlotte to Valentina has turned up with gin and Maltesers – there's something strange about the whole thing. I've never been surrounded by so many people. But I've never felt so alone.

Chapter 100

'Can I get you a drink?' he offers as we find a table in a quiet part of the bar.

'A glass of white wine would be great,' I say.

'Coming up,' he replies.

When he returns to the table, he's clutching an ice bucket and a bottle of champagne instead.

'What's all this about?' I ask. 'Have you won the Lottery? If you'd mentioned it earlier, I'd have agreed to go out with you ages ago.'

'I just thought we ought to be celebrating,' he says, smiling.

'Oh?' I reply. 'Celebrating what?'

'Celebrating the fact that two friends have been reunited,' he says.

'Were we friends?' I ask. 'I don't remember it like that.'

'No,' he says. 'You're right. Two *lovers* reunited.'

344

It's nice being out with Seb. I know I told myself I wasn't interested, but things have changed since then. And one thing's for sure, I can't spend another moment moping around my flat waiting for Jack Williamson to call, even if it has been good for my standards of household cleanliness.

It's been almost two weeks now. Two weeks of moping, crying, hating myself, hating *How Clean Is Your House*. But enough's enough now. He hasn't phoned, he's not interested and there's only one thing for it. I've got to pick myself up and start again.

'So, I know you work for a building society,' I say, 'but tell me again what your job involves exactly?'

'Well,' says Seb, and starts to tell me again.

I'm aware I already asked him about this at Georgia's wedding. But when you're in a profession like mine, where you've got something visible to show for your efforts at the end of the day – even if it is sometimes only three nibs about library opening hours – trying to get your head around a job which involves 'determining regional strategy' and 'finding synergies to improve overall efficiency' is a bit weird.

'... so you see,' he concludes, 'it's all quite straightforward really.'

I get a flashback of Jack telling me about his job when we first met, but push the thought out of my mind immediately. So what if Jack helps impoverished families in famine-hit regions of Africa? Big deal. Determining regional strategy and finding synergies to improve ... whatever it is Seb improves, is probably just as interesting – only in a different way.

'You know, I was really gutted when we drifted apart at uni.' One side of his mouth turns up flirtatiously. 'You were probably too good for me anyway.'

I don't let on how much it means to me, but it is genuinely nice to hear Seb saying this sort of thing. My self-esteem has never felt as battered and bruised as it has recently, and Seb being so lovely tonight has gone a long way to cheering me up.

'Anyway, I won't hold it against you,' he continues, with a teasing wink. 'We've all grown up since then, haven't we? Things change.'

He's right about that one. A few months ago, the closest I'd ever got to commitment was deciding on a new colour to paint my living-room walls.

But – and I say this in all seriousness – things are different now. I have come to the realization that the only way I'm ever going to end up in a serious relationship is by trying harder, criticizing less and being much more tolerant.

Chapter 101

We end up in a venue of Seb's choosing, a city centre club which, judging by the clientele, is where the beautiful people come.

The look here is all never-ending legs and hair, long eyelashes and designer shoes that probably cost more than the deposit for a house.

As we pass the doormen, Seb nods in acknowledgement and I immediately get a sense of how Charlotte must have felt six months ago. There are some women here so skinny that dozens of regurgitated dinners are probably swilling about in the lavatory system.

'I must remember to book in for some liposuction before my next visit,' I mutter.

'You're gorgeous as it is,' says Seb, sliding his arm round my waist.

As we walk past the dance floor and Seb heads for the bar, I spot someone who, despite the regulation hot pants and strappy heels, makes me do a double-take.

'Beth,' I say, feeling very wobbly all of a sudden. 'Er, hi.'

I might have known this would be the sort of place she'd come. Although she immediately looks as awkward to see me as I am to see her.

'Hi, Evie,' she says, flicking back her long dark hair.

I smile as naturally as possible, which I think in practice is about as convincing as someone on a particularly poor chewing-gum advert.

'Sorry to hear about you and Jack,' she says.

'Right, yes,' I say casually. 'Georgia told you about it, did she?'

'No, it was—' she says, then immediately looks like she regrets it. 'I mean, yeah. Georgia told me about it.'

I scrutinize her expression. You don't have to be Sherlock Holmes to work out that Georgia didn't tell her at all. Was it Jack himself? I feel a stab in my chest. So I was right all along.

'Well, nice seeing you,' I say, forcing myself to smile again.

'Yeah, you too,' she says, and away we both go to separate ends of the dance floor.

As Seb and I start dancing, I give it my best but it's hard to get in the mood under the circumstances. Besides that, dancing here just doesn't feel as much fun as it used to, camping it up to 'Native New Yorker'. Or even singing Ruby Turner as appallingly as I managed to. I push the thought out of my head and tell myself that now, more than ever, I've got to forget about Jack.

After a while, Seb somehow gets us into the VIP room. He

finds a seat in a private, tucked-away booth and orders a cocktail from the waiter.

'I'll need something to wash this down with,' he says, taking something out of his jacket pocket and putting it onto the table.

I watch in silent astonishment as he proceeds to chop and line up a pile of white powder with the side of his credit card, roll up a new twenty-pound note and snort it. This is accompanied by sound effects you'd expect from a warthog with a congestion problem.

Seb leans back with a grin on his face and powder stuck on the end of his nose as if he's dipped it in a sugar bowl.

'Er, you've missed a bit,' I whisper.

He brushes it off with a finger and snorts that up too.

'Here, let me set a line up for you,' he says casually.

'Oh, no,' I say hastily. 'Honestly, I'll stick with my cocktail. Besides, aren't you worried someone will see?'

'Not in here,' he chuckles. 'This is the VIP room. Everyone's at it. Come on, I don't want to party by myself.'

'Really, I'd prefer not to,' I say.

He looks at me as if he's suddenly got Miss Jean Brodie sitting opposite him.

'Oh, come on,' he frowns. 'It's just a bit of fun. It'll help you loosen up.'

'No. Honestly, Seb, I'm loose enough – really,' I say, although I suddenly feel the opposite.

Mercifully, the waiter appears with our cocktails and, despite his bravado, Seb scrambles to put his paraphernalia away. But over the next couple of hours, he proceeds to take his little packet of magic dust from his inside pocket to perform the same ritual three times.

'Did you enjoy Georgia's wedding?' I ask, trying to ignore what he's doing.

'Yeah,' he says. 'Yeah, I did. It was good to see some of the old gang again. You in particular.'

I smile.

'There were some pissed people on that dance floor by the end of the night though, weren't there?' he adds.

'Aren't there always at weddings?' I say.

'Yeah, but did you see that guy in the stripy jacket with his missus?' he adds, shaking his head and smirking. 'Those two looked like they needed locking up.'

I feel a surge of heat rising to my cheeks as I realize that the couple he's referring to are Bob and my mother.

'You're talking about Bob,' I say. 'Bob and, er . . .'

'Oh, do you know them?' he says, before I get a chance to finish. 'I hope I haven't offended anyone.'

'Er, well – no, you haven't offended anyone,' I say, shifting in my seat. 'But it was my mum and her husband you were talking about.'

'Shit!' he says, laughing. 'Christ, talk about the wrong way to impress your date!'

I laugh too. Seb wasn't to know who he was referring to. And, let's face it, it's nothing I haven't said myself.

'I have to say though,' he continues, 'I've never seen a pair of tights quite like the ones she was wearing.'

'No, you're right,' I say, chuckling. 'She's got unusual dress sense.'

'And that hat. *Jesus*,' he adds, rolling his eyes.

'Er, yes,' I say, starting to feel a bit uncomfortable.

'Listen, I'm just glad you haven't inherited your mother's sense of taste – or lack of,' he adds. 'You look amazing tonight.'

The compliment somehow doesn't have the same effect as his earlier ones.

'Yeah, okay, Seb,' I find myself saying with an agitated tone. 'So my mum looks a bit unconventional. But that's the way I like her.'

'Whoa,' he says, holding up his hands. 'Just having a little joke. Didn't mean to offend.'

I untense my shoulders and suddenly feel a bit silly.

'No, I'm sorry,' I say. 'I didn't mean to snap.'

'That's okay.' He winks at me. 'I'll forgive you.'

I shift uneasily, but remind myself how grateful I was that he asked me out.

I'm just thinking about this when he leans over and, taking me by surprise, kisses me on the lips. I say he kisses me, but Seb's manoeuvre reminds me of a giant octopus pouncing on its prey. He goes from nought to sixty in seconds, with full-on tongue and not a great deal of opportunity for the small matter of breathing.

I pull away, gasping for breath, and lean back on my seat. I know it's only because of the way I've felt since Jack and I split up that's making me react like this. But I still can't help it.

'What's up?' he says, agitated.

'Oh, nothing.' Then I look up and spot Beth on the other side of the room.

'I mean, I don't know,' I add.

But as Beth looks away, I realize I do know. Of course I know.

Chapter 102

I'd almost given up on Uncle Benno's story about Pete Gibson, the angelic pop star with a secret penchant for cocaine and orgies.

After phoning Benno three times a week for the last two months to see whether the business with the dodgy copper has been sorted out, so I could go ahead and write my story, I started to fear that the whole thing was going to come to nothing.

Not least because I couldn't believe the nationals hadn't picked up on it yet. If I'm entirely honest, despite how desperate I have been for this story, I've also had other things on my mind more recently.

However, this evening, I get back from work after an early shift, slump in front of the television with a bowl of reconstituted noodles which look barely fit for human consumption, and the phone rings.

I recognize the voice as Uncle Benno's immediately.

'What are you up to?' he asks.

'Eating rubbish and watching telly,' I say.

'Well, you need to tear yourself away from both and get yourself down here with a snapper,' he announces. 'You're about to get your story.'

'Really?' In my excitement, I throw my bowl down on the couch next to me.

'But before that I want a favour,' he adds.

My heart sinks. 'You know we don't have much of a budget,' I say.

'Tsk, I know *that*, love,' he replies. 'I've seen the car you drive. No, you know my step-daughter?'

'Of course,' I say. 'How is Torremolinos?'

Uncle Benno's new wife Tina had followed in the footsteps of Victoria Beckham and named her first child after the place in which she was conceived.

'She's great! Fifteen now, believe it or not. And she wants to be a journalist. So I was just wondering if you'd be able to sort her out with some work experience or something.'

On these occasions I'm supposed to say that there's a long waiting list and she'll have to write to the Managing Editor. But this story is just too good and, even with the threat of a bollocking from Simon, I make an executive decision.

'Uncle Benno, I'll get her some work experience. In fact, I won't rest until she's editing the *Sunday Times*.'

Chapter 103

GREEN'S GYM, LIVERPOOL,
THURSDAY, 28 JUNE, 8.20 P.M.

We're printing the story about Pete Gibson in tomorrow's paper. In the event, the constable he was attempting to bribe was having none of it and turned out to be one of the good guys, after all. Which is fine by me, because, by itself, the fact that one of the saintliest pop stars in the UK is actually a cocaine dealer who regularly organizes celebrity orgies has got to constitute one of the scoops of the year.

The only thing is, I'm so nervous about it all, I'm now experiencing the sort of nausea I once had on a nine-hour ferry crossing in high winds. At work, they call it *the fear*, that horrible feeling journalists have just before a really big story breaks. It's a peculiar mixture of blood-pumping adrenaline because you know something amazing is about to be printed, and total knicker-wetting terror in case you've written something that will land the Editor in court. Which is not good for anyone's career prospects.

I've covered all bases on this three times over – as have the paper's lawyers – but these are serious allegations and there is no doubt that a large helping of the brown stuff is going to hit the fan tomorrow.

So, here I am at the gym with Charlotte, trying to take my mind off things. Only it's the first time I've done any exercise in weeks and I'm starting to wish I'd brought a note from my mum to let me sit it out.

We start on the treadmills and I optimistically, and very foolishly, plump for a setting called 'World Endurance'. I plan to start off slowly, but somewhere along the way, manage to find myself in the middle of a K2 climb, along with the sort of gradient that shouldn't be attempted without crampons.

I frantically stride upwards in a movement reminiscent of Basil Fawlty's impression of the Germans and, with a mixture of panic and near-exhaustion, begin hitting the buttons like a hyperactive seven-year-old let loose on a fruit machine.

'Bloody hell!' I squeal, before slamming my hand against the emergency Stop button. The machine grinds to a halt and I lean over to rest on the side of the treadmill, feeling like my lungs are about to explode.

Charlotte giggles and when I get my breath back, I giggle too. We're both laughing now in a weird, hysterical kind of way. People are starting to look at us like we've been taking hallucinogenic drugs.

'How are you feeling these days, Evie?' she asks, when I finally manage to find a more sedate setting.

'Apart from nearly killing myself on a treadmill, you mean?' I grin.

'You know what I mean.'

'Oh, fine,' I say. 'Absolutely fine. Bit nervous about my story, but fine really.'

I know full well she's not talking about the story. And if the truth be told, my jitters over that – even when they're making my stomach churn like it's on a spin cycle – still aren't a patch on the feelings about Jack.

But her question takes me a bit by surprise because people have stopped asking me about Jack recently. I guess three weeks after we split, it's becoming old news. Plus, it's not like I've ever given anyone much of an insight. I've only ever said the same thing as I say to Charlotte now. I'm fine. Couldn't be finer. I'm as fine as fine can be. Really, I'm very, very fine indeed.

'Well, if that's true then I'm glad to hear it,' says Charlotte, but she looks unconvinced.

'Why do you look like you don't believe me?' I ask.

She slows her treadmill down.

'We all just knew how much you liked him, I suppose,' she tells me.

'You mean you think I'm a sad act.'

'Course not,' she says. 'People just don't know what it's like to be in love with someone when it's not reciprocated.'

I frown.

'They don't, Evie,' she stresses and I suddenly realize that she looks really unhappy.

'What's up?' I want to know. 'I thought I had the monopoly in personal misery these days.'

She shakes her head. 'I'm just pre-menstrual, that's all. I get upset at the slightest thing these days.'

'Come on, shall we go for a drink?'

'I'll never say no to a Diet Coke,' she says.

At the pub, we order two drinks and talk for the rest of the night, predominantly about my story. It feels good to get some of my nervous tension off my chest. Then, when last orders have been called, Charlotte brings up the thing I've been avoiding.

'Were you in love with Jack?' she asks, out of nowhere.

I feel my jaw tense.

'If I admitted that to myself, I really would be a dead loss, wouldn't I?'

'What do you mean?'

'I mean,' I say, 'that if the only man I had ever fallen in love with turned out to be someone who didn't want me ... well, that'd be tragic.'

'Hmm,' she says.

'Besides, I'm having a nice time with Seb,' I say.

'*Nice?*' she echoes, and I realize I sound about as convincing as Jack the Ripper's defence lawyer.

'I guess I've discovered one thing,' I say, 'that sometimes, no matter how much you want someone, no matter how much you love them, no matter how desperate you are for them . . . sometimes you just can't have them. It hurts like hell. But sometimes you just can't have them.'

I look up at Charlotte and she's wiping her eye. Then I remember something – what she said at my mum's wedding, her hints that she'd kissed someone.

I'm just about to bring this up when the landlord comes over.

'Haven't you two got homes to go to?' he grumbles. With the exception of a German Shepherd polishing off a packet of cheese and onion crisps at the other end of the bar, I look round and see that we're the last ones in the pub.

Chapter 104

The Editor's PA asks me to go and see him just after the first edition of the paper has come up from the press hall the next day. When I knock on the door, Frank is on the phone, but beckons me in.

'I don't give a toss about how much work your fella's done for charity, Diamond,' he says. 'He should have thought of that before he let his crotch do his thinking for him.'

He's talking to Dale Diamond, celebrity agent and staunch advocate of the What They Don't Know Won't Hurt Them school of public relations. By the sound of the protestations I can hear coming from the telephone receiver, Mr Diamond doesn't appear to be very happy with today's splash.

'You'll go to the Press Complaints Commission?' laughs Frank. 'On what grounds? Causing undue distress to a dirty old drug dealer? Sorry, but I need to go. Right on deadline.

Thanks for your call,' he says unconvincingly, then slams down the phone.

He walks round the desk and heads to the conference table, where today's paper sits.

'Evie,' he says, jabbing the main picture of Pete Gibson being arrested outside his multi-million pound mansion, 'this is brilliant. Absolutely fucking brilliant.'

Frank Carlisle has many qualities as an Editor, but being able to get through a sentence without using at least one expletive is not one of them.

'Thanks,' I say, wondering if I should remain standing here like a schoolgirl in the Headmaster's office, or just sit down.

'Take a seat,' he says, as if reading my mind, and I pull out a chair from around his huge conference table.

'I've been impressed with your stuff lately, Evie,' he tells me. 'You've got balls, and I like a reporter with balls.'

'Er, that's nice of you to say, Boss,' I say.

'Now, the thing is,' he goes on, 'you know we're about to lose Sam to one of the nationals?'

'Yes, of course.' Sam Webb, the crime reporter, has landed a job working for *The Times* and is due to leave in less than two weeks.

'Well, that leaves a gap,' Frank continues.

'Right,' I say.

'I only want someone in an "acting" capacity, of course,' he warns me. 'But we can review that in a couple of months' time.'

'I see,' I say.

'So, I've got two questions for you,' he goes on.

'Okay,' I say.

'Do you want the job?' he says. 'Or do you want the job?'

Chapter 105

Valentina said that only a small core of the main protagonists would be here for her wedding rehearsal, which by my count today means about sixty of us. As well as seven bridesmaids, there is an entire army of people fussing over the music, the flowers, the choreography, the reading and just about anything and everything, in fact, to ensure that the Big Day tomorrow is stage-managed to perfection.

'Did you hear how one of Valentina's stylists took the vicar to one side to request that he does his hair differently tomorrow?' whispers Grace.

I shake my head in disbelief.

'So now even the seventy-year-old curate has got to look like he's just stepped out of *Vogue*?' I say.

'Don't feel too sorry for him,' chuckles Grace, digging me in the ribs. 'He apparently asked them if they could put in some highlights for him.'

I laugh, but the truth is, neither I nor Grace – nor, for that matter, Charlotte – are in the mood for this today. Grace is putting a brave face on things, but she's undoubtedly still having trouble at home and Charlotte, well, Charlotte is just acting very strangely.

As for me, I'm trying not to mope these days, I really am. And in many ways I've got absolutely no reason to do so. Work is going brilliantly. I've landed a good job – no, a *great* job – which, as far as my career is concerned, means the world is my oyster. But there's something about being here today, when I'd originally imagined I'd be here with Jack, that is preventing me from really getting into the swing of things. Thankfully the bride-to-be is getting into the swing of things enough for everyone.

'Now,' says Valentina, who has somewhere along the way acquired a clipboard, 'I'd like to practise the entrance again. I'm a bit concerned about the posture of some of the bridesmaids, *naming no names . . .*' she says, glaring at me.

'Subtle, isn't she?' I mutter to Grace.

'Come on, girls, off we go to the back again,' orders Valentina. She'd almost make a convincing headmistress, if she weren't wearing her Balenciaga baseball cap and four-inch wedges.

'Do try not to slouch, Evie,' she says briskly. 'I know you

don't have a natural sense of grace, but if you *could* just make an effort?'

The church is surprisingly modest. I suspect Valentina would have preferred Westminster Cathedral, but apparently this is where generations of the Barnetts have married, and it was Edmund's one and only request.

He got St Nicholas's Church, she got four wedding co-ordinators, a contract with *High Life!* magazine and a dress costing more than the GDP of some small states. I think, on balance, she did quite well out of the deal.

When we're at the back of the church, Valentina links arms with Federico, a former male stripper turned model and her mother's thirty-one-year-old boyfriend. He's the one who will be giving her away tomorrow.

Valentina has only met him once before and didn't particularly like him then, but given the Barnetts' fondness for tradition, she felt strongly that she needed someone – anyone, in fact – to walk her down the aisle. Well, anyone she'd never slept with, which obviously narrowed it down. A bit. So Federico it was.

'Can you take over here, Jasmine,' Valentina says, foisting her clipboard on one of her planners. 'I'm needed for the important bit.'

Jasmine gives a nod to the organist and the church is filled with the opening bars of Mendelssohn's 'Wedding March'. Valentina flicks back her hair, grabs Federico by the arm and begins her walk down the aisle with a smile that says she couldn't be more pleased with herself if she'd made it to a Wimbledon final.

'Remember, not too fast,' warns Jasmine, but Valentina has no intention of speeding this up.

Even with the pews only half-full with wedding organizers, she is obviously enjoying herself too much to do anything other than a slow, dramatic walk that allows everyone the opportunity to look at her for as long as they might wish.

Valentina's mother, Mrs Allegra D'Souza, is in one of the adjacent pews and as they walk past, she lifts a glamorous hand and blows Federico a kiss through the most luminously white dental veneers I've seen in my life. Federico winks back, prompting Valentina to tut and tug at his arm like a disobedient puppy.

It takes a good few minutes to get to the altar, before Valentina turns around and supervises her bridesmaids, shuffling into place at the front one by one.

'Very good, Georgia, and you too, Grace,' she says. 'Evie, *really*, if you could just take a leaf out of Grace's book, you'd be fine.'

I bite my lip and glance sympathetically over to Edmund as he stands at the front with Patrick – his best man – next to him.

We go through the vows four more times until, finally, Valentina is happy with everything.

'Now, everyone,' she concludes, 'I'll see you all tomorrow,

Bridesmaids

and don't be late. That includes you, pumpkin,' she adds, flashing a smile at Edmund. He leans over and kisses her on the nose. He is clearly besotted.

As people start to head for home, Valentina makes a bee-line for Grace, Charlotte and me.

'Can I just say that I don't know what the matter is,' she snaps, 'but all three of you look like you're rehearsing for a funeral, not a wedding. And, yes, that includes you, Charlotte.'

'I'm just a bit tired,' she says. 'I've had a busy week at work.'

'I hadn't thought working at the Inland Thingumijig was particularly pressurized,' Valentina says.

Charlotte simply shrugs.

'And, Evie,' Valentina goes on, '*buck up*, will you? You've just been promoted, for goodness' sake! I mean, correct me if I'm wrong, but doesn't that mean that it might not be long before you can go and work for a proper newspaper?'

I am considering whether or not to dignify this with an answer when Valentina turns to Grace.

'Now, Grace,' says Valentina, 'what on earth have you got to be down in the dumps about? You managed to bag a lovely husband before any of the rest of us.'

'I'm all right, Valentina,' says Grace. 'Honestly. I'm just tired, like Charlotte. I'll be fine tomorrow. We all will be.'

Valentina frowns. 'Well, I do hope so,' she says, turning on her heels. 'God knows what the *High Life!* team will think otherwise.'

Chapter 106

'Does anybody want a lift?' asks Grace when we get outside the church.

'I've got my car with me,' I tell her.

'No, it's okay,' says Charlotte.

'Come on, Charlotte,' Grace urges. 'We go right past your flat. How are you going to get home otherwise?'

'Oh, I feel like the walk,' says Charlotte. 'Honestly.'

'Don't be daft, it's starting to rain. Tell her, Patrick, it's no trouble.'

Patrick is standing at the driver's door of his Audi, ready to go. 'Actually, I could do with getting straight back, Grace,' he says.

'What are you on about?' says Grace. 'It's on the way.'

'Really,' Charlotte interrupts. 'I'm fine.'

'See? She's fine,' says Patrick. 'Now, come on.' He gets into the car and slams the door.

'Well, if you're sure,' says Grace, looking bemused. 'I'll see you tomorrow then. Bye, Evie.'

When Grace is in the car, it reverses and speeds out of the church grounds like Lewis Hamilton is at the wheel.

'Christ, he's in a hurry,' I say. 'Why didn't you want to go with them?'

Charlotte shrugs. 'I really could do with the walk,' she says.

'In this rain?' I query. 'All that diet food must have got to your brain.'

She smiles.

'You're welcome to come with me, if you want,' I offer.

'Well, if you don't mind,' she says, slightly to my surprise.

'You'll just have to move a few McDonald's cartons first,' I tell her. 'And don't let my mother know you've seen them, she'd disown me.'

As I reverse out of the car park and head in the direction of Charlotte's flat with her in the passenger seat, I turn the radio on low enough for us to be able to talk over it.

'So what do you reckon?' I say. 'Are you and I always going to be the bridesmaids and never the brides?'

I'm trying to be jolly but the way it comes out sounds as miserable as sin.

'It's looking increasingly like it,' she says, trying to smile.

'But, hey, single isn't that bad, is it?' I say with the forced enthusiasm of a primary school PE teacher. 'In fact, it's quite fun, I think. I *enjoy* being able to go out when I like and with whom I like, whenever I like, and not have to justify myself to anyone else, thank you very much.'

'Hmm,' she says.

'I mean, who wants to get married anyway?' I continue. 'All you're doing is condemning yourself to a lifetime of conversation with the same person. How dull must that be?'

'You're probably right,' says Charlotte reluctantly. 'Being single isn't that bad.'

'And all this wedding malarkey,' I rant. 'I mean, at the end of the day, it's just a bloody big expensive party, isn't it? All that money, thrown away on one party! Think of all the other things you could buy.'

There's a silence.

'Like what?' says Charlotte finally.

'Well,' I say, determined to prove my point, 'you could go on holiday. A *brilliant* holiday. God, you could go anywhere – and fly first-class too. You could sit at the front sipping champagne and getting your bunions massaged, while the oiks in Economy battle with the lids of their in-flight meals and get snotty remarks from the flight attendants. Fantastic.'

She nods. Then says: 'By yourself though.'

I frown. 'I thought we were agreed there was nothing wrong with *by yourself*,' I say. It's only as I say this that I realize how much I mean this. I think back to my date with Seb and wonder why exactly I haven't been practising my own advice.

'Look, let me think of a better example . . . just think of all the shoes you could buy,' I offer.

'You sound like Valentina,' Charlotte giggles.

I groan. 'Fine, then you could give the money to help starving children in Africa.'

I'd meant it to be flippant, but the second I say it, we both know I couldn't have picked a worse example to illustrate the point than something my ex-boyfriend does every day. As I continue driving silently, I look over at Charlotte, who is staring straight ahead with a very peculiar look on her face.

'Is everything all right?' I ask.

It takes her a moment before she says anything. 'Can I tell you something, Evie?' she asks.

'Of course,' I say immediately. 'Go on.'

'I'm in love,' she says.

She couldn't sound more matter-of-fact if she'd just told me she was off to the shops to buy some turnips. My mouth drops open in amazement.

'Hey, that's fantastic!' I exclaim. 'Who with?'

She hesitates then takes a deep breath, before turning to look straight at me.

'With Patrick. I'm in love with Patrick.'

Chapter 107

Starsky and Hutch have got nothing on the manner in which I swerve my VW Golf to the side of the road. I pull the handbrake on and turn to Charlotte, barely able to believe what I've just heard.

'Patrick who?' I ask, in the vain hope there has been a terrible mix-up and she's actually referring to some bloke who works in her local chip shop – and not our best friend's husband.

'*Patrick* Patrick,' she says.

'*Patrick* Patrick who?'

'Patrick *Cunningham*.'

I shake my head, unable to compute this piece of information.

'Let me get this straight,' I say, frowning. 'You're telling me that you are in love *with Patrick?* With *our* Patrick? With *Grace's* Patrick?'

'I know it sounds hard to believe.'

'Hard to believe? Charlotte, he's married. To our best friend.'

'*Your* best friend, Evie,' she mutters.

My eyes widen. 'So not only are you in love with her husband but Grace is now no longer your friend?' I ask, incredulous.

'I didn't *say* that,' she replies.

I stare straight ahead, gripping the steering wheel.

'Well . . . how long have you felt like this?' I ask, trying to stay calm.

'From the moment I met him,' she tells me. 'Seven years, to be exact. I've felt like this ever since I first set eyes on him. I've never stopped loving him.'

The last sentence makes my blood run cold. How could I have not seen this? How could any of us have not seen this? My mind is a whirl of thoughts, not least how matter-of-fact Charlotte appears to be about the situation.

'But, Charlotte,' I say, my voice torn between sympathy and exasperation, 'Patrick loves Grace. And Grace loves Patrick. They have a *family*. Whatever your feelings for him, you need to put a stop to them now. For your own sake. Because, Grace and Patrick – they're solid as a rock.'

She gives a snort of derision.

'What was that for?' I ask, shocked.

'You don't know the half of it, Evie.'

'What on earth do you mean?'

'Well, I'm just saying,' she continues. 'You speak as if the very idea of me and Patrick being together is ridiculous.'

'It *is* ridiculous,' I tell her, my voice rising uncontrollably. Now Charlotte looks really annoyed.

'It might have been six months ago, Evie,' she says. 'But I'm as good as anyone now. I'm thin, and fashionable and pretty and—'

'What the hell has that got to do with anything?' I say.

She frowns. 'I'm just saying, the idea is *not* so ridiculous any more,' she says, her fury palpable.

I can't believe what I'm hearing. I think about Grace and the kids. I think about how distraught she's been about Patrick. I think about the fact that they've only been married a couple of months. For the first time ever, my feelings towards Charlotte are not entirely positive ones.

'Charlotte,' I say, 'you losing a load of weight has got nothing to do with this. The idea is a ridiculous one – not because you're not pretty enough for him – but because you're talking about our friend and her husband. About Grace and Patrick. Where's your loyalty?'

She looks out of the window and snorts dismissively. Which, to be honest, slightly sends me over the edge.

'Listen, Charlotte, you need to forget this whole thing. Because you are *not* going to get together with Patrick, do you hear me? *Not ever.*'

The blood is rising to Charlotte's cheeks now.

'That, Evie, is where you're wrong.'

'What?'

'I said, that's where you're wrong,' she continues, her face flaming. 'Patrick and I *would* get together. In fact, Patrick and I already have.'

Chapter 108

'What are you talking about?' I ask, dreading the answer.

'At your mum's wedding,' says Charlotte. 'You know I kissed someone? It was Patrick. In fact, we didn't just kiss ...'

'What do you mean?'

Charlotte is clearly wondering whether or not she should go on. But there's no going back now – and she knows it.

'I'd ... I'd gone for a walk to clear my head,' she says, her voice wobbling. 'I was feeling a bit drunk and – well, I found him doing the same thing. Just sitting – clearing his head. And so we started to talk. We talked and talked. And he told me things that you haven't got a clue about, Evie. That *Grace* hasn't even got a clue about.'

'And?'

'Then ... well ... it just happened. We started kissing.' She pauses, unsure whether to say any more.

'And?'

She sighs. 'One thing led to another, as they say. And ... we ... we ...'

'You what?'

'We had sex,' she says defiantly. 'There – you happy now? Patrick and I . . . *we had sex.*'

My eyes nearly pop out of my head.

'In the field?' I say, appalled. 'In the field when my mum's wedding reception was happening next door?'

Charlotte's lip is still wobbling, but she's not backing down. 'Yes, in the field,' she says, determined to hold her head high. 'Yes.'

'I don't believe you,' I say. But, actually, I do.

'It's true,' she replies. 'Ask him yourself if you like. But it's absolutely true.'

Words are failing me. I find myself just sitting, struggling to reach for the right thing to say.

'How could you?' I finally blurt out. 'How could you do this to Grace?'

'I couldn't help it,' she whimpers, less defiant now. 'I mean it, Evie, I really couldn't help it.'

'Of *course* you could help it!'

Her eyes blur with a film of tears. 'Let me put it this way. What you're feeling about Jack at the moment – the heartbreak, the intensity, the pain – well, you've felt like that for a few weeks now. I've felt like that for seven years. *Seven years.* You just couldn't begin to imagine what it's been like.'

I close my eyes. 'I don't think I know you very well any more, Charlotte,' I whisper. It's all I can think of.

She grabs my hand.

'Don't say that, Evie,' she pleads. 'You're my best friend. Please try to understand.'

'Do you even recognize what you've done is wrong?' I ask.

Charlotte sighs. 'I know what I've done isn't right,' she says, 'given that they're married and have kids. But doing the right thing has got me nowhere in life, Evie. Absolutely nowhere.'

I look into her eyes. 'Charlotte,' I say, 'you are one of my oldest friends. You know that I would do anything for you. But if you're responsible for breaking up that marriage, I don't know how I'll ever forgive you. I really don't.'

She puts her head in her hands and sobs silently. She sobs and she sobs, for I don't know how long. Finally, she lifts her head up.

'I won't break up their marriage,' she says.

'How are you so sure?'

She sniffs. 'Believe me, I'm sure,' she says, taking another pause for breath. 'He . . . he . . . made us stop almost immediately.'

'Go on.'

She shakes her head.

'That's how quickly he regretted it. God Almighty. I've been trying to kid myself into thinking it might have been the start of something. But I managed to make someone regret sleeping with me before it was even over.'

'So what happened?' I ask reluctantly, not particularly wanting the gory details but knowing I've got to hear them.

'He was so drunk,' she confesses. 'Not just drunk, actually, he could barely stand up. I can still picture him now, fumbling to zip his trousers up and virtually running away from me. And now, well, he's not even spoken to me since it happened. He *hates* me.'

Charlotte is sobbing hysterically, but I can barely bring myself to look at her. Then something else strikes me.

'I've got to tell Grace, you know,' I say.

She turns to me with panic in her eyes.

'Don't do that,' she says. 'Please don't do that.'

'She's my best friend,' I say. 'I've got to tell her.'

Charlotte starts shaking her head.

'No. No, you can't,' she gabbles. 'She's got two children. A family. You telling her is only going to be the fastest way to destroy that.'

I hesitate, biting one of my nails.

'But how *could* I keep this a secret from her?' I ask.

'All you would be doing is unburdening yourself,' she says. 'Tell her, and their marriage won't last the year.'

'How did you become so concerned for her and Patrick all of a sudden?' It comes out before I can stop myself.

'Hate me as much as you want, Evie,' she says dully. 'But what I'm saying is the truth.'

We sit in silence again.

'I don't hate you, Charlotte,' I tell her. 'I just can't believe this is happening. And I can't see how I can keep this from Grace. I'd feel like an accomplice.'

'Listen,' she says, 'don't say anything tomorrow at the very least. Not on Valentina's wedding day. It'd ruin everything. Just sit on it for a few days, then you'll realize what I'm saying is right.'

I don't know what the hell to do. Going along with Charlotte now is not something I feel particularly inclined to do. But she's undoubtedly right about Valentina's wedding day being the wrong time and place.

'A few days, then,' I decide. 'I'll think about it for a few days – that's all I'm promising.'

'Okay,' she says. 'Good.' She wipes her eyes.

'There's one thing I don't get though,' I say, partly wondering why I'm even telling her this. 'Patrick's been acting strangely since well before my mum's wedding. He's been . . . odd . . . for months now.'

Charlotte bites her lip.

'I think I might be able to shed some light on that,' she mumbles.

'Oh?'

'This is what our talk was about. Our long talk, before . . .'

'Well, what?' I say. 'Come on, spit it out.'

'Okay, okay,' says Charlotte, taking another deep breath. 'Patrick has lost his job. He hasn't told a soul. He's broke. *They're* broke. And Grace hasn't got a clue.'

Chapter 109

'I want to wear my bra,' whines Polly.

'You can't, I've told you,' says Grace, grabbing some baby food out of the microwave with one hand and brushing her hair with the other. 'Five-year-olds do not wear bras.'

'I bet Evie will be wearing a bra,' Polly replies. 'Won't you, Evie?'

'Well, yes,' I tell her. 'But I'm a 34B – and you're not.'

Polly pouts.

As usual, Grace's kitchen looks like the set of *It's A Knockout*. The theme to *Peppa Pig* has been blaring out for the last half-hour while Grace has galloped around ironing Polly's outfits, locating bottles of Calpol and entering into intense telephone negotiations with her mother about whether or not Scarlett should be eating with a knife and fork yet.

Grace plonks Scarlett in her high chair and starts shovelling a spoon into her mouth with a concoction on it she insists is lentil bake – but looks more like something you'd find splattered on the floor outside a nightclub at 2 a.m.

Patrick wanders in, looking for something with which to polish his shoes. At first, I can barely look at him I'm so furious with him. Then, I study his face. He looks about as happy as you'd expect for someone who's secretly unemployed and has recently had a drunken quickie with one of his wife's oldest friends ... and didn't even manage to finish that from what Charlotte said.

'Well, I have to say I never thought Valentina and Edmund would end up together, did you?' Grace asks, looking at Patrick hopefully to see if he might answer her.

'Hmm,' he shrugs, pulling a duster out of the cupboard under the sink.

As best man, Patrick is due to meet the groom at his house in about twenty minutes. It won't be a minute too soon, as far as I'm concerned: just being in the same room as him and Grace, with the knowledge that I have but she doesn't, is making me feel distinctly twitchy.

'God knows what sort of marriage they'll have,' Grace ploughs on. 'I can't help thinking she'll walk all over him.'

'Maybe,' he says.

Grace flashes me an almost apologetic look as if to say: This is how stimulating our conversation gets these days. I look away immediately and start studying the nutritional information panel on the back of a packet of Cheerios.

'How does she get on with his parents?' she asks.

'Fine, I think. Don't know, really,' he grunts, and I feel another wave of loathing. He should be going out of his way to make up to Grace. Instead, he's clearly wrapped up in his own problems.

'Bernard probably loves her,' she continues, 'but Jacqueline . . . I don't know, I suspect she'd have preferred it if Edmund had brought someone a bit less exuberant home.'

'Hmm,' I say. 'Like Madonna.'

Patrick puts his duster back into the cupboard under the sink and walks towards the hallway, saying nothing. I hear the door to the loo shut just as Polly arrives wearing her lovely pale pink dress, through which her 'bra' – which is actually the top half of a bikini – is perfectly visible. '*Polly*,' says Grace wearily as Scarlett starts hurling her plastic bricks across the kitchen. 'What did I tell you?'

'I can't remember,' she says.

'I told you you couldn't wear that thing, didn't I?' says Grace.

'But—' she interrupts.

'No buts,' Grace says sternly.

'Yeah,' I add, starting to tickle her. 'Or we'll call Supernanny.'

Polly collapses into reluctant giggles, forcing their way through despite her being absolutely determined that she's going to sulk.

'I'd better get going,' says Patrick, appearing again.

'Daddy,' says Polly, 'can I wear my bra for the wedding? It's not a real bra, it's only a pretend one. And Grandma bought it for me because she thought it was nice. So can I, Dad?'

Grace and I listen to this and exchange glances. If Polly is like this at five, what on earth will she be like when she's fifteen? Machiavelli?

'If Grandma bought it for you, then I don't see why not,' says Patrick, grabbing his car keys.

'Patrick!' protests Grace. 'No, she can't wear it!'

'But Daddy said I could,' says Polly, pulling a face.

'Daddy didn't mean it,' says Grace. 'Did you, Daddy?'

Patrick flashes her a look.

'I *thought*,' he says indignantly, 'that Mummy and Daddy weren't supposed to contradict each other in front of the children.'

'You're right,' says Grace, with equal indignation, 'they're not. But Daddy obviously doesn't realize that *he's* just done exactly that.'

'Right,' he says, his tone getting firmer, 'but Mummy must surely accept that Daddy isn't psychic and therefore could not have been aware of whatever it was exactly that she'd said earlier.'

'Mummy *does*,' says Grace, 'but given Daddy now knows what Mummy's views were, she would be very grateful if he would back her up on this.'

He looks on the verge of throwing another comment so acidic it could melt the furniture, when his phone rings. He pauses to answer it.

'So,' says Polly, 'now that Mummy and Daddy have had a chat about it, I'm okay to wear my bra, aren't I?'

'No!' shouts Grace.

She and Polly continue their battle, as Peppa Pig chirps on and Scarlett whines for her next spoonful while banging plastic bricks on the table of her high chair. But, although so much is going on in this place you barely know where to look, I can't help focusing on one person. Patrick. Patrick is the only one who is silent, and as he listens to whoever is on the other end of the phone, he remains so, draining of colour.

Eventually, he puts the phone down. 'Who was that?' asks Grace.

'Evie,' he croaks. 'Sorry . . . but could you leave us to it?'

'What's the matter?' asks Grace.

'Seriously?' he pleads to me. 'I need to speak to Grace about something. I need to speak to her alone.'

Chapter 110

Valentina is dressed from head to toe in the most expensive bridal couture money can buy, and she is wearing a tiara that would out-dazzle a Buckingham Palace chandelier. But something is not quite right: the bride isn't smiling.

'I don't know what I expected from the *High Life!* magazine team,' she pouts, as we pose for the first photographs of the day, 'but it wasn't one old slime ball taking the photos and a seventeen-year-old work experience girl doing the interviews.'

We're in the sweeping grounds of Knowsley Hall, one of the most impressive ancestral piles in the North of England and where – except for the church service – most of the action is taking place today.

'She is eighteen, apparently,' I tell her.

'Who?' asks Valentina.

'The interviewer. We were chatting earlier. She's called Drusilla – Drusilla von Something. Her dad's a Count somewhere in Europe who knows the magazine's owner.'

But Valentina isn't interested in Drusilla von Something's dad.

'Now listen,' she is saying to the photographer, 'how about one of me getting into the carriage with my bridesmaids close by?'

'Dear,' he snarls, 'you concentrate on looking pretty and I'll look after the pictures. Then we'll both get on just fine. Now, I think one of the bride and her father before they leave for the church would be nice. Where is your father exactly?'

'I am 'ere,' says Federico, sidling up to Valentina and putting his hand around her waist.

'You are *not* my father,' she tells him. 'He is *not* my father,' she tells everyone else.

'I know I am not *usually*,' says Federico, 'but I thought just for today, just for ze 'ere and now, zat's what I am to be.'

'You're giving me away, that's all,' she hisses. 'That doesn't alter the biological fact that you and I have nothing whatsoever to do with each other. You are here to decorate my arm, okay?'

'Okay, okay,' he says, holding his hands up. 'I get ze idea. You are so 'arsh sometimes, Valentina. But I like zat in a woman.'

Insistent that *High Life!* magazine has sent him with a list of instructions – including returning with a picture of the bride and her father – the photographer forces a reluctant Valentina to pose for a photo with Federico. The latter slings his arm low around her waist again in a pose that somehow doesn't look very paternal, given the proximity of his palm to the top of her buttock.

There is no doubt about it, Valentina has put some truly spectacular finishing touches to this wedding. The cake has been handcrafted in white Belgian chocolate and, at over five foot, it makes Michael Douglas and Catherine Zeta Jones's effort look like something from Marks & Spencer.

There are semi-detached houses in parts of the country you could buy for less than the cost of her dress. And the look, according to Valentina, is elegant, but also sexy enough to ensure Edmund's pulse is just the right side of coronary failure the moment he sees her.

Of all the finishing touches though, none is more jaw-dropping than the one we're standing in front of now: her Cinderella carriage. Embedded with crystals and with four white horses at the front, I'm afraid Valentina's sense of taste has in this particular case been railroaded by her equally well-developed sense of exhibitionism.

As the bridesmaids – with the exception of Grace – wait in the background, I take Charlotte to one side at the first opportunity I get.

'Was that you who phoned Patrick earlier?' I demand.

Her face flushes, but she looks defiant.

'Yes,' she says, gripping her bouquet.

'What did you say?' I ask.

'I told him that you knew,' she says. 'I told him that I'd told you everything.'

I frown.

'I had to,' she says. 'I couldn't risk you telling Grace first.'

'I told you I wouldn't, didn't I?' I whisper. 'At least not until after the wedding.'

She sniffs and shrugs.

'Whatever happens now happens,' she says, 'he knows how I feel. The ball is in his court.'

I shake my head, unable even to contemplate what could be happening at Grace's house at this moment in time.

'Ah, excuse me, ah,' says Drusilla, the *High Life!* journalist, stepping forward.

'Ah, do you think I could do my, ah, interview, yet?' she says.

'Absolutely,' says Valentina briskly. 'Fire away.'

'Ah, yah, well, okay,' she says. 'So, did you and Mr Barnett meet at a party?'

'He was best man at another wedding, actually,' Valentina tells her. 'That of two of my dearest friends, Grace and Patrick. That might be too much detail, but you don't have to mention them if you don't want. However, it might be nice if you did mention that I have many friends. Many dear, dear friends.'

'Ah, yah, okay,' says Drusilla, taking down shorthand notes at a rate of about six words per minute. 'And, ah, now, ah . . . do you like parties?'

'Well, yes,' says Valentina. 'Of course I do – who doesn't?'

'Right,' says the girl. 'And what kind of parties do you go to?'

'Well, all sorts of parties,' Valentina continues. 'But what have they got to do with my wedding?'

'Oh, ah, well, I'm not sure really,' says Drusilla. 'But my Editor said I should always ask about parties. She said if I make sure I ask about parties I won't go wrong.'

'You're not aiming for a Pulitzer Prize with this article then,' says Valentina.

Chapter 111

Georgia is starting to look a bit concerned. But not, I suspect, as concerned as I am.

'When do we need to head off to the church?' she asks.

'Not for another hour,' I say.

'Has Grace turned up yet?'

'Erm ...' Georgia glances up to see whether Valentina is listening.

'You mean *no*, don't you?' Valentina shrieks. 'You'd think on today of all days she might have made the effort to turn up on time.'

'I'm sure she won't be long,' says Georgia. 'You know what she's like. She's always late – but she always makes it in the end.'

'That may be,' says Valentina. 'But there's *no way* Andrew Herbert is going to be able to do her hair in this amount of time. The man may be a genius with colour, but time travel is not one of his skills, as far as I'm aware.'

'Look,' says Georgia, 'why don't you come inside and have a glass of fizz with the rest of us?'

'Fine,' says Valentina, marching off towards the main house. 'I'd had enough of David Bailey and his intrepid reporter anyway.'

When we reach the drawing room, we each take a glass of champagne and it's not long before everyone starts to relax. Even Valentina. And even me. And soon, the place takes on the hint of merry excitement that every wedding should have. As I sip my champagne and look across at Valentina, glowing with happiness and about to commit herself to one man for the rest of her life, I feel compelled to say something. 'I'd like to propose a little toast.'

Everyone stops what they're doing. 'Well, Valentina,' I say, 'we've all known you for over six years and, like any friendships, there have been ups and downs. But there's little doubt that you are one in a million. And luckily, you've found a man who's one in a million too. Someone who absolutely adores you and someone who's determined to never let you go. And that is one of the most . . . well, it's one of the most amazing things in the world.'

Emotion rises into my throat and my mouth suddenly goes dry, as I am overwhelmed with thoughts of how complicated love can be. I think about Grace and Patrick and Charlotte. I think about my mum and dad and Bob. But, above all, I think about Jack.

I look upwards and pretend to check my mascara as tears

well into my eyes. A vivid image of his kind, generous smile flashes into my head and I sniff sharply.

'Are you all right, Evie?' asks Georgia, but as she puts her hand on my arm, the gesture just seems to make it worse. I pull myself together and nod.

'I am, thank you. Now let's raise our glasses. *To the bride!*'

'*To the bride!*' everyone cheers, clapping as she laps up the limelight.

'Oh look,' says Georgia, glancing out of the window. 'Here's Grace now.'

'Well, thank God for that,' says Valentina. 'Although I hope she knows she can't leave her car there in the middle of the driveway. I don't want a three-year-old Audi in the wedding photos.'

But as Grace's footsteps approach the room less than a minute later and the door bursts open, it's quite obvious for all to see that the wedding photos are the last thing she's interested in right now.

Chapter 112

Grace looks about as ready to be a bridesmaid as someone who has just mucked out a farmyard. But it's not just the jeans, lack of make-up and general state of dishevelment that is the most striking thing about her. It's the look on her face. As if she's about to explode.

'You,' she says, pointing at Charlotte. 'You and I have got some talking to do.'

'Grace!' shrieks Valentina. 'There's no time for talking – we need to get your hair in curlers!'

'I'm sorry, Valentina,' says Grace, 'but I've got something more important to do at the moment than get my hair done.'

'What could *possibly* be more important than getting your hair done?' asks the bride-to-be. 'The service is in less than forty minutes.'

Grace turns back to Charlotte.

'Do you want to do this here, or outside?' she demands.

Valentina looks horrified.

'Listen, Grace,' she says, 'I know how difficult Evie can be sometimes, but really, can't you just put your differences aside for the moment? At least until the *High Life!* team has gone home.'

Poor Valentina obviously thinks it's me Grace has fallen out with.

'Well, Charlotte, what's it to be?' asks Grace.

Charlotte's entire face and chest have turned so red it looks like she needs extinguishing.

'Grace,' she says, her mouth quivering as if she's about to say something. But nothing comes out.

'Right,' says Valentina, taking charge. 'Enough's enough. What's going on?'

Grace's face crumples.

'How could you, Charlotte?' she says. 'How could you do it after being my friend for so many years? After seeing my children growing up? After being my bridesmaid?'

Now Charlotte looks at the floor silently, her lip still quivering.

'You've acted like Miss Sweetness and Light for as long as I've known you, Charlotte. But tell everyone what you've done. Go on.'

Charlotte doesn't move and still doesn't say anything. 'No? Well, let me tell everyone instead,' Grace says.

'Charlotte has been trying to steal my husband from me.'

'What?' says Valentina. 'Grace, have you been drinking?'

'Just ask her,' Grace says. 'Ask her about attempting to seduce Patrick – at your mum's wedding, Evie.'

I bite my lip and look at the floor, suddenly aware that Patrick hasn't told her that I know. I have about 0.2 seconds to feel relieved, when Grace does a double-take.

'You knew!' she yells at me.

'The thing is, Grace . . .' I begin to protest.

'You bloody knew!' she continues. 'Jesus, I don't believe this.'

'*I* didn't,' stresses Valentina. 'Why am I always the last to know these things?'

Charlotte, shaking and red, suddenly looks defiant. 'Okay, Grace,' she says. 'How could I? Well, I'll tell you how.'

The whole room is suddenly very, very quiet.

'Because I love him,' she says.

Valentina looks like she's going to pass out.

'I love him more than I suspect you've ever loved him,' continues Charlotte. 'I'd do anything for him. I'd die for him. Can you honestly say that?'

Grace's face contorts with horror.

'No,' says Charlotte. 'I didn't think so.'

Grace falls back into a chair.

'If it means anything,' Charlotte adds solemnly, 'I did feel guilty – about you and the children. It wasn't as if I didn't think about you and them at all.'

Grace, her face filled with emotion, stands up again and walks towards Charlotte. For a second, it looks like she's about to hug her. But when she gets within a foot of Charlotte, she punches her square in the face.

Chapter 113

'I 'ad no idea English weddings were zis exciting,' says Federico as we trundle along in the horse-drawn carriage.

'Oh shut up,' says Valentina, as Georgia puts a supportive hand on hers.

The carriage has the sort of suspension you'd expect from the back end of a tractor, and whoever hired the horses at the front just may have found the four most flatulent beasts in Britain. On the plus side, however, Valentina is somehow slightly calmer now, even though we're downwind of the most horrendous whiff outside the elephant enclosure of Chester Zoo.

She's even managed to stop hyperventilating about the fact that she's now one bridesmaid down, having had to dispatch Charlotte to Accident and Emergency. And the fact that three of her other bridesmaids now have the slight but unmistakable splatter of blood – the resulting debris from Grace's punch – across their dresses.

Jane Costello

Mine is the worst, with a big gory blob right on the front of my skirt that was only made worse by a frantic amount of scrubbing. But if I position my bouquet in a certain way I can almost cover it, and Drusilla from *High Life!* has assured Valentina that they'll be able to airbrush any excess off before they go to print.

'Grace,' I say, as we bump up and down, negotiating a section of road with more pot-holes than a third-world dirt track, 'can we talk about this?'

'Yes, please do,' insists Valentina. 'Make friends, for God's sake. Or at least start smiling like you're all meant to.'

'I'm too angry and upset to talk about it,' says Grace, close to tears. 'Now isn't the time.'

'No,' says Valentina. 'No, you're probably right. No more drama today, thank you. But *do* smile, won't you? *Please.*'

We slow down at a set of traffic-lights, but before we get a chance to stop, the carriage starts to make a strange sound. A cracking sound.

Valentina's eyes widen and we all look at each other in alarm. Then, all of a sudden, the noise gets louder and one corner of the carriage plummets to the ground, catapulting bridesmaids and posies and satin shoes and veils and tiaras into all directions.

'What the—' cries Valentina as she bangs her head on the windowframe, completely forgetting her role as the demure bride.

'What ze 'ell is going on?' shouts Federico.

We climb out of the carriage and the sight before us doesn't look promising at all.

'The goddamn bloody goddamn wheel has broken,' screams Valentina, apparently directing this tirade at the driver.

He scratches his head and looks exceptionally calm about the whole thing, which is completely inappropriate in the circumstances.

'Oh dear,' he says.

'Well, what are you going to do about it?' she asks hysterically.

He shrugs. 'Not sure really,' he says. 'You can't just call the AA with one o' these.'

Valentina fans her forehead.

'So how do you propose I get to the church?' she growls. He shrugs again. 'You could always hitch-hike, love.'

Chapter 114

We'd thought at first he was joking. But with everyone we know already in church with their mobile phones switched off and not a taxi in sight, hitch-hiking suddenly became the only option.

So we split ourselves into two parties, and my group piles into the rear of a van belonging to a fish merchant just on his way back from the wholesalers. Having left the house smelling of Vera Wang, we arrive at the church smelling of *eau de haddock*.

But for the other group – the bride and her 'father' – we reserve a vehicle we all agreed would *almost* pass for a wedding car – if the *High Life!* photographer and the video man catch her at the right angle, that is.

'You might need to do a bit of editing of this,' I tell him as we wait outside the church for them to arrive.

'Why?' he says. 'What is it she's coming in exactly?'

'Er. . . just do your best with this video, will you?'

As Valentina and Federico's vehicle comes into the driveway

head on, nothing at all looks amiss from a distance. It's only when it has to make a right turn to park that all becomes clear. The videographer and the *High Life!* snapper gasp.

'Tell me she's not in a hearse,' breathes the *High Life!* photographer. 'She *can't* be in a bloody hearse, surely?'

'Like I said,' I tell him, trying to retain a sense of calm, 'if you photograph her getting out from the front, it could easily look like a wedding car.'

'But what about the flowers in the window?' he asks. 'They're arranged to spell out RIP BILLY.'

'I know, I know,' I concede, realizing we must be presenting one of the biggest challenges to his professional career to date. 'But they've said we can shove those in the back with the coffin for a couple of shots. Come on, we'll have to be quick.'

As Valentina emerges from her hearse, beaming from ear to ear and apparently unfazed by the fact that she's just shared her journey with a corpse *and* Federico, I start to see her in a whole new light.

'I'm impressed,' I say to her as we stand at the back of the church, ready to go in. 'You're taking all this incredibly well.'

She smiles.

'Well,' she says. 'It suddenly struck me on the way here: I'm about to get married. Why would I let anything else bother me?'

It's the first bit of sense I think I've ever heard come out of her mouth.

Chapter 115

I strongly suspect that I'll never be able to go to a wedding again without thinking about Jack.

It's not just the fact that our brief but sweet courtship both started and finished at occasions just like these. It's also that everything weddings are meant to represent – love, commitment, happiness – are things I now honestly believe I'm never going to find with anyone else.

I know that doesn't sound very positive but I'm just being realistic. I mean, why would I find love with anyone else when I hadn't even come close beforehand? I had my chance and I blew it. Simple as that.

'What's up with you?' Seb asks when we get to the reception. 'You looked as miserable as sin throughout that whole service.'

'Nothing,' I say. 'I'm fine. Absolutely fine.'

'Well, I wish you'd cheer up. You're putting *me* in a bad mood,' he says.

'Sorry,' I mutter.

'Don't worry,' he says, leaning over and whirling his tongue around my ear with all the subtlety of a St Bernard devouring a lamb chop. 'You can make it up to me later.'

He puts his hand on my backside and squeezes it as if he's trying to determine the ripeness of a melon.

'Don't, Seb,' I grimace. 'Not at a wedding.'

Not wanting to be groped is something I can only partly put down to the occasion. It's also because, despite trying very hard to make this work, I can now barely look at Seb without wishing he was somewhere else. Like Outer Mongolia.

But it's at that moment that something strikes me. This time, I don't think it's *just me*. I don't think this can solely be attributed to me having a commitment problem.

Turns out, I just *hadn't* met the right person.

That being the case, what exactly am I doing with Seb? If I can't have Jack, I don't want anyone else.

I want to be single, because being single really *is* okay, for reasons that go far above and beyond those I listed to Charlotte that time.

'I'm just going to the gents for a bit of a pick-me-up,' whispers Seb, winking. 'To get me through the speeches.'

And then he disappears as the guests start to pour into the main dining room of Knowsley Hall.

It quickly becomes evident that the bride and groom's camps aren't mixing. I'm not sure why it happens exactly and I'm sure they're not doing it intentionally. It's just that those in the groom's party seem to feel a little ill at ease speaking to anyone who isn't wearing a twinset and pearls; ditto the bride's party and anyone without a facelift.

'Whatever happened to Charlotte?' I look up and find my mum approaching, in a purple velvet culotte suit and matching Robin Hood hat, the feather of which made several guests sneeze throughout the entire ceremony.

'It's a long story,' I say.

'Well, as long as she's okay,' Mum says.

'She will be,' I reply, not entirely confidently.

When Seb returns, he looks slightly taken aback to come face to face with my mum. She often has this effect on people, but they don't usually greet her with quite the same look of distaste.

'Hello,' she says brightly. 'I don't think we've met. I'm Sarah, Evie's mum.'

'Hi,' he says dismissively, and grabs the last glass of champagne for himself from a passing tray.

'I think you were at Georgia's wedding, weren't you?' Mum continues, smiling. 'You might not remember me, but I was there too.'

'I remember you all right,' he sniggers, and turns away.

At first, Mum looks a little thrown by his comment. And I'm so startled that, for once, I can't think of anything to say.

'Well,' she says, forcing a smile, 'I'm sure I'll see you later. Enjoy the rest of the day.'

When she's out of earshot I turn to Seb.

'Don't take the piss out of my mum,' I say, in a tone that makes it clear he's unlikely to get his tongue anywhere near my ear canal again.

'Oh, come on – all I said was I remembered her,' he says carelessly.

'You said: *I remember you all right*,' I tell him.

'Well, Christ, how could I not have, the way she looked?'

'Why are you so obsessed with the way people look?' I ask. 'My mum is a wonderful person – and if you'd bothered to speak to her, then I'm sure you'd have discovered that.'

'What-*ever*,' he says, sounding like a stroppy teenager. 'Christ, when did you become such a bloody drag? Anyway, it was just a joke.'

He takes another swig from his glass, apparently finding the whole thing more entertaining than a trip to the seaside. 'I know,' I say matter-of-factly. 'But the thing is, Seb, I just don't get your jokes.'

The smile is wiped off his face in a second.

'I suppose,' I continue, 'I don't want to see you any more. I'm sorry.'

'You're dumping me at a wedding?' he asks, incredulous. 'I haven't even had my dinner yet.'

'I'm in love with someone else,' I say, and it's only as the words are out of my mouth that I realize they're true.

'You?' he sneers. 'In love? Ha – don't make me laugh. Evie,

405

it'll last five minutes, just like they all do.' He turns on his heel and I watch as Seb storms across the room heading for the door, before I sense someone next to me and turn to look.

The videographer is happily filming away as if he's gathering footage for a David Attenborough programme.

'Do you *mind*?' I snap. 'Can't a girl expect a little privacy when she's dumping someone these days?'

'Oh, sorry,' he tells me. 'I was just told to film as much action as I could.'

Chapter 116

Grace is clearly avoiding me. I've spent the last half-hour searching for her, desperate to talk things through, and all without success. Then, just when I'm starting to think she might have left, I spot her across the other side of the room, talking to Bob. I make a beeline for them but am stopped in my tracks by a familiar voice that is about as pleasing to the ear as chalk scraping across a blackboard.

'Evie! Looking amazing.'

Gareth outside on the terrace, sucking on a Marlboro.

'I don't want to talk to you, Gareth,' I say.

This is the first time I've seen him since he decided he was going to tell Jack all about me, my past and those bloody earrings.

'Why not?' he says. 'Not over that business with the earrings? And your, well, your *commitment problem*. I hope I didn't put my foot in it.'

'You did, Gareth. And I think you did it deliberately.'

Gareth shrugs, trying to look cool, but the vigour with which he's scratching his face again suggests he's feeling anything but.

'I just didn't think he was right for you.'

'Why – because I liked him more than you?'

'You don't suit being angry, Evie,' he says, wagging his finger at me.

'Gareth,' I begin, deciding maybe I do want to talk to him after all, 'can I speak to you bluntly?'

'Of course,' he says.

'I've tried to be nice,' I tell him. 'I tried to let you down gently. I tried not to have to tell you that if you were the last animal, mineral or vegetable left on the planet I'd still rather spend Saturday night in watching *Casualty* all by myself. I've said I'm sorry for dumping you countless times and, quite frankly, I'm not going to say it again. Because now I'm not sorry. Now I'm *glad* I dumped you. I just wish I'd realized earlier what a sneaky little toad you were.'

He looks wounded. 'You're saying you really won't agree to go out with me again? Like, really?'

I snatch the cigarette from his hand and drop it in his drink.

'I think we're finally starting to understand each other.'

Chapter 117

As I approach Grace and Bob, she straightens her back defensively.

'Evie!' says Bob when he spots me. 'Grace and I were just comparing honeymoons. Our three weeks in Colombia sounds rather different from the Maldives. We loved it, of course. I'm secretly rather jealous of their flushing toilet.'

'I bet,' I nod.

'By the way,' he adds, 'I saw you talking to Gareth there. I finally found out why he left work in such strange circumstances.'

'Oh, why?' I ask.

'You know I told you there was something funny going on between him and Deirdre Bennett, my colleague? Well, it turned out they'd had a fling.'

'Wasn't this the lady with the big bottom and terrible teeth?' I ask.

'Um . . . it sounds unkind when you put it like that,' says Bob.

'*You* put it like that!'

'Oh. Anyway, by the time he left, he was virtually stalking her. Even bought her some strange rubber underwear from one of those funny shops – you know the ones. That was when the Vice Chancellor stepped in to tell him to either put a stop to it or leave. Fortunately, he decided on the latter and Deirdre hasn't heard anything from him since about when you started dating him actually. I think you'd do well to steer clear, personally.'

'I think you're right, thanks, Bob.' I glance at Grace. 'Is there any chance I could speak to Grace for a second? By ourselves, I mean.'

'Of course,' replies Bob. 'I was about to go and find your mother anyway. I'd left her telling one of Edmund's aunts all about the wormery we're installing. I'm not sure it was quite Lady Barnett's thing.'

As soon as Bob is out of earshot, I get straight to the point.

'I'm sorry for not telling you, Grace,' I say frantically. 'I really am. But I only found out last night and, well, I just wanted to get the wedding over so that it didn't ruin things.'

She sighs. 'It's a bit late for that now.'

'I know,' I say.

'So you *were* going to tell me?' she asks.

'Well, yes, I think so,' I say, realizing immediately that I could have made life easier by just saying yes.

'What do you mean *you think so*?' she says. 'You're supposed to be my best friend. Best friends can't keep secrets like that from each other.'

410

'I know, I know,' I mutter. 'I'm sure I would have told you. But it wasn't as simple as that. I was worried about what it would do to you and Patrick. I mean, I knew things had been ... tricky ... recently and I was scared that just coming out and telling you might have – well, made things even trickier.'

'Don't worry about it,' she says, sniffing. 'You're not the only one who finds it difficult to tell me what's going on.'

I hesitate. 'You're talking about Patrick losing his job, aren't you?'

'Oh,' she says despondently. 'You knew about that too.'

'Sorry,' I say, lowering my head. 'That's all I know though. I don't know why or what it's all about or anything.'

'He confessed everything earlier,' she says. 'He lost his job months ago, just after our wedding. That's what's been wrong with him.'

'But why?' I ask.

'They made him redundant,' she sighs. 'I couldn't believe it – he's always been such a high flyer. I just assumed he'd be the last to go if they ever started reshuffling. But he was called in one day, told there had been a downturn in business and the firm needed to do some cost-cutting. Then he was out on his ear. Just like that.'

'God,' I say lamely.

'He's been picking up the odd bit of freelance work,' continues Grace, 'but nowhere near enough to pay the bills in the long term. So he kept this secret. That's what's really killing me. I hate him for what he's done . . . but part of me wonders what sort of wife I must be that he couldn't even bring himself to tell me.'

'Don't be *ridiculous*,' I insist. 'You're a brilliant wife and Patrick loves you. He doesn't *deserve* you, but he does love you. You know that, don't you?'

She sniffs again and doesn't answer.

'You know exactly what happened between him and Charlotte, don't you?' she asks.

I nod. 'Yes. She told me. She also told me it was over in seconds and he couldn't get away from her fast enough. Not that that makes it much better.'

Grace's lip starts trembling. 'No, it doesn't. It doesn't change the fact that he had sex with one of my friends. I honestly don't think our relationship could ever get over something like this. I think it might be over between me and Patrick, Evie. What do *you* think?'

I put my arm around her and take a deep breath.

'Maybe it *doesn't* need to destroy your marriage. Maybe you can work it out. But then . . . maybe not,' I shrug. 'Only *you* can reach that decision, Grace. And I want you to know that, whatever happens, I'll be with you all the way.'

As I say it I don't completely know whether what I'm telling her is good advice or not. I mean, she's right. Her husband had sex with her friend. How could anyone forgive that? One thing I *am* sure of though is that she shouldn't do anything hasty.

'I guess I've got a lot of thinking to do,' she says. 'It's still so raw. I need to have a long think about what I'm going to do.'

'Well, for God's sake blow your nose first,' I say, and lean over to hug her.

She wraps her arms so tightly around me, I'm struggling to breathe.

'Thanks, Evie,' she says. 'I love you.'

'I love you too, Grace,' I say.

Suddenly, Patrick is by our side. He looks terrified – of Grace and of me.

'Do you mind if we have a moment, Evie?' he says. 'I've got some serious making up to do.'

Grace looks up at him furiously.

'I'm not taking anything for granted,' he says, 'but I will do anything – *anything* – for you to stay with me. For you to forgive me. I know I don't deserve you, but I'm nothing without you.'

'Then perhaps you should have realized that earlier,' she replies.

Chapter 118

'Well, it's a hell of a wedding, anyway,' says Georgia, as we share her make-up bag in the ladies'. Her cosmetic collection is a combination of £3.99 Rimmel lipsticks and face powders that probably cost more than gold dust.

'Makes yours look distinctly tame, doesn't it?' I say, sweeping a blusher brush across my cheeks in an attempt to revive some colour in them. 'No physical fights, no coffins, no marital bust-ups. It was all a bit boring, really.'

'Thank God,' she laughs. 'Although, give Valentina some credit. She's really taken it all on the chin. Speaking of which, how are you feeling these days, Evie?'

'How do you mean?' I ask.

'Well, I heard you were still a bit upset over Jack,' she says. 'And we've not really had a chance to talk about it, have we? I haven't even seen you since your mum's wedding.'

'I'm fine,' I say. 'Honestly, Georgia. These things happen.'

'Well, if it means anything,' she continues, 'Beth said he's been moping around work ever since it happened.'

I pause.

'Beth?' I repeat.

'Yes, Beth. You know – my cousin,' she says.

'Yes,' I say. 'I know your cousin Beth. I just thought you said "he'd been moping *around work*".'

'I did,' says Georgia. 'They work together.'

'Really?' I am slightly confused. 'I hadn't realized. I mean, I'd worked out they were seeing each other, but—'

'Seeing each other?' echoes Georgia. 'Evie, they're not seeing each other.'

I frown.

'They *work* together,' she explains. 'Only since very recently, mind you. Beth's always wanted to work in the voluntary sector and she got chatting to Jack about the charity he works for at our wedding. He told her there was some administrative position coming up, so she phoned him on the Monday and started work there about a week later.'

'So, she's still working for them now?' I ask.

'Yes,' says Georgia, 'but there's nothing going on between the two of them, I promise you. I know that for certain because Beth has fancied him from day one but he's refused to even acknowledge it. He clearly just isn't interested in her. And she does nothing but complain about it.'

I shake my head.

'But why wouldn't he have told me she was working with him?' I ask.

'Probably because he's a man,' Georgia says dismissively. 'Pete's had deaths, pregnancies and a sex change among his colleagues without bothering to keep me up to date.'

That might explain the phone number exchanges. And the missed calls on the mobile.

'But that doesn't explain something else,' I tell Georgia, as she zips up her make-up bag. I tell her about the call from Beth that I picked up during my mum's wedding. About how she'd left her top at his flat that morning. How could she explain *that*?

'I really don't know,' she says, looking puzzled. Then: 'Hang on, this was the night of your mum's wedding, wasn't it?'

'Yes.'

'Well, she couldn't have been with him the night before, because we were all at my Uncle Tom's fiftieth birthday party. I was with her all night. In fact, we stayed at the hotel.'

My heart sinks. I don't know what the explanation is for what she said on the phone. But I do now know that I publicly accused Jack of two-timing me when he was completely innocent; did so when he'd just discovered I'd lied to him about my past, and then failed even to pick up the phone afterwards to say sorry.

I have an overwhelming urge to burst into tears.

Chapter 119

Edmund has given Valentina the biggest and best wedding money can buy, but he's saved the thing that will probably mean most to her for last. He's been taking ballroom dancing lessons.

Naturally, she's chosen the tango. And as the dance ends to rapturous applause, with her and Edmund nose to nose, she pulls a rose from between her teeth and kisses him like a comic-book heroine who has just been rescued from a marauding gang.

The guests pour onto the dance floor, including Bob and my mother, whose particular brand of dancing immediately terrifies some of the elderly and infirm in the party.

I pick up my bag and decide to go outside for a walk in the grounds. The breeze is soft and warm and when I find a decent log, I plonk myself down on it and look into the sky. Tears prick into my eyes again as I think about what Georgia told me earlier.

'You lot have got it easy,' I say, between sniffs, to a couple of sheep munching away at some grass in front of me. 'You don't have to deal with having your bum groped in front of other wedding guests and being stalked by psychotic ex-boyfriends. And certainly, you don't have to deal with screwing things up with the one man who ever meant anything to you. At least, I don't think you do.'

I really have lost it now. I'm sitting here, blubbing and talking to a group of farm animals. I think this might constitute a breakdown.

I don't know how long I sit here for. Certainly it's a good while, and somewhere along the way the two existing sheep are joined by another handful.

I am just starting to feel like Little Bo Peep when suddenly I hear voices behind me. When I turn around, Valentina, Grace and Georgia are marching towards me.

'I hope there aren't any cow pats around here,' says Valentina, holding her hem up in disgust. 'These shoes are Louboutins.'

'Valentina,' I say, 'aren't you meant to be mingling or something?'

'Yes, Evie,' she says, 'I am. But we're here because we're worried about you.'

'Me?' I repeat, waving them away. 'Surely I'm the least of everyone's worries today. Really, I'm fine.'

'Well, we don't think you are,' says Georgia. 'In fact, we think you're less than fine.'

'We think you're pining,' says Valentina. 'For Jack.'

'You make me sound like a Labrador,' I say. 'Anyway, whether I'm pining or not, there's nothing you can do about it. I've buggered it all up – big time.'

The three of them exchange glances. 'Maybe, maybe not,' says Georgia. 'I've just been in touch with Beth. The top she was referring to when she spoke to you on the phone was actually a charity T-shirt that she needed for a fun run the following day. That top *hadn't* been left at Jack's flat. It had been left in Jack's office.'

I groan. 'Do you have to even tell me this? I mean, I feel like enough of an idiot anyway without having all the horrifying details rubbed in.'

'I just thought you'd like to know,' says Georgia. 'That, and something else.'

'Oh God,' I say.

'According to Beth,' continues Georgia, 'for two weeks after your row, Jack spent the whole time pacing up and down the office, agitated, and clearly pretty upset.'

'So why didn't he phone?'

'One might say that should have been up to you,' she points out gently. 'The misunderstanding was all yours – not his, Evie.'

'Fair point.' I slump back onto my log.

'The thing is, he might have,' Georgia persists, 'but something put a stop to that once and for all.'

'What?' I ask.

'My little minx of a cousin told him about you and Seb. About her seeing you in that club.'

I cast my mind back to the club and Beth witnessing Seb's big sloppy kiss. It sends a shiver down my spine just thinking she might have relayed that back to Jack.

'Do you really have to go on?'

'Well, we have got something *good* to tell you too,' Grace pipes up.

'Please do.'

'It's possible, indeed *probable* that Jack is quite into you,' she says coyly. 'In fact . . . Beth thinks he loves you!'

'Oh, I wanted to say that bit,' protests Valentina.

I scrunch up my nose. 'I don't think so, somehow.'

They all look at each other again, each grinning from ear to ear.

'The thing is,' continues Georgia, 'once I'd spoken to Beth, we weren't going to leave it there, were we? I mean, what sort of friends would we be to just not do anything?'

'So . . . what did you do?' I ask, slightly hysterically.

'We phoned someone,' says Valentina, clapping her hands. 'In fact, we phoned—'

'Why don't you just come with us and see,' interrupts Grace, grabbing me by the hand.

Chapter 120

The first thing I notice when I walk into the ballroom is that the music has stopped; virtually the only thing I can hear is my own heartbeat, which is now hammering away as if I'd just run up five flights of stairs.

The next thing I notice is Jack. Standing there, on the other side of the room, and the only person in the place wearing jeans, a T-shirt and, most bewilderingly, holding a microphone. I can see some guests out of the corner of my eye exchanging baffled looks and I glance at them for a second as if to say: 'I haven't got a bloody clue what's going on either.'

'What . . . what's happening?' I splutter.

'You'll see,' says Grace, grinning.

Then the music starts, the unmistakable opening bars of a song I recognize instantly. Jack lifts up the microphone and feedback screeches through the sound system, prompting a sharp collective intake of breath from everyone in the room. 'Sorry,' he says, and I suddenly realize that he looks terribly nervous. 'Although you might think that sounds good compared with what you're about to hear.'

Georgia giggles.

'Evie,' says Jack, 'we haven't spoken for a while now. And . . . well, I want to change that.'

He's right across on the other side of the room, but our eyes are locked as if we're inches apart. I try to swallow. I can't. I'm frozen to the spot, exhilarated and pumped with emotion.

'I think after what's happened that I need to do something to prove just how I feel about you. And, although it's a shame that the only thing I could think of makes me look a complete and utter prat, there really is only one way to do it.'

Every guest in the room is enthralled.

I flash a look at Grace and she grins. Jack starts slowly walking towards me and, as lightning races through my veins, Ruby Turner's backing singers launch into song.

Then, to my complete amazement, so does Jack.

Jack Williamson, a man who *never* sung in public – a man who *swore* he never would – is singing. He's singing to *me*.

His voice is deep and ever so slightly off-key, but I don't think I'd care right now if he sounded like a castrated seagull.

As Jack sings, the guests who were initially wondering what the hell was going on, now start to get into the swing of things – and one or two even stand up and begin swaying, as if they're at a Queen concert. Someone actually holds their lighter up.

By the time Jack has walked all the way over to me, I am unable to determine whether I should laugh, cry or pass out with the sheer insanity of it all.

Jack looks into my eyes to sing the final line and we're so close now I can see the contours of his face in the sort of detail that I never thought I'd see again.

'*Nobody . . . but . . . you.*'

He places the microphone down on the table next to me and pulls me towards him as I wipe away my tears. With applause echoing through my ears, Jack leans forward and our lips meet.

It is the sweetest, deepest, happiest moment in my twenty-seven years on this earth. And right now, right at this moment, I know I'm going to say something I thought I'd never say to anyone. Ever.

I pull back and I look at Jack, my Jack, my shaking hands clutching his, while I search for my voice and whisper three, unprecedented words.

'I love you.'

THREE YEARS LATER

Epilogue

'You know,' says Valentina, admiring her profile in the mirror, 'I had my doubts about wearing a bridesmaid dress at eight months pregnant, but I think we can conclude that I've carried it off.'

I can't help smiling to myself. Valentina may have been married for three years and be about to bear her first child for Edmund, but some things never change. So are you a little bit surprised? That they're still together, I mean? Well, don't worry – I suspect a few others are too.

Let's face it, when they first met, it didn't take a cynic to recognize that Valentina appeared to be as romantically attached to Edmund's Gold Card as she was to Edmund himself. But, somewhere along the way, a funny thing happened: she seems to have fallen for him. Whether it was when she witnessed him saving a man's life on their honeymoon, or when they found out baby Paris (Orlando if it's a boy) was on the way, I'm not entirely sure. But it happened all right – and the Barnetts couldn't be happier. Which from Valentina's point of view is fantastic, because divorce is *so* last year.

The door to our hotel suite opens and Polly walks in.

'Where's your mum?' I ask, slightly nervously. I may have been fully expecting Grace to be late, but it doesn't make me feel any less jumpy about it.

'Just coming,' says Polly, who at eight is so grown up now. 'You didn't really expect us to be on time, did you?'

'Soooo sorry!' says Grace, bursting through the door and ushering Scarlett in with one hand and her bags in with another. 'I've been trying to get out of the house for an hour but my mother phoned to ask if I wanted anything from Debenhams while she was in there. Then she phoned to ask if I wanted anything from M&S. Then John Lewis. Then she phoned back to ask was I absolutely sure I didn't want anything because M&S had some lovely pâté in – she knew it was lovely because Maureen Thomas from church had some the last time she was round there and it had real Cointreau in and ... Oh look, the upshot is: *sorry*. Now, where do I get changed?'

They got off to a shaky start, but Grace and Patrick have somehow managed to move on from the early events of their marriage. If you catch Grace at an unguarded moment, she'll tell you that, once your husband has done something like Patrick did, you can't ever love and trust them in the same way as before. But to be absolutely fair to him – and, believe me, that was the last thing I thought he deserved at the start – he has worked hard at proving himself to Grace. Once he'd got a new job and she moved to a new law firm (with a female boss who couldn't be less like her old one), things seemed to slot into place. It seems to be a good place – and all I can do as her friend is hope that it stays that way.

'Right,' says my mum, straightening her turban – which along with the three-quarter pants she's wearing makes her look like she's just appeared out of a magic lamp. 'I can't be hanging round here all day. I've got guests to greet. See? See how responsible I can be?'

I go over and kiss her.

'You're right,' I say fondly. 'At least about you needing to get going. The responsible bit I'll reserve judgement on. And make sure Bob gets here on time, will you?' Georgia brings the champagne over to top me up again.

'Bloody hell, not too much!' I say. 'Or I'll be doing the splits on the dance floor later – and I'm leaving that to Valentina.'

'You don't think the fact that she's eight months pregnant might stop her this time?' asks Georgia.

'Of course not!'

Georgia laughs – and I realize it's a while since I heard her do that.

She and Pete separated last month, something that would make any future bride – even one certain she's doing the right thing – think twice. Apparently, they'd drifted apart;

they wanted different things; they realized they were better as friends, not husband and wife. Neither have been bitter, nor acrimonious, just sad. And, I'll be honest, I was completely shocked. I suppose it goes to show that two good people don't always make for a good marriage.

With twenty minutes to go, I head into the bathroom to touch up my lipstick and Valentina follows me with her own extensive cosmetics collection.

'One of the hotel staff just passed this in for you,' she says, handing me an envelope.

I put down my lip brush and open it, while Valentina starts tonging her hair for the fifth time today.

'God,' I say, reading it.

'What is it?' she asks.

She leans over to read with me.

Dear Evie

Well, it's been a long time, that's for sure. I'm sorry about that. I know you kept trying to get in touch with me after Valentina's wedding and I'd like you to know how grateful I was about that. But I also hope you understand why I didn't return any of your calls and emails. Things were very difficult. Emotionally I was a mess – and more importantly, I began to realize that what I'd done was unforgivable. That was why I took that job in Scotland and left without saying goodbye. I just needed to put some space between me and, well, everyone really. Anyway, Valentina phoned and told me about today and I could have jumped for joy when I found out (except I've put all that weight on again now so it's not so easy any more!). The point is, I was delighted – more than delighted, in fact – ecstatic. And while that doubled when I received an invitation from you, I hope you understand why I had to decline. It wouldn't have been fair on anyone – particularly Grace – for me to have come. That said, I wondered if you'd like to meet for coffee sometime, just you and me? I miss you terribly and I'd love to catch up, next time I'm back in town, although I'll understand if you don't want to after all this time. My mobile number is still the same.

Anyway, nobody deserves to be happier than you, Evie. So good luck, and all my love, Charlotte. x

'Oh, Charlotte! Do you think I've got time to phone her now?' I ask.

'Absolutely not, there's only a few minutes left,' says Valentina, fiddling with my hair. 'Do it later, or tomorrow. After this long, one day isn't going to make any difference.'

The bathroom door opens and Scarlett and Polly poke their heads around it.

'You two have got the prettiest dresses I've ever seen, no competition,' I say.

'Come on, Auntie Evie,' says Polly. 'It's time to go. Bob's here to take you down the aisle.'

I walk out into the hotel room and look at the clock. She's right. Two minutes to go.

'You look beautiful, Evie,' says Bob, appearing at my side. 'I feel so proud.'

We link arms, and with my bridesmaids behind us, we head downstairs until we reach the door to the room where the ceremony is taking place. I can already see Jack standing at the front waiting for me, and my heart leaps.

'Well, you've proved someone wrong, anyway,' says Grace, straightening my veil.

'Oh?' I ask her.

'My mother,' she says, grinning. 'She said this morning she never thought she'd see the day when Evie Hart walked down the aisle.'

A hush descends on the room and the music starts. My skin prickles with excitement.

'Actually, Grace,' I whisper, 'I couldn't agree with her more.'

Acknowledgements

As *Bridesmaids* was my debut novel, I'll be forever grateful to my former agent Darley Anderson for spotting my potential and encouraging me to write on.

Thanks also to the team at Simon & Schuster UK who first published this book, especially Suzanne Baboneau, Julie Wright and my first editor Libby Vernon. It was the start of a wonderful, long relationship with the publisher that continues to this day.

Thanks to Sheila Crowley for the phenomenal new direction in which she's taken my new career writing as Catherine Isaac.

Thanks also to my parents, Jean and Phil Wolstenholme, my husband Mark and my three sons, Otis, Lucas and Isaac, around whom there's never a dull moment.

A letter from Jane Costello

I've been writing novels under my pseudonym Jane Costello for more than a decade. But when I came up with the idea for my next book, *You Me Everything*, it immediately felt different from my romantic comedies.

Still uplifting and full of humour, but this time it dealt with a subject that was bigger and more important than anything I'd tackled before.

Since I wrote the novel, it's been bought by publishers in the UK and US, will be translated into twenty languages and, most excitingly, has been optioned for a movie by Lionsgate and Temple Hill.

This worldwide interest underlined the fact that this book was very different from my previous work and, as such, it would make sense to publish it under a new name.

So my first novel writing as Catherine Isaac was published in Spring 2018. *You Me Everything* is an incredibly special book for me. I can't wait to hear what you think.

Jane / Catherine
x

Turn the page for an exciting extract
from Catherine Isaac's

YOU
ME
EVERYTHING

Prologue

Manchester, England, 2006

Sometimes life takes the best and worst it has to offer and throws the whole lot at you on the same day.

This probably isn't an uncommon conclusion to reach during childbirth, but in my case, it wasn't the usual cocktail of pain and joy that led me to it. It was that, although I was finally about to meet the tiny human who'd shared my body for nine months, those eight agonising hours were also spent trying to reach his father on my mobile – to drag him away from whatever bar, club or other woman he was in.

'Did you remember to bring your notes, Jessica?' the midwife asked after I'd arrived at the hospital alone.

'I've got my notes. It's my boyfriend I've mislaid,' I said, through an apologetic smile. She glanced up at me from under her eyelashes as I leaned on the reception desk of the delivery suite, waiting for the searing pain in my belly to pass.

'I'm sure he'll be on his way soon.' Sweat gathered on the back of my neck. 'I've left him a couple of messages.' Twelve, to be exact. 'He's at a work event. He probably can't get a signal.'

At this stage, part of me was still hoping this was true. I always was determined to see the good in Adam, even in the face of clear evidence to the contrary.

'We never used to have men here,' she reminded me. 'So if we need to do it without Dad, we'll be just fine.' *Dad*. I couldn't deny the biological facts, but the title sounded wrong when it was applied to Adam.

The midwife looked reassuringly matronly, with stout legs, a bosom you could stand a potted plant on and the kind of hair that had been in foam curlers overnight. The name on her badge was Mary. I'd known Mary for about three minutes and I already liked her, which was good given that she was about to examine my cervix.

'Come on, lovely; let's get you to a room.'

I went to pick up the overnight bag that the taxi driver had helped me with, but she swooped in and took the handle, staggering under its weight.

'How long are you hoping to stay?' she hooted and I did my best to laugh until I realised another contraction was on its way. I stood in mute agony, screwing up my eyes but determined not to be the woman who terrified everyone else by screaming the place down.

When the pain subsided, I slowly followed Mary down the

over-lit corridor, pulling out my phone to check again for messages. There were a dozen texts from my mum and Becky, my closest friend, but still none from Adam.

It wasn't meant to be happening like this.

I didn't want to be on my own.

No matter how worried I'd been about our relationship in recent months, right then I'd have done anything to have him with me, holding my hand and telling me everything was going to be all right.

I'd discovered I was pregnant the day after my twenty-second birthday. Even though it wasn't planned, I'd convinced myself in the nine months that followed that I'd be a confident mum. That suddenly felt like a fragile bravado.

'All right, dear?' Mary asked as we arrived at the door of the labour room.

I nodded silently, despite the real truth: even in her capable hands, I felt alone, terrified and certain that this feeling would continue until Adam arrived to do his brow-patting, hand-clutching duty.

The room was small and functional, with thin patterned curtains that gave it the air of a dated Travelodge. The sky outside was the colour of treacle, black and impenetrable, a pearlescent moon reclining into the shadows.

'Hop on,' said Mary, patting the bed.

I followed her directions to lie back and open my legs. She then coolly declared, 'Going in,' before manoeuvring her hand up my unmentionables as my eyes popped and I lost the ability to breathe.

'Four centimetres dilated.' She straightened up, smiled and snapped off her latex glove as the contraction started building. 'You're in labour, Jessica.'

'Exciting,' I replied, too polite to mention that this didn't feel like a revelation; I'd already christened my kitchen floor with amniotic fluid hours earlier.

'The best thing to do is get on the birthing ball and let gravity help us out. I'm going to check on the lady next door, but don't hesitate to use your call button. Is there anyone else who could join you? A friend? Or your mother?'

Becky didn't live far, but Mum was always the only choice, as humiliating as it had been to call and explain that Adam was AWOL.

'I've got my mum on standby. If I haven't heard from my boyfriend by two a.m., she's going to drive over.'

'Excellent,' she said, before leaving me alone with my half-formed space hopper, an iPod full of Jack Johnson songs and a gas and air machine that I'd forgotten to ask how to use.

I called Mum on the dot of two. She arrived at six minutes past, in slim-legged jeans and a soft linen blouse, the whisper of Estée Lauder *Beautiful* clinging to her neck. She was carrying a massive gym bag, which contained her last-minute 'birthing kit'. This consisted of a compact video camera, a goose down pillow, a tube of toothpaste, a copy of *Woman & Home*, some Neal's Yard hand cream, a bunch of grapes, two large Tupperware boxes containing a selection of recently baked cakes, some pink towels and – I kid you not – a cuddly toy.

'How are you?' she asked anxiously, dragging up a chair as she tucked a wisp of short, blonde hair behind her ear. She wore the softest hint of make-up; she had good skin so never needed much, and her brilliant blue eyes were luminous.

'Okay. How are you?'

'I'm great. Over the moon to be here, in fact.'

Her foot was tapping against the bed as she spoke, the metallic sound clanking through the room. Mum always kept her head in a crisis, but I'd noticed her nervous tics lately; that night her leg had a life of its own.

'It can't have taken you six minutes to drive from home?' I said, trying a suck of the gas and air for the first time, before coughing as it caught at the back of my throat.

'I've been in the car park since midnight. I didn't want to get stuck in traffic.'

'If only Adam had been so thoughtful,' I muttered.

Her smile faltered. 'Have you tried texting him again?'

I nodded and attempted to hide how upset I was. 'Yes, but clearly, something was more important than being here.'

She reached over and squeezed my fingers. She wasn't used to hearing me sound resentful. I hardly ever got *really* angry with anyone or anything, with the possible exception of our crappy broadband connection.

But you wouldn't have known it that night.

'I hate him.' I sniffed.

She shook her head as the pads of her fingertips stroked my knuckles. 'No you don't.'

'Mum, you don't know the half of what's been going on lately.' I dreaded filling her in, because that would've burst the bubble, the idea that my family life with Adam could ever compare with the one she and Dad had given me. I looked back on my childhood as largely blessed – secure and happy, even accounting for some difficult periods that were by now all in the past.

She exhaled. 'Okay. Well, don't get yourself worked up about that now. You're never going to get this moment back. Are you hungry?' She opened up one of the Tupperware boxes.

I managed to smile. 'Are you serious?'

'No?' she said, surprised. 'I was starving when I had you. I got through half a lemon drizzle cake before my waters had even gone.'

My mum was a brilliant birth partner. She made me smile between contractions, kept me calm until everything felt so out of control that I couldn't stop myself from screaming.

'Why haven't they given you something for the pain?' she said under her breath.

'I told them I didn't want an epidural. I did a natural birth plan. And . . . I've done yoga.'

'Jess, you're trying to push another human being out of your vagina, I think you need more than breathing exercises and a candle.'

She turned out to be right. By the time I'd vomited for the umpteenth time I was in the grip of such incomprehensible agony that I'd have sucked on a crack pipe if it'd been available. A muted sun began to blur through the window and a different midwife – who'd probably introduced herself earlier, when my mind was on other things – stooped to examine me.

'Sorry, my love, you're too far along for an epidural. You can have a pethidine injection if you want, but this baby is going to be born very soon.'

My legs started shaking uncontrollably, the pain catching my breath, robbing my ability to speak properly, or think rationally.

'I just want Adam here. Mum . . . *please.*'

She frantically fumbled with her phone to try and call his number. But she dropped the handset, cursing her clumsiness as she scrambled on the floor, chasing it around like a bar of soap in the bath.

Events after that are vague because I wasn't concentrating on phone calls or the needle in my thigh; I was delirious with the terrible and miraculous force of my own body.

It was about a minute and three pushes after the pethidine was administered that my baby made his entrance into the world.

He was a thing of wonder, my boy, with chubby limbs and a perplexed expression as he blinked his eyes and unscrunched his little face when the midwife placed him in my arms.

'Oh my God,' gasped Mum. 'He's . . .'

'Gorgeous,' I whispered.

'*Massive*,' she replied.

I'd always thought of newborn babies as delicate and help-less, but William was a 9lb 4oz bruiser. And he didn't cry, not in those first moments, he just curled into the warm curve of my breast and made everything all right.

Well, almost everything.

As I pressed my lips against his forehead and breathed in his sweet, new scent, the door crashed open. There was Adam, entirely disproving the theory that it's better late than never.

I don't know what was more overpowering as he approached us, the smell of another woman's perfume, or the bitter reek of stale booze. He was still wearing last night's clothes. He'd failed in an attempt to wipe the lipstick off his neck, leaving a violent, slut-pink smudge that started by his ear and ended on his shirt.

I suddenly didn't want him anywhere near me or our baby – no amount of antibacterial hand gel would've changed the fact that he was a complete mess. In more ways than one. I wondered desolately how long ago I'd come to that conclusion.

'Can I . . . can I hold her?' he said, extending his arms.

Mum winced as I drew a sharp breath. 'It's a *boy*, Adam.'

He looked up, surprised, and withdrew his arms. He sat looking at us, apparently unable to say anything, let alone the right thing.

'You missed it,' I said, brushing away the sting of new tears. 'I can't believe you missed it, Adam.'

'Jess, listen . . . I can explain.'

Chapter 1

Ten years later, summer 2016

I don't know when I became so bad at packing. I was good at it once, in the days when I had the time and headspace to stock up on inflatable travel pillows and mini toiletries. It's not volume that's lacking; my old Citroën is bursting. But I have an unshakeable feeling that I've forgotten something, or several somethings.

The problem lies in the fact that I didn't make a list. Women of my generation are led to believe that lists are the solution to everything, even if the world around them is falling apart. Right now, I'm beyond lists – there comes a point where there's so much to do that stopping for something as indulgent as *list-making* feels like pure folly. Besides, if I've forgotten anything I can just buy it when we get there – we're only going to rural France, not the Amazon basin.

If my packing has been haphazard, I'm not sure what you'd

call William's. The contents of his bag largely involve Haribos found under his bed after a recent sleepover, books with names like *Venomous Snakes of the World*, several water pistols and a selection of heavily spiced toiletries.

He's only recently begun taking an interest in the latter after his friend Cameron decided turning ten was the time to start wearing deodorant to school. I had to gently point out to my son that walking round in a mushroom cloud of Lynx Africa wouldn't get him very far in France without any actual trousers.

I jump into the driver's seat, turn the key and experience the usual flicker of surprise when the engine starts. 'Are you sure you've got everything?' I ask.

'Think so.' The flare of excitement on his face makes my heart twist a little. He's been like this ever since I told him we'd be spending the summer with his dad. I lean over to give him a quick kiss on the side of his head. He tolerates it, but the days of him flinging his arms round me to declare, 'You're the best mum I've ever had' are long gone.

William is tall for his age, gangly almost, despite an enormous appetite and the recent obsession he's developed with *Domino's*. He got his height from his father, as well as those liquid brown eyes, skin that tans easily and dark hair that curls at the nape of his neck.

As I'm five foot four, it won't be long before he towers above me, at which point he'll probably look even less like he belongs to me. My skin is pale, freckled and prone to turning pink in the slightest heat. The blonde hair that skims my shoulders doesn't curl like my son's, but it's not straight either; it has a kink that used to annoy me in the days when that was all I had to worry about.

'Who's going to look after the house while we're away?' he asks.

'It doesn't really need looking after, sweetheart. Just someone to pick up the post.'

'What if someone burgles it?'

'They won't.'

'How do you know?' he asks.

'If anyone was going to break in to a house on this street ours would be the last one they'd choose.'

I bought our tiny terrace in south Manchester thanks to a financial leg-up from my dad shortly after I'd had William and – fortuitously – before the neighbourhood became trendy.

I've never joined in the ironic bingo nights in the falafel bar at the end of the road and must've only bought one quinoa-laced sourdough since the artisan bakery opened. But I'm all for these kind of places, as they've made house prices soar.

It does mean, however, that I am probably the only thirty-three-year-old single parent on a salary like mine who lives round here. I teach creative writing at our local sixth-form college, which has always offered more in the way of job satisfaction than in financial rewards.

'Jake Milton was burgled,' William tells me sombrely as we

turn down the street. 'They took all his mum's jewellery, his dad's car and Jake's Xbox.'

'Really? That's awful.'

'I know. He'd got to the final level on *Garden Warfare*,' he sighs, shaking his head. 'He'll just *never* get that back.'

It will take four or five hours to reach the south coast to catch our ferry, but we're leaving early to make a stop-off, not far from our house.

We arrive at Willow Bank Lodge ten minutes later and pull into the small car park at the front. The building looks like an oversized Lego house from outside, with uniform mud-brown bricks and a grey tiled roof. But then, nobody chooses a care home for the architecture.

I key in the code for the two doors and sign us in as we're hit by the smell of over-roasted meat and mushy vegetables. Inside, the place is clean, bright and well-maintained, even if its interior designer must've been colour blind. The swirly wallpaper is a thick avocado green, the floor covered in patterned navy and red carpet tiles, and the skirting boards tinted with a marmalade varnish that someone misguidedly must've thought looked like natural wood.

The sounds of lunchtime drift out from beyond a set of double doors and the television area, so we head in that direction, instead of turning down the corridor towards Mum's room.

'Are you all right there, Arthur?' I ask gently, as one of

the long-term residents wanders out of the bathroom with an expression like he's just stepped into Narnia. He straightens his back defensively. 'I'm looking for my pans. Have you taken my pans?'

'Not us, Arthur. Why don't you come and try the dining room?' I'm about to rescue him before he steps into the broom cupboard, when the double doors open and one of the nursing staff, Raheem, appears to offer him a reassuring arm and guide him away.

'Hiya,' says William. In his mid-twenties and of Somalian descent, Raheem also owns an Xbox, so they always have plenty to discuss.

'Hey, William. Your grandma's about to have lunch. There might be some pineapple turnover left if you fancy it?'

'Yeah okay.' My son never declines an offer of food, unless it's something I've gone to enormous effort to make, when he invariably looks at it like I've presented him with a plate of steaming industrial waste.

As Arthur shuffles through the door, followed by Raheem, the figure of a man appears in their place. The skin around his temples is etched with years of spiralling pressure, which has surely had a more potent effect on his health than the fact that he's a reformed alcoholic.

'Granddad!' William's face erupts into a smile and my dad's pale grey eyes sparkle into life.

Chapter 2

It's one of the small miracles of my world that, even in the face of unimaginable strain, every bit of my dad smiles when his grandson is around. 'Are you all set, William?'

'Yep. Packed and on our way, Granddad.'

Dad ruffles his thick, curly hair and steps back to examine him. 'I could've taken you for a cut before you left.'

'But I like it long.'

'You look like a burst cushion.' William chuckles, even though he's heard this quip more times than he could count.

'How many minutes in four and a half hours?' Dad challenges him.

'Hmm. Two hundred and . . . seventy.'

'Good lad.' He pulls him in briefly for a hug.

That my son is on a Gifted and Talented register for maths is not something for which I can take credit. Arithmetic is definitely not my forte and the only figures at which Adam excels are the hourglass variety.

But then my dad, an accountant, was always more of a father to William than Adam ever was. My parents' semi is only ten minutes away from where we live and it was a second home to William before he started school, the place he'd puzzle over jigsaws with my dad and bake fairy cakes with Mum.

Even later on, it was Dad who'd wait at the school gates and take William back to their place to supervise homework or ferry him to karate club, while I finished up at work.

Everything's changed in the last couple of years.

My mum is no longer the grandma she once was, someone who, seven or eight years ago would be the first in line to shoot down the big, wavy slide in our local soft-play centre, with William on her knee. She was never concerned about looking like a big kid; she just kicked off her shoes and got stuck in, as William shrieked with delight and other women her age – who hadn't had the diagnosis she'd already had by then – remained at the sidelines, sipping their lattes.

'Let me give you something to spend,' Dad says, rooting in his trouser pocket.

'You don't need to do that,' William murmurs unconvincingly as my father thrusts a twenty pound note in his hand.

'Buy yourself a comic on the ferry.'

'Could I get some Coke?'

'Of course,' Dad replies, before I can say definitely not.

'Thanks, Granddad. I really appreciate it.' William skips

into the dining room to find his grandma, while I hold back to talk to Dad.

'You should've gone straight off for your ferry, love,' he tells me. 'You didn't need to stop here on the way.'

'Of course I did. I wanted to give Mum lunch before I go.'

'I'll do that. I was only popping out to buy a paper.'

'No, I'd like to do it, if you don't mind.'

He nods, inhaling slowly. 'Well, listen. Try and relax in France. You need a holiday.'

I smile dubiously. 'Is that what you're calling it?'

'You'll enjoy it if you *let* yourself. And make sure you do. For your mum's sake, if it makes you feel any better. She really wants this, you know.'

'I still think it's too long to be away.'

'We've lived with this for a decade, Jess. Absolutely nothing is going to happen in five weeks.'

booksandthecity.co.uk
the home of female fiction

BOOKS | NEWS & EVENTS | FEATURES | AUTHOR PODCASTS | COMPETITIONS

Follow us online to be the first to hear from
your favourite authors

bc
booksandthecity.co.uk

books and the city

@TeamBATC

Join our mailing list for the latest news, events and
exclusive competitions

Sign up at
booksandthecity.co.uk

'Terrifying. A heart-pounding thriller'
Cosmopolitan

'The suspense is electrifying'
Publishers Weekly

'Gritty, realistic, packed with action
. . . heart-stopping thrills along with
heart-wrenching revelations . . .
promises much and delivers'
Mystery Scene

By Dean Koontz and available from Headline